TORN

BREATH OF FATE

I

TORN

BREATH OF FATE

I

ANGELINA J. STEFFORT

TORN
BREATH OF FATE BOOK 1

First published 2020

Copyright © by Angelina J. Steffort 2020

Print: ISBN 9783903357051
Ebook: ASIN B08LJPY3S1

Typeset int EB Garamond

MK

www.ajsteffort.com

For the ones who are scared … and still yearn to love.

1. Cas

Darkness arrived before me. And how I adored the shadows that traveled alongside me. My safe haven.

I leaned against the wall while darkness slowly dissolved and observed the struggle of the woman in red who was writhing on the artsy carpet at my feet. Her dress was short, exposing long legs in tasteless tights. How I despised the fashion of the current era. The tight pants and short skirts left so little to my imagination that sometimes it wasn't even worth dreaming about what lay beneath.

My eyes fell on a photograph on the wall above where the woman was fighting her fate. It was her face, maybe fifteen years younger. Pretty, eyes sparkling with anticipation of a future that lay ahead, and I wondered what that future had been ... what her life had been like since that picture had been taken.

With a gentle push, I straightened away from the wall, eyes following the arrangement of pictures.

The woman on the floor gurgled as she fought for air, her hands clutching her throat.

I lifted my leg and stepped over her, making my way toward the artifacts of her past. There were several of her, in a prom dress, her holding a trophy, her surrounded by other women, equally pretty and equally smiling, their faces empty despite their grinning lips.

None of them nearly interesting enough that I'd have considered courting them... not that I ever could. My existence was bound to go unnoticed, and that meant no rendezvous, no proms, no courting... I'd long gotten used to the fact that I would never feel a woman again—at least not the way I had a long, long time ago. Too long to think.

The woman rolled onto her back, and I tore my attention away from my own thoughts to focus on her instead. Her eyes were already growing distant, body too weak to struggle much longer. I didn't know exactly what the cause had been— poison maybe or an overdose of drugs. The only thing that was relevant to me was that she wouldn't be going anywhere after tonight. Once I had done my job, she would have arrived where her entire life had been leading her.

"Hello, Cynthia." I bent down and ran a finger over the woman's cheek as she gasped for her last breath. Of course, she couldn't see me or hear me. That was the beauty of it. When the moment came for me to give them a lift, they had no idea what was coming for them—or who.

Cynthia's lips were turning blue, and she exhaled a last painful gust of air before her heart gave out. I studied her fine features. Not older than forty. Lines of laughter spread from her eyes, allowing me to believe she'd had her happy moments in life—more than a fair share. Something in my stomach twisted, and I decided not to look too closely. After all, this body of hers was no longer her home.

"There is someone waiting for you at the place I'm taking you," I whispered. She couldn't hear.

Sometimes I wondered if I should be grateful they didn't know it was me who delivered them to hell or if I should be upset that no one ever knew what a great job I was doing.

I made their transition swift, painless. There was enough pain waiting for them down there; I didn't need to add to it.

"Come now." With a motion so familiar after ages of executing it, I bent forward, lowered my mouth over the woman's face, appreciating that she must have led a life of mostly bad choices. I told myself that that must have been her life or they wouldn't have sent me to pick her up.

As I blew a breath of death upon her, her soul split from her body, floating out of her as if it were to evaporate. But my breath caught it and bound it. I sucked it in, letting it settle within the hollow chambers of my chest.

"Let's go."

2. LANEY

As I flipped the pages of our English textbook and sighed audibly, from his desk across the aisle, Leon shot me a look.

I was doing it again.

"Sorry," I mouthed.

To my luck, no one else had paid attention, and while my mind was drifting elsewhere—anywhere—the others were studying intently the content of the pages.

I gave an apologetic smile, allowing my eyes a moment of rest from the tedious material I was supposed to study and read Leon's familiar features instead.

After a long school day, my body was ready to sprawl on my bed with no other task than reading a good book—not a textbook. But the week wasn't over yet, and I needed to get up to speed with things before Mom and I left for the weekend. One of the trips on which Leon didn't come.

Leon winked, and I rolled my eyes toward the ceiling, sending a short request to whatever lay above—miles and miles and miles above, where the stars sat, watching over us, I hoped—that the day would be over soon. The response was our teacher's grumbling stomach. The sound tugged on the corners of my mouth, and yet again, when I glanced to the side, I found Leon's eyes on me, his own lips mimicking my smile. His eyes seemed to say 'just a couple more minutes'.

So I dipped my nose back into my book and absorbed the paragraphs before me until the merciful sound of the bell announced our freedom.

Leon was on his feet and beside me before I could even close the book.

"I'll drive you?" he offered.

Behind me, Avery said something about what a waste of Leon's time I was, and the boy turned just enough to put her out of his field of vision before he draped his arm over me, half-pulling me out of my chair.

It was easier not to question Leon's devotion. After basically growing up together, he had taken a special interest in me after last summer when ... I didn't want to even think of it.

He was there for me. Just there. Even if I had nothing to give back to him. Yet, he spent his days by my side and his nights... I had no idea how he spent his nights. And I was inclined to not think about it too much.

I let Leon pull me through the rows of desks until we found more room to breathe in the hallway. Most students were already filing out the orange front doors, and with the weight of Leon's arm on my shoulders, I felt more comfortable to linger while the others made their escape.

"What's different today?" Leon eyed me through his white-blond hair, his face lowered just enough to make me feel that he was ready for any answer... as long as it was the truth.

I looked around. The people looked the same as every day. The walls were the same boring hue of beige. Even the sounds, laughter and chattering interwoven with some cursing and shouts, were the same as every day. "Nothing." I glanced up at him, finding his eyes sparkling with interest.

There was something about the way he kept looking at me, not just today but every day; as if he was waiting for something. And that alone made the day more the same than anything else. "I think," I added for his sake, and his lips curled in a smile I couldn't fully read.

"You want to talk about it?" he offered and tucked me a tad tighter, the fabric of his shirt scratching over my neck under my ponytail.

There was nothing to talk about, really. And even if there was...

Leon stopped us right before the door, waiting for a group of giggling girls to pass by, then said, "Whenever you're ready."

"That may be never," I responded, flashes of faces going through my mind—faces I should have never been able to see.

He only smiled—"Never it is."—and led me through the front door and across the parking lot, aiming for his truck.

As we passed our classmates, most of them weren't even paying attention. Leon and I had become such a familiar sight that their teasing and guessing had stopped. Except, of course, for the girls who had been hoping Leon's attention would eventually move on and find them. The only girl who waved at us was my friend Jo, who was also the only girl who still talked to me like a normal person. I lifted a hand and waved back.

We had reached the white truck when Leon tensed, his body stiffening beside me as if he had turned into solid rock.

I glanced at him to find his eyes distant.

"Everything all right?"

He didn't react.

I tugged on his sleeve. "Leon?"

It took half a second for him to return to normal, a slightly distant look in his dark eyes the only thing that gave away he'd had one of his moments.

He smiled. "Let's go."

As he slid his arm off my shoulders and reached for the passenger door, he rubbed his face with his free hand as if he was trying to wipe away a memory.

I didn't push him. It was as much part of our silent pact that I didn't ask too many questions as it was that he didn't push me about... I shoved down the memory of the faces. Too many of them. All hovering above the street...

With a deep breath and long exhale, I sent those memories flying and got into the car, letting Leon shut the door behind me—behind them.

On the way home, we stopped by the small nursing home which lay on the outskirts of the small town. Gran would be expecting me as she did every day. And every visit represented a challenge in itself. I knew I didn't need to be afraid of the building, of the people who lived there, spending their final years in good care. But my fear wasn't from them. It was from the people whose last hour had arrived. A fear which had not been there a year ago but now manifested whenever I was confronted with death—

Leon eyed me with a frown as he pulled into the parking spot in silence, and when the door clicked loudly as I opened it to wordlessly get out, he leaned forward to study my face through the open door. He knew the expression there too well. Fortunately, he refrained from commenting. Part of our silent pact. A pact which we had established almost exactly a year ago...

"Should I come with you today?"

Leon asked this every day, an offer of comfort, and every day, I shook my head. The time with Gran was sacred to me. I didn't want or need to be under observation when I was with her. But today, something in Leon's eyes was different. An urgency, an almost burning depth that made me change my mind. I nodded.

Leon's eyes widened in surprise. "You sure?"

Again, I nodded and started walking. He was beside me within seconds, jogging around the car and linking his arm with mine. I didn't pull away.

"She knows about me." He more assumed than asked.

Again, I nodded. Even if I hadn't told Gran about the kind boy who continued keeping me company, Glyndon was a small town, and there was hardly any news that didn't travel more than one route.

The path up the ramp to the entrance door was easy compared to the corridors that lay behind.

"Good afternoon, Miss Dawson," a young nurse greeted as we entered the neon-lit foyer which spread into three hallways.

I gave a smile and asked if Gran was in her room.

"She's in the garden," the nurse informed me and eyed Leon with shuttering eyes. "I see you brought company today. She'll be happy to see both of you."

Something about the nurse's expression made me wonder if everything was all right with her.

Leon just grinned and tugged on my arm as I thanked the nurse. He led me right toward the glass doors at the end of the middle hallway, which made me wonder for a moment how he knew where to go, if he'd been here before. Then, I noticed the sign on the eggshell-colored wall, pointing toward the garden.

Most doors to the residents' rooms were left open during the day, and I caught a glimpse of some of them as they chatted with visitors, played cards with their neighbors... But some of them were alone, every day, all year, whenever I visited.

And some rooms, which had been occupied the day before, were empty today, the name beside the door removed.

I swallowed.

"You look nauseous." Leon tightened his arm around mine.

I shook my head. Now was not the time to go there...

"Another time," I answered, aware that it didn't make sense.

He nodded anyway, his gaze following mine as it lingered on the empty bed in the room we were passing by.

Gran's room was just by the garden door, and as we walked past, in the room across the hall, Mr. Frank waved at us.

"Hi, Mr. Frank." I returned his wave and popped my head inside the room, Leon letting go of my arm and standing aside for once. "You're looking better," I noted as his face was less pale than yesterday.

"I'm recovering." He shrugged, his frail shoulders moving awkwardly. "Or it's the body's final push against death..." He smiled at me, reaching for the control panel to get himself more upright.

I flinched at his joke but put on a brave face and returned his smile.

"I'm indestructible, Laney," he winked as he noticed he'd made me uncomfortable.

But his body, weak from old age, just having overcome another broken hip...

"Tell your grandmother to come visit me later," he said and waved.

Grateful to be released from the conversation, I waved back and dipped my chin.

Leon stood beside the threshold, watching me the entire time, face unreadable.

"Mr. Frank is Gran's neighbor," I explained and pointed at Gran's room just across the hall.

Leon pulled in his lower lip as if he was keeping in words he was dying to say.

"Are they close?" he eventually got out, and we continued walking.

"They've been spending a lot of time together in here." I glanced at him, trying to figure out the meaning of his suddenly glum tone.

Instead of meeting my gaze, he surveilled the garden as we stepped outside.

The fauna was lush around this time of the year. Hortensia blossoming in all colors of the rainbow, and the neatly trimmed hedge, which enclosed the small outside area, was deep green by now. Gran sat in a wheelchair near the patio, face turned toward the sun, her white hair tinted in soft hues of pink and orange by the afternoon light.

She didn't notice us until I stood beside her, eyes on the flowerbed before us.

"Lovely, aren't they?" Gran looked up at me first, and then her eyes twinkled.

I nodded and hugged her by way of greeting.

"Hello there," Gran hugged me back with one fragile arm, her head turning enough so she spotted Leon behind me. "And who is your friend?"

Leon reached out one hand to greet her, acting very little like the casual Leon I experienced on a daily basis, and I had to stifle a laugh as he sounded as if he were convincing a girl's father he'd return her safe and unharmed after prom-night.

"So you're the one who keeps my granddaughter company when I can't." Gran winked at Leo, who shrugged stiffly, his white shirt wrinkling on his collarbones and blond hair dancing on his forehead.

"Doing my best, Mrs. Dawson." He curled his lips on one side, making his face equally intriguing as the action made it handsome. I let go of Gran and pulled a chair from the white-painted iron table before us. "Naturally, I can never live up to the standards you set during Laney's visits."

They shared a glance.

"You've been hiding him from me for too long, my dear," Gran eventually chuckled and shot me a look that made clear I was to bring Leon every day from now on.

We chatted about school, the weather, and nothing in particular, the way we did every afternoon. But the time we spent together was a sanctuary, reminding me of my childhood, of rainy summer afternoons filled with stories and hot chocolate, of Gran's garden, which had returned to being a wild patch of grass and emerging bushes since she had moved here.

My heart gave a small ache as I eyed her while settling down into a chair; Leon followed my lead and took a chair beside me. It would never again be like that. Her house was where Mom and I had moved to, and slowly, day by day, her spirit retreated from the rooms. That was why I came here every day. While Mom was busy with work, I had the time to visit and listen to her stories.

"You are pensive today," she noted. Even with her thick glasses, there was no detail she didn't miss.

Leon's eyes were on me as I searched for something to say and failed.

"You know, Laney," Gran began, the way she did when she started a new story, "Long before you were born, I knew a gentleman who looked just like Leon." Leon stiffened beside me, his smile not as at ease as usual as we both eyed him.

"I look just like my grandfather when he was young." Leon ran a tan hand through his hair, making it look as if sand was trickling through his fingers. His eyes darted to me, trying to read me.

Gran's gaze followed his as if she was trying to figure something out.

And for a tense second, neither of us spoke.

Then, Gran leaned back in her wheelchair and sighed, eyes wandering back to Leon. "Dean Martin," she said as if she finally figured it out. Both Leon and I stared at her. "You look just like Dean Martin."

While Leon chuckled as if she'd made a joke, a mild shake going through his body, I wondered if there was something wrong with Gran's memory.

She watched Leon as if trailing back into the past, and Leon got to his feet, excusing himself.

I watched him stroll up the ramp and in through the glass doors as Gran grabbed me by the hands in a sudden surge of energy.

"Don't bring him here again." She stared me in the eye, her own eyes suddenly bright and unclouded as if the frailness of old age had fallen off of her.

I started.

"And stay away from him, Laney." She pulled me forward, forcing me to listen. "Do you hear me? Stay away."

I had no idea what she was talking about. But I nodded, so in shock that I didn't have another option.

And just as I wanted to ask why, Leon emerged from the doors, making his way back toward us.

Gran let go and slipped back into her wheelchair, her lips pulling into a benevolent smile.

"We were just talking, that it's time for me to get back inside," she cooed and folded her wrinkled hands in her lap. "Would you mind rolling me up the ramp, Leon?"

3. Laney

On the way out, I waved goodbye to Mr. Frank while Leon, yet again, skipped past his door after he rolled Gran into her room.

Her words resonated with me the entire drive through the sparsely populated area between the nursing home and the main part of the village. *Stay away.*

Leon glanced at me from the side, both hands on the steering wheel, which was wrapped in dark leather so fine it didn't seem to belong in his pickup. Returning his gaze, I studied him as he turned back and focused on the road.

No matter how hard I looked, there was nothing remotely dangerous about Leon Milliari. Not his dark eyes, which had become a refuge whenever the past threatened to catch up with us; or his arms, muscled and gentle, which protectively tucked me against him when we walked; or his humor...

Leon caught me staring. "You can as well tell me what's on your mind," he prompted.

I shook my head, and he gave me a half-smile, which expressed that I didn't need to. At least for now.

"Your grandmother seems nice," he changed the subject, making it hardly any better for me, but I nodded all the same for lack of anything to say. "I could come with you again tomorrow."

For a heartbeat, I didn't know what to tell him. That I didn't want him to come? That wasn't true. I did. But after Gran's warning... The words of an old woman who was slowly losing it, or the words of someone with enough life experience to tell a rotten apple from a good one?

My hand flicked to my lips, and I chewed on my nails instead of thinking of something to say, letting generous silence spread between Leon and me. His driving style was cautious as if he knew that the images of last year were still haunting me. Not one rough break or one turn that he didn't take with utter gentleness. Almost as if he was telling me, by the way he steered the car, that something like *that* would never happen when he was behind the wheel.

I didn't need reminding. I didn't need reassurance. I needed to forget already.

"You seem absent," he murmured as he took the final turn to the main road back to Glyndon.

I shrugged. There were no words for what I was trying to ban from my memory. None—

The tires squealed as Leon stomped on the break just in time to avoid crashing with a sleek black sports car. My body strained against the seat belt, which almost cut off my air supply as it pressed against my chest and shoulder, and I braced myself against the glove box.

My heart jumped into my throat, and one by one, the images came back, letting the momentary pain fade to the background. The heap of scrap metal. The firemen and ambulances. And then there had been the dead—

I shot Leon a look, but his eyes were still on the street where the car had almost hit us, his breathing unnaturally fast. From the frozen expression on his face, I could tell that he remembered them, too. Even if we never spoke about it. Our little secret.

It had been the day of the accident that Leon had practically attached himself to me, becoming a willing protector, a friend far beyond what I'd known until then.

"That was close." The words whistled from my lips as I managed to straighten in my seat and take a breath.

Leon simply nodded, his white-blond hair shifting into his forehead. He brushed it back with a shaky hand, revealing his eyes which—to my surprise—held not shock but raw anger. The expression made me cringe back into my seat.

Leon's fingers, knuckles white, loosened their grip on the steering wheel the second he noticed the way I was eyeing him, and his face softened, returning to the familiar warm coffee brown.

"Good reflexes," I praised, ignoring the sense that there was something more burdening him than that we'd just escaped probable death.

Mom wasn't there when Leon dropped me off a couple of minutes later. He hesitated as I waved at him before closing the car door behind me.

"Is your mom home?" he asked cautiously through a lowered window—his tone one I'd heard less and less often over the past months from sunny Leon.

I leaned down to see his face and shrugged. "Probably still stuck at the office." She was most of the afternoons, making me a devourer of microwaved lasagna and a friend of the quick-boiling veggies of the season.

Leon ran a hand through his hair and nodded. "Then let me help you make dinner."

He didn't wait for my response before he cut the engine and hopped out of the car, and I didn't object, lingering images of the car crash a year ago giving me a migraine.

We walked up to the door in silence, and it was only when we were getting to work on the lasagna—enough for two, my mom was always prepared for Leon—that he asked, "You're still having nightmares about it, aren't you?" His voice was a golden thread through the haze that formed in my head at the memories of the street, the cars, the dead. Not bodies but whatever it was that left their bodies after they had been squished between the metal and concrete. I swallowed.

"You don't need to answer." He didn't look up from the tomato under his knife.

I just watched him slice into the red flesh of the fruit, not remotely ready to answer. Knowing Leon, he already had gotten all the answers he needed from my momentary frozen silence.

Leon didn't come to the nursing home with me the next day. On the way to Gran's room, I noticed more staff in the corridors than usual, their conversations huffed as they all seemed to gravitate toward Mr. Frank's room. I passed by the closed door, wondering what was going on, but noticed that one of the nurses turned into Gran's room in a hurry.

Automatically, my pace quickened, and I made it to the room just in time to see the nurse taking Gran's pulse and blood pressure.

As I entered, she gave me a wide smile, and I waited by the door until she finished taking the vitals before I joined them by the bed.

"Hello, bear," Gran huffed, her skin a shade paler than usual.

"Is anything wrong?" I asked by way of greeting, unable to shake the feeling.

Gran smiled and shook her head, but the nurse took her hand and said, "Your grandmother is undergoing emotional stress. It's not good for her heart."

"My heart is just fine," Gran said with a defiant smile.

Somehow I didn't believe her.

The nurse pulled me aside, letting go of Gran's hand, and whispered, "Mr. Frank died last night."

A jolt of pity ran through my stomach as I glanced at Gran, who had rested her head back against the thick, white pillows and closed her eyes, the smile faded from her lips and her features relaxed except for the crease on her forehead.

Her heart wasn't fine at all. It was weak. I shuddered. Mr. Frank had been her friend for many years, and now ... he was gone. Overnight. Just like that.

I nodded my understanding at the nurse and joined Gran by her bed again, sitting on the edge of the mattress, and waited for the woman to retreat from the room.

"I'm sorry," I told her and reached for her hand.

But Gran shook her head. "We are all old here," she murmured, her voice filled with some humor, making my shudder run deeper.

"Not you," I said, attempting to mirror her tone. "You'll live forever."

She nodded, her eyes bright and open as she lifted her head from the pillows.

"He's in a better place now. And I'll follow someday." There was no humor in her voice though, and I could no longer keep up the smile.

"What happened?" I asked, hoping it would help her to speak about it. But she just shook her head.

"Let's not talk about death, my dear. Life is too short to ponder the inevitable." She sat up in her bed, using the triangle above her to straighten herself. "Have you ditched Dean Martin?"

Something in the lightness of her tone was disturbing. As if her friend's death meant nothing to her—at least nothing that would make it worth mourning.

I shook my head.

Maybe the shock hadn't set in yet. How could I possibly know—

She cocked her head, slowly enough to make it look almost comical, and gave me a long, measuring look.

I remembered her question. All night long, I had been wondering what she might have possibly meant by *dangerous* when she had warned me about Leon. Now that I was sitting there by her side, I somehow felt anxious to know and terrified of the answer all at once.

"Leon?" I squeezed her hand and glanced at the window on the other side of her bed. She had a beautiful view of the garden. "I have been wondering what you meant yesterday."

She gave me a wistful look. "That's a long story," she sighed. "A story for another day when there is less going on." Despite her light tone and playing down Mr. Frank's death, a sudden tiredness had entered her body, making her eyelids droop.

"Today, I think I need to rest." She raised her eyebrows an inch and leaned back into her pillows. "At least, that's what Nurse Peters says."

Before I could respond, her eyes had closed and her breathing became even.

For a while, I sat and held her hand while she slept, wondering what that *long story* was that she wasn't ready to tell me today, until Nurse Peters entered the room with a soft knock to announce her presence and ushered me out, repeating what Gran had just said.

I didn't object—only took a moment to kiss Gran's forehead before I left, navigating through the still rushed movements in the corridor where now two men clad in dark uniform were rolling a stretcher with a covered body.

I gulped down a breath of air, avoiding the inclination to look left or right if I could help it. Last time I had seen a body, I had seen the spirit—or soul, whatever one wanted to call it— leave the mangled mortal remains. It couldn't happen again. It wouldn't. My heart was racing in my chest all the way to the yellow front door, my thoughts embedded in a haze like that day a year ago, since which I had been questioning my sanity.

I stormed down the ramp to the parking lot and didn't slow down until I was halfway to my car. Only then did I dare take in my surroundings; the soft sunlight of the late afternoon, the small cloud framed in orange brightness there on the azure sky. The breeze was playing with my hair like invisible fingers, making a shiver run down my spine, and for some reason, I had the feeling as if I wasn't alone—almost as if a set of eyes had been following from the moment I had seen the coroners. Out of instinct, I turned left and right now, almost at my car, trying to pinpoint the eerie presence that seemed to hover like a ... I didn't allow myself to think it. But I found nothing other than the nursing home behind me, windows reflecting the warm light, wide gardens stretching out to each side before the first neighboring building came into view, and the parked vehicles around me.

With sweaty hands, I fished for my keys and unlocked the car, sliding in and settling in the driver's seat. *There is nothing to be afraid of. Nothing.* I kept chanting it like a mantra. *Nothing.* The way I had been chanting for months since the accident Leon and I had witnessed a year ago—

For a long moment, I just sat there, breathing in and out, trying to flush the memories from my mind and to calm myself enough to be able to drive. But each time the air filled my lungs, a hollow feeling accompanied it, and my hands flew to my chest to soothe the ache as I coughed it out again.

Until eventually, when dusk was already settling, my hands stopped shaking, and the danger of driving agitated seemed like less of a risk than the prospect of staying here after it turned dark.

4. LANEY

The reason the other girls avoided me wasn't my excessively blue eyes but the fact that *he* was with me. Everywhere I went, he came. And they didn't like it. Even more than they hated that he wasn't with them.

I ducked the cold gaze of Avery Macmillan, Leon following behind as I vanished around a corner.

"One day, I'm going to kill them." Leon grinned as he dropped his bag on the floor and settled next to it, resting his muscled forearms on his knees.

"You won't," I reminded him. "And they're just giving me the evil eye because..."

I didn't like to speak about it, the silent pact between Leon and me—

It was the same reason I hadn't told him about Mr. Frank's death and the strange sensation in the parking lot. It would have required bringing up the accident. And our pact with each other was put into place to prevent that exact thing from happening. Those months I had been chanting my mantra that there was nothing to fear out there had made me socially awkward in the worst of ways. Sometimes I even wondered why my other best friend, Jo, stuck with me. I understood Leon; he had seen what I had seen. But Jo ... she had just patiently endured my *phase*.

"Because..." He turned his head, grinning up at me as I leaned against the wall beside him, white-blond hair dancing into his eyes. Eyes like Italian coffee.

I shook my head and slid down beside him, savoring the coolness of the wall as I rested my back against it. His gaze met mine, and there was that look ... that look I had been avoiding acknowledging for the past months—and the way it made me feel.

"You coming tomorrow?" he asked, his eyes resembling the dark roast that made you stay up all night.

With a flutter in my heart, I nodded. He wanted to drive to Towson to get some new books, and instead of telling me he won't be there after my visit at the nursing home, he had invited me to come. It was an offer tempting enough. So I had said yes, knowing that Gran—herself an avid reader—would understand if I skipped one afternoon to spend between neatly packaged and beautifully covered stacks of paper. "Wouldn't miss it for the world." My voice remained—without a trace of what had been bothering all night—surprisingly humorous. So did his gaze. "If you promise me to be at your best behavior."

Leon laughed ... one of those deep laughs that gave away he was intending the exact opposite.

I peeked over my shoulder. The chatter of Avery's minions had faded enough to tell me they had proceeded toward the gym.

Using Leon's white sleeve to pull myself back up, I exhaled the stuffy air of Glyndon High and readied myself for another afternoon of tedium.

Leon walked me to the gym before he turned the corner to the boys' locker room. As I watched him disappear, I couldn't help but admit that I didn't fully understand the nature of our relationship. Yes, Leon was with me all the time. Sometimes, my mother was surprised he didn't insist on staying overnight—he hadn't done that once. And yes, he was heartbreakingly handsome. And yet, there was nothing between us. For some reason, we enjoyed each other's company more than that of the evil-eyed Avery Macmillans of this world.

I chuckled to myself as Leon lifted a hand to wave without even bothering to look back. He knew I'd be watching him the same way I knew he'd wave. We were a team, he and I. A package deal. A package without a label.

As I slipped into the girls' locker room minutes after the bell rang, I was already missing Leon. P.E. was one of the few times during school hours that he and I were separated. Sometimes, I wondered if that was what having a twin brother felt like. And then I remembered the color of his eyes and how he always glanced at me through those unearthly blonde strands of hair. Nope. Not brotherly.

Jo waved at me from the other end of the gym when I made it there a minute later, having changed into my sports uniform so fast it made me wonder if I had just slowed time.

"He didn't let you go?" she asked with a significant look.

I rolled my eyes. "You know Leon." It was enough explanation for me, but Jo shook her head.

"That's the thing, Laney," she started, not without humor as she shoved her glasses further up her nose. "No one really *knows* Leon." She pursed her lips. "No one but you."

She was referring to the summers Leon and I had spent together as children before Dad had left and we'd moved to Glyndon. And the almost twenty-four-seven we spent together ever since Mom and I had moved here for good.

"He's Leon," I explained with a shrug. "He doesn't care if I forget where I am or what I wanted to do." Which frequently happened, and Leon regularly saved me from ending up in the wrong classroom.

Jo raised an eyebrow and tugged on her chin-length chestnut hair, eyes stern behind her glasses. She was one of the few not to care if Leon was charming and radiant and left most girls gaping. She didn't envy our friendship. On the contrary, if there was a reason Jo complained, it was because Leon monopolized me and left little space for our rare girls' nights.

I shrugged again and started running laps as the coach gave us a sharp look, ignoring the chatter and the stares of the others. Ignoring them had become my routine.

Yes, Leon was demanding, time-intensive, but there was no safer place than with Leon. After what had happened... A shudder spread over my shoulders and up my neck to my hairline, as if it was happening again. But I glanced around, and there was nothing unusual there. Just the girls staring and talking. As if a year wasn't enough time to find a different topic to obsess over.

The truth was that they didn't avoid me because Leon preferred my company over theirs but because he—besides Jo—was the only one who didn't care that after being relatively sociable and easy to be around, from one day to the other, I had turned into a distracted odd-ball who stared into blank spaces, on the constant watch for more of them—souls. I liked to think of them as souls. It was easier to give them the name rather than something from a horror movie.

Leon had seen them, there at the accident, too. I wasn't crazy. Just—preoccupied in my mind. And on constant guard of drifting back into those memories.

I thought of Leon's smile and felt the cold on my neck fade.

"Laney?" Jo's voice and uneven breathing brought me back to the present.

I nodded. Everything was fine. *Nothing to be afraid of.*

With a few strong kicks, I launched myself into a faster pace, waving Jo along with me.

She gave a grin of relief as I acted normal, and she ran with me.

The next day, after school, Leon walked me to his pickup, playing with the car key ... and oddly silent.

He had been thoughtful most of the day since he'd picked me up in the morning. He hadn't grinned or winked. His humorous side had not yet shown today even when I had doodled weird animals on my notebook during classes—something that usually entertained him.

There was a frown on his lips that was highly unusual—even for his worst days—as he unlocked the door and watched me climb in and settle in the passenger seat. He closed the door behind me and reluctantly got in the car.

"We don't need to go," I told him, wondering if he would talk to me if I asked what was wrong.

He glanced at me with a look that was almost offended and started the car without taking his eyes off me. "That's the only thing I am looking forward to today," he said with a half-smile. "You don't want to rob me of our afternoon, do you?"

Returning his smile, I shook my head. "Not if I can help it."

For a moment, there was something in the air ... an electric current as he held my gaze, frown dissolving entirely into a full-lipped smile.

"Not if *I* can help it, either." He slid one hand off the steering wheel and took mine from my lap where I was clasping my backpack. "Ready?"

I nodded, letting him, squeezing my fingers not affecting me. Friends. He was my best friend and confidant. The sensation in my palm as he touched me didn't mean a thing.

At least, that was what I told myself.

Leon didn't let go as he steered the car out of the lot, taking us right to the main road that took us out of the small town that had become my mother's and my refuge. The warmth of his fingers wasn't something I wasn't used to. Just the feeling of his skin on mine triggered something today—

For a while, I watched the old houses as we passed out of the town, the white fences of the farms, the meadows dotted with horses ... it was a beautiful, peaceful place that was just right for my mother and me.

"What are you thinking?" Leon leaned over just a bit as if he was asking me to share a secret, his face still holding the smile from before as he glanced at me with interest.

I shrugged. "How beautiful it is here," I told him the truth. He nodded and fell silent again.

So I studied him from the side—the white-blonde hair, the dark lashes, and sun-kissed skin. I frequently forgot that my best friend was also the most beautiful boy in my high school. Watching him drive in silence, focused on the road, and with his smile gradually fading into the pensiveness from earlier, I nodded at my own assessment. He truly was.

But his quietness was new. Even after the accident, when we had made the pact not to speak about what we had seen on the street, he had resumed his cheerful nature quickly—trying to be happy enough for both of us, it sometimes seemed.

"What are *you* thinking?" I asked, forcing nonchalance into my tone.

He glanced at me and met my gaze for a fraction of a second before turning back to focus on the street.

He didn't speak until we made it to Towson where he pulled into the parking lot at a bookstore near the city center. There, he gave me a long look, cutting off the engine and turning to face me as he spoke, "I don't know if I should tell you this, but..." He let his voice trail off, his eyes lingering on mine, drinking in the questions in them.

"Tell me what?" I prompted, my body suddenly very much aware that he had never let go of my hand.

His fingers closed more tightly around mine, his gaze lost. "I shouldn't," he came to his own conclusion and reached for the door, letting my hand slide out of his grasp as he unfolded from the car.

I followed his lead, for once frustrated with my best friend. We didn't have secrets. That was the whole point of our friendship. We had gone through the same shit last year. We had gotten over it together even if we had never truly talked it through. We had both seen dead people, and I wasn't speaking about the corpses—those, too—but about the essence of the people who would never again wander the earth.

Leon had taken me away from the accident so fast that I couldn't tell what had happened to those souls. If they had simply dissolved into thin air, if the ground had opened beneath them and swallowed them; I would never know. Maybe it was best not to know. It allowed me to hope for something better after this life.

As we walked into the bookstore, his face had smoothed over, his smile back in place as if he had never tried to stammer words he wasn't ready to speak.

5. CAS

Her breathing was low, labored, silver-gray hair pasted to her sweating forehead, heart struggling with every weak beat as it galloped toward the certain end.

It would be moments, mere seconds before it was over. I watched her, my breathing half-speed of hers, taking in her features, the wrinkles around the eyes that spoke of the happy moments of her life, and the stark, edged lines between her brows that told me she had spent a majority of her years worrying. Each line told a story, each experience, each thought, positive or negative, permanently marked on her face. An interesting face for sure. And one that had hidden secrets over the span of decades.

I couldn't say I enjoyed waiting for her heart to stop beating, but, most certainly, it was better than being the one I was going to take.

Her heartbeat stuttered.

Any second now.

It was early in the morning, the nursing home quiet except for the muffled voices in the staff room where the night nurses were handing over protocols to the day shift. I smiled as I realized I could as well have been in my visible form, and no one would have seen me but my target.

A few more thuds, and Mrs. Parker's heart would stop for good... or for bad if she came with me.

Surprisingly, none of the others had appeared. *Others* meaning the ones who ensured a good soul went to heaven. While I—

Mrs. Parker tore open her eyes and looked at me, right at me. Not the wall behind me, or the ugly, eggshell-and-pink curtain, but *right* at me.

I froze. Turning to see if I had missed a human, if someone had snuck past me as I had almost dozed off, waiting for her to come around.

Her eyes widened as she recognized me for what I was, and her lips trembled as if she was going to say something— not scream but tell me something, let me in on a secret...

Her heart faltered, and her last breath left her a moment later, eyes still staring ... and staring.

I squared my shoulders and got out of the chair where I had been lounging for the past hour. Time to get ready for work.

With a glance around, I made sure there was no one else there to claim her soul. Even if the old lady might deserve to go with one of them rather than with me—at least, to give her a choice—none of the Lightbringers had come.

I didn't know about her life, but it was likely that she hadn't done all bad.

I glanced at the clock on the wall. 7:39 AM. It had almost been a minute when finally one of them showed up. A boy hardly eighteen, dark eyes ferocious as he noticed me standing by the woman's bed.

From the way his eyes locked on mine as he stalked up to me, I knew what he was, that he saw me.

"Lightbringer," I greeted him, a common courtesy among our kind.

He nodded in return, not half as civilized as our relationship with the other side usually was.

"I was wondering when one of you would show up." I straightened, my eyes drifting back to the woman whose struggle was over—at least the struggle of her body. Her soul was still there, hovering within the tissues of her dead flesh.

The Lightbringer stepped to the other side of the bed, squaring his shoulders, shaking back his ridiculously blond hair. With a quick look, I assessed whether he was a real opponent if it came to a fight.

Wearing a loose white shirt, faded jeans, he was fashionable, young, good looking, I had to admit. But the expression on his face was nothing like the other Lightbringers I had met. There was more about this soul than just wanting to outsmart a Shadowbringer. For him, this was personal.

"I'll let you take the next one, kiddo." I smirked at him and was ready to breathe upon the old lady, flushing her soul out of the lifeless body where it seemed to be cowering, waiting, reluctant to meet its fate—whether it was to go with the infuriated Lightbringer or me.

"No." His tone was dark—the opposite of the shiny bright strands dancing on his forehead—as he held my gaze, leaning in himself, ready to hijack the soul if I dared breathe.

"Okay, the next two," I offered playfully, no longer interested whether this soul deserved to go to hell or to heaven but with annoying the Lightbringer who seemed so prone to letting the situation escalate. My code bound me to not attacking unless I was attacked. It was the one thing that kept the peace between the two sides of the afterlife.

Negotiating for a soul, however, was something that was as common among us as it was for humans to bargain for goods in a market.

"No." His eyes were a dark shade of brown and hard as stone as he answered.

This Lightbringer wasn't ready to bargain.

I stared him down, inhaling deeply, readying myself to do my task regardless of what the boy's claim on the soul was. I had been there first, sent to harvest the old lady and carry her back to the fiery pits of hell. So here I was. That boy wouldn't get in my way, not unless he was ready to give something up for it.

6. Laney

It was about the one-millionth time I wished the clock would stop ticking so I could spare myself walking out into the first truly cool morning of this fall—

This time it did.

I started from the bed to check on the antique alarm-clock on the plain wooden nightstand, hardly believing my own eyes.

"Shit," I whispered as I hit my toe on the stack of books beside my bed, and I crouched down to find myself sitting on top of *Wuthering Heights*.

I would apologize to the book later, but for now, all of my attention was captured by that second hand, which no longer was doing its job.

My hands were shaky as I picked up the heavy metal piece and reached behind it, fingers searching for the small wheel that allowed me to adjust the time and then further up to the bigger, wing-shaped thing that was meant for restarting the clock when it died.

I twisted and let go, expecting the second hand to pick up its duty at release.

But it sat still as the dead.

At 7:38 AM.

I cursed again as I realized that I had almost as much time to get to school as it took to drive half the distance there. Being late wouldn't help the unnoticed entrance I'd been planning.

"Breakfast, Laney!" My mother's call—the same urgent call as any morning—made me abandon my little project and aim for the closet instead.

"Coming!" My jeans were still only half-buttoned as I rushed down the stairs, stumbling over a laundry basket and stack of newspapers.

Mom had a bowl of cereal ready for me, and my hands, just having finished the buttons on my pants, darted out to grab it when Mom's phone rang and I glanced at the clock above the kitchen table.

I halted. 7:38. It was 7:38 there too. It should at least be 7:43.

Mom's lovely face turned to stone as she listened intently.

"What is it?" I whispered to her without failing to keep an eye on the clock. The second hand wasn't moving; the minute hand wasn't moving.

Mom shook her head, nodded, and then she lowered the phone just in time for me to see who the caller was before they hung up.

"Gran passed away." Mom's features were smooth, frozen, no tears freeing themselves—yet.

But I could tell from the way she pulled on her short, coffee-brown hair that she was using her lawyer mask to keep her emotions contained.

And while she remained the image of serene composure, my own eyes grew moist.

"Let's go," she ordered, and I put down my bowl to pick up my jacket, forgetting 7:38 AM as we walked out the door to see my grandmother for one last time.

We were out the door and in the car within a minute and then on the road, winding through the morning traffic.

My stomach tightened at the thought that I had missed my last afternoon with Gran to go book shopping with Leon. Leon whom I saw every day at school, who was available any time, night or day if I needed him. And Gran ... I had stood her up for him.

I pulled my phone out, texting Leon that I would be late for school today, and shoved it back into my bag. Even if Jo would wonder where I was if I didn't show up today, she wouldn't call before the lunch break to check in. But Leon ... he would probably walk out of the school by the end of the first class and drive through the town until he found me if I didn't let him know I was all right. That was how protective he had become since that accident. Even if we hadn't been scathed.

"It's okay, Laney," Mom said and rested her hand on my forearm as she drove, her face still calm and composed. "I'll call the school for you later and let them know you're not coming in today." Her voice was still that of the lawyer, her words almost cold as if there weren't any emotions under that calculated face of hers. It was her protective mask. The mask that got her through the day when she negotiated for clients when she fought their battles. When she was the strong, independent woman she had chosen to be.

And she was the best. I could tell from her stories. She won for a living.

I swallowed, watching her brave face and wishing I had only a fraction of that courage.

Mom pulled into the parking lot at the nursing home and took a deep breath. "We can do this," she said and gave me a look with her electric blue eyes—the same color as mine. The same as Gran's.

I nodded. And something other than the sorrow of losing Gran crept up on me as Mom got out of the car and we headed to the yellow doors, Mom breaking into a jog as if being there a minute or two sooner would make a change. As if Gran wasn't already dead. As if we could somehow save her. Fear filled me. Fear that seeing a dead body meant seeing a soul.

Wrapping my arms around my torso to brace myself for what awaited us inside the building, I followed Mom as she picked up her pace so she wouldn't have to face Gran alone. So I wouldn't walk in there alone.

Mom's mask had crumbled by the time we crossed the threshold, and when the nurse welcomed us with a grave face, tears were running down her rouge-blushed cheeks. I looped my arm around my mother's and gritted my teeth against the fear—and the grief that was already filling my body head to toe. Mom needed me.

The relationship between my mother and my grandmother hadn't always been easy, but I knew how much they loved each other. Saying goodbye would break Mom's heart, and I needed to be there to hold her hand.

The clock on the wall said 8:17 AM when we turned into the corridor that led to Gran's room. Our footsteps echoed along the tiled floor, the pale yellow walls, the framed pictures of flowers and landscapes rushing by as the seconds trickled on.

"She didn't suffer," the nurse said as she stopped before the door, her hand resting on the yellow handle. Everything seemed too yellow for my taste, something I hadn't noticed until today. "When we checked in this morning, she had passed on."

"How do you know she didn't suffer?" My words came out uncontrolled, harsh. As if it was the nurse's fault Gran had finally surrendered to her condition.

The nurse squeezed my arm with a gentle hand and smiled, pity in her eyes. "Your grandmother has been struggling with her heart insufficiency for a long time. Our staff checked with her every hour or two during the nights with her since Mr. Frank's death." I remembered how affected she had been when he'd died. "She was fast asleep when I did my last round. She probably didn't even wake up."

Mom's breath hitched beside me. "Can we ... can we see her now?"

The nurse nodded, releasing my arm and pushing down the door handle. "We left everything as it was so you can say your goodbyes."

Mom nodded at her and stepped through the door, one hand resting lightly at her throat, the other sliding out of my arm as she rushed to Gran's side, picking up the gray hand of what had once been her mother.

On sluggish feet, I followed her into the room but didn't get far, for by my grandmother's bed, two young men were hovering, both of them seemingly unaware of my mother sitting right beside them as they loomed over Gran's body with an eagerness of a scene of nightmares. One with fair hair, his shape familiar, standing with his back to me, and the other with hair black as the night, his eyes locking on mine in shock as he noticed I was staring.

7. LANEY

For a long moment, I just stood, heart racing as I stared, unable to tear my gaze off the dark pits that were the boy's eyes. But I wasn't the only one who seemed to be in shock. The boy's face was pale with the shock of being caught doing—what was it that he was doing there?—but there was also excitement in there, brightening his eyes as he stepped back from the bed and leaned against the pale yellow wall. He lifted a finger to his lips, gesturing for me to be quiet, and braced a foot behind him as he crossed his arms over his black-clad chest.

I swallowed and blinked as he freed me from his gaze, finally able to take in the second boy. The familiar one who had looked up at the other's sudden retreat.

"Leon," I whispered, and horror filled his eyes as he saw me there.

Mom didn't react, probably not having heard me. She didn't seem to notice the two boys either, her attention fully on the dead body.

Leon crossed the room and joined me by the door so fast it was impossible to follow his movements. "What are you doing here?" he whispered and glanced nervously back over his shoulder at the black-haired boy, who was watching intently and with no lack of amusement now.

I shook my head. "That's what I was going to ask you," I responded and wondered if I was hallucinating.

Mom looked up, her gaze finding me easily, unbothered by my tall, blond best friend who was partly blocking her from view. "What were you going to ask?"

Thick black lines of smeared mascara were now streaking down her cheeks.

I looked at Leon then at Mom and back at Leon. He shook his head at me, a plea in his eyes.

What was going on?

"Nothing, Mom." I glanced over my shoulder as I stepped past Leon, who was holding out a hand as if to comfort me, but I didn't let him touch me. There was something very wrong.

If Mom couldn't see them—she obviously couldn't, for she hadn't even stopped a second to acknowledge Leon, nor his storm-eyed companion, who was smirking from behind the bed, head now resting against the wall as he played with some strings of leather attached to his sleeve.

Cold rushed through me as I stepped beside my mother and finally turned my eyes away from the boys, taking in Gran's ashen face, her closed eyes, relaxed, peaceful features.

No pain, the nurse had said. I dearly hoped for Gran that the woman had been right.

I more felt than saw Leon behind me, drifting closer with soundless steps.

"I will explain everything, Laney," he whispered, and again, Mom didn't react. And I did my best to ignore him. If Mom couldn't see them, and I could, that meant that they couldn't really be here. A wishful thought maybe, that Leon was here with me to wrap his strong arms around me as my tears were falling. But the other boy—

Maybe they both weren't here—not really. Not the way I was, or my mother, or the nurses out in the hallways. Maybe they were dead just like after the accident—

A cold so icy that I started shivering ran through my body.

If Leon was dead ... something terrible had to have happened between when he had dropped me off after our trip to Towson last night and this morning when he was supposed to sit beside me in English class.

My gaze lifted to study the other boy, who seemed to have overcome his shock completely and was now giving me a lazy grin before he caught Leon's eye over my shoulder.

"You owe me," he said to Leon before he pushed away from the wall and sauntered out of the room, tilting his head and winking at me as he passed by the bed.

I didn't know what to think, what to believe as I watched the boy, who was there and yet seemed to be visible exclusively to me, disappear through the closed door as if the principles of physics didn't apply to him at all.

I gave Leon a questioning look as Mom's quiet sobs faded to a background noise that reminded me there was a reason I was here, and it wasn't to witness something I wasn't supposed to be able to see.

"Are you dead?" I whispered, hardly believing I was speaking the words.

Mom didn't look up, her hand wrapped around Gran's, murmuring to her as if she could still hear us.

Leon shook his head again and opened his mouth, about to speak, but stopped before even a word came out, his eyes darting to Gran.

My head whipped around, my gaze following his, curious and frightened at the same time to see what had caught his attention.

There, where Gram's body was lying, lifeless and quiet, on the bed, her shape had started moving away from her ... not her shape. A second version of her, translucent and glimmering, slightly silver as she peeled herself from her body.

I sucked in a breath at the sight, my hand automatically searching for Leon's, but he had disappeared from behind me, now standing on the other side of the bed, eyes intent on the flickering form hovering over Gran's dead body right between us.

Mom hadn't moved, probably hadn't realized there was something more going on here. Not too absorbed in mourning her mother but oblivious to what was happening.

Leon pinned me with his gaze. "I am sorry for your loss, Laney," he whispered and leaned in toward Gran's soul, blowing a gust of air onto the translucent form.

The cold in my body eased for a moment, but only because I was so violently shaking that I had started sweating from the strain. This was worse than the accident. There were my best friend and my grandmother, invisible to my mother, and I couldn't find it in me to simply turn away and pretend this wasn't happening, the way we had done with the accident. All I could do was stare at Gran's soul as she opened her eyes and looked at me fiercely before saying, "Be careful who you give your heart to, Laney." Her words were still lingering like a thread of silver as her form began to collapse into a shimmering star, which hovered between Leon and me.

Leon gave me a wary look as he leaned closer to the star. "Look away, Laney," he said and waited for a second. But I couldn't look away. I had to see what was happening. I had to see—every little detail.

He opened his mouth and inhaled deeply, and Gran's soul slipped in between his lips, disappearing, until Leon's gaze was no longer the deep brown of Italian coffee but flickered with the silver light that was no longer filling the room.

"I will explain," he promised, scrutinizing my frozen features for another moment before he dissolved into thin air before me, leaving me to the suddenly deafening sobs of my mother and the empty shell that used to be my grandmother.

8. LANEY

The door banged as I barged from the room, tears streaming from frustration as much as from grief.

"Laney!" Mom's voice was a weak tether struggling to hold me back as she called my name over and over again.

I kept walking. And walking. And walking. Until I was out of the building that now no longer seemed friendly with its flowerbeds in the gardens and its sunshine-yellow doors, with its smiling staff and the cozy room where Gran had kept pictures of Mom and me on the tiny bedside table. Until I was walking from the parking lot out into the street, following it with surprising energy.

There was only one image in my mind: Gran's flickering, silver soul looking me in the eye.

Be careful who you give your heart to, Laney.

Were those the last words from her? Her final message for me when she realized I could see her. Not, *I love you.* Or, *Take care of your mother.* Or, *I wish we had more time.*

No. *Be careful who you give your heart to, Laney.*

And I had been too petrified to say anything. To tell her 'thank you' for those final years, thank you for countless conversations. To tell her how much I loved her. To ask her why she had warned me about Leon...

Well, it seemed that was a secret that, as of today, was no longer a secret. *What* had he done to her?

The image of him inhaling her soul before he disappeared wouldn't leave my head.

A car honked loudly as it rushed past, making me jump into the grass and pause for a moment.

The nursing home already lay a good half-mile behind and I wasn't certain if the shapes in the parking lot were even truly visible—to the rest of the world. I could no longer tell if anyone I saw was alive or was a ghost, a soul, whatever.

I scrubbed my fingers over my face, trying to wipe away what had happened, what I had seen—and Mom obviously hadn't.

Dirt covered my sneakers as I trudged forward on the grass, no longer daring to step onto the road itself, my fingers clammy from clutching my bag against my chest, and the chill air caressing my tear-wet cheeks like the fingers of a ghost. I shuddered.

It took minutes, maybe longer, before a car stopped beside me, and Mom's voice sounded through the open window, "Hop in, Laney, and let's talk about it."

What should I talk about? She had no clue what had happened to Gran.

I gingerly stepped around the car and climbed into the passenger seat anyway, my eyes on my bag, finding the gray and purple pattern suddenly more fascinating than anything else.

"You scared me there for a minute," Mom said, her voice calmer than before at the nursing home, "when you ran out."

I didn't look up—not yet—unable to face her grief. The same grief I should be experiencing when all that I could muster was frustration and fear of what I had seen. Disbelief.

"Sorry, Mom." It was all I could bring myself to say.

"I'm sorry, too." She reached over with one hand and stroked my cheek the way she used to when I was a little girl. "She loved you so much, you know." She smiled a smile punctured by the pain of loss.

I nodded.

"What now?" I wondered. It was the one question that applied to both Gran's death and what I had witnessed in her room.

Mom pulled in at Santoni's on the way back to town, parking right by the white pillars at the entrance, and turned to face me, one hand still on the wheel. "Now, we take a deep breath and have breakfast before we do anything else."

I saw the tears returning to her eyes now that she no longer needed to focus on driving, but she wiped them away with the back of her hand and reached into her bag to dig out her phone.

As she dialed the number of the school, I sat, immobile, and watched her brave the situation the way she braved her war rooms at work. I listened to her calm voice explaining to the dean that I wasn't going to come in today and promising him that she would make sure I got my homework assignments from Jo or Leon.

Jo, I wanted to scream, anxious to avoid Leon now that I no longer knew who or what he was. I remained silent.

When Mom was done, she motioned for me to get out of the car, and I followed her into the store, right into the bakery section where she ordered two raspberry Danish and two coffees—something we sometimes ordered when we were too lazy to cook breakfast at home on weekends. My attention drifted as we were waiting for the order, eyes grazing over the rows of shelves just to have something to do while the emptiness in my chest started spreading.

Right between the popcorn and the display of delicious spreads, a shadow appeared almost as if I were looking through smoky glass. My pulse quickened, fingers digging into my forearms as I clutched them before my stomach, half-expecting to be punched in the guts.

In the background, I acknowledged Mom telling the staff about Gran's passing. Some of them knew her from before she moved into the nursing home. I heard their condolences and their comforting tones, but I couldn't bring myself to look away from the spot where the shadows thickened and began winding as if testing the air.

"Laney?" I hardly heard Mom as she held out my coffee but turned as she touched my shoulder. "Are you all right?"

With slow fingers, I took the takeaway cup from her and nodded my thanks. I lifted the cup to my lips, ready for the hot latte, something to ground me, when behind her shoulder, a familiar face peeked through the shelves.

It took me a second to realize it was the same young man with shadow-gray eyes who was observing me from the shadows of the aisles.

I cringed as hot liquid trickled onto my hand instead of into my mouth, at the sight of the second boy who had stood by Gran's bed.

You owe me, he had told Leon. Owe him what?

I tried to look away, but the dark intensity of his gaze pinned me, his lips curling slightly as if he found something particularly amusing.

For a moment.

When he realized I was staring right back, his smirk faded, replaced by something more, something cold, hostile.

I was lifting a foot to take a step in the boy's direction, not knowing exactly what I was going to do or say once I made it to the aisle. But Mom's hand offering a raspberry Danish on a small paper plate made me hesitate before I set the foot down. It was one moment too long. One moment during which the shadows dissolved and the boy was gone.

It took me half the day to shake the sense of paranoia. In every dark corner, I saw him. His pale features—not in detail, for I hadn't seen him from up close, just a stark contrast of black and chalk white. And his amusement, which I could have picked up from a mile away.

But he wasn't the only one I was scared of seeing. Leon had texted me about a hundred times since I had left the nursing home, not to mention as many missed calls. At some point, I had tossed the phone into the plain, black dresser that stood against the teal wall across from my bed.

After our Danish-breakfast, Mom and I had spent the day sitting on the couch, talking about Gran, about the stories she used to tell when Mom was little, the ones that Mom had told me, too. About Gran's love for black-and-white movies, our afternoons together...

Tears had flowed until we both were devoid of any of them and were just grieving in silence and bitter-sweet smiles.

Now that the sun was setting, I could no longer ignore that this was all true, that Gran was dead. Truly dead. That someone—Leon if he truly had been Leon—had sucked her soul into their lungs with a simple breath and vanished, taking her God-knew-where.

I shuddered as I curled up in bed, pressing my pillow against my chest, and the images of a year ago washed through me.

Cars running toward each other, too fast to avoid a crash. The deafening sound of the impact. The sudden silence as they came to a halt after spinning into the field beside the road. Leon's hand grabbing mine as he froze beside me. The people, too many. As many as there were seats available in two cars. Not really the people, for their bodies had been crushed, mangled, twisted, torn, but something else. Some half-translucent version of human shapes flickering in the light of the afternoon sun as they hovered above the street, waiting ... turning toward us ... waiting ... waiting ... waiting as if they were expecting us to help them. The relief when police had shown up and interviewed people who had witnessed the accident from closer by. The moment we had decided to leave ... the emptiness in my chest, my fingers clutching the front of my shirt as if I could soothe the hollow feeling, smooth it out somehow. Our footfalls, loud on the concrete as we walked away ... Leon's face as he realized I had seen what he had seen ... and the conversation that followed.

I shook the memories away.

If I was honest with myself, seeing Gran's soul leave her body shouldn't have shocked me the way it did. It should uplift me to know that there was something after death other than a black hole of oblivion.

It didn't. It gave me a headache. It made me want to scream. To thrust my fists into my mattress the way I had a year ago after Leon and I had shared what we had seen and decided no one in their right mind was going to believe us. When we had decided silence was the only way to deal with it. To make it un-happen again.

Now. There was no way I could deny any longer either of the things that had happened. Gran's death and the emptiness it left in me; no more afternoons together, no more discussions about her favorite movies, about the best way to pot plants in spring. And the knowledge that there were things—invisible things—that had been there at the nursing home. Gran's soul. But something more. Leon, who had been invisible to Mom but not to me, and the other boy who seemed to have had some kind of conflict with my best friend.

I sat up, no longer comfortable with the coziness of the bed. Anything too comforting could no longer be true if Leon wasn't who I had believed him to be. He had been the perfect companion over those past years. My sunshine. My friend. And now, what was he—?

Stay away from him, Laney. Gran's words echoed in my mind. *Be careful who you give your heart to.*

Had she known something was different about him? She hadn't seemed surprised to see him there when her soul left her body. She had known I saw her.

I flung my hands to my head, attempting to contain the headache unfolding as my thoughts circled helplessly around the image of her flickering shape, dissolving into a silver star ... and Leon inhaling her in a deep breath, disappearing into thin air.

A buzz sounded from the dresser, making me unfold from the bed and open the sock drawer where my phone was ringing again, the display showing the face of my white-blond friend in a white Henley, and his name in a simple, clean font: *Leon Milliari.*

9. Laney

"Are you okay?" he asked by way of greeting, his voice so familiar and yet not. That of a stranger, of an invisible man, of a soul sucker.

I frowned at the wall, noticing the tiny fissures in the paint where I had been too lazy to do a second round when I had redone the room last year.

"Laney?"

It cost me all my strength to say hello and try to remember what he had asked me before. All I could see was how the silver star had disappeared in between his lips.

"I was with Mom all day," I said, feeling that it sounded like an excuse, not an explanation.

"And now?" There was concern in his voice; even over the phone, it was obvious.

"I am debating if I should go to bed early." A glance at the setting sun told me that I wouldn't be able to get a minute of sleep until the darkness of night swept me away—or exhaustion.

"I need to talk to you."

I couldn't respond. He needed to talk to me.

I will explain.

Was that what he intended to do? Was I ready for it? The icy cold from the nursing home overcame me once more, and I closed my eyes with a sigh.

"Can I come over?" he asked as I didn't respond. "Or will your mom throw me out?"

I heard the real question in his tone. *Will* you *throw me out?*

My fingers were suddenly slippery as I thought of the prospect of him being in the same room with me. Of the invisible boy who had taken my Gran somewhere. Gran had warned me about him. To stay away...

"You don't need to drive all the way here," I said, unable to predict if fear was going to outmatch my curiosity. For the moment I had picked up the phone, I had felt it tingle in my chest, the pull of the secret that he had to share, that I had witnessed, to talk about everything that had been bottled up for a year, banned from our thoughts as well as possible. It was as if his voice had torn open the pit in which we had buried it.

"I don't need to drive," he said with something like unease in his tone, making me wonder if he was afraid to face me.

I sure was to face him.

"What, you are already here at the door?" I prompted, half-afraid to hear the answer.

"No." I could picture him shaking his head at the phone as he spoke, blond strands dancing on his forehead. "But now I am here."

I stumbled into the dresser as I turned around at his voice, no longer in the speaker of my phone but right behind me.

My knee hit the black wood, and I gasped in pain, turning on one foot and cursing under my breath.

"Hello," he whispered, face unreadable, sending me into nervous hyperventilation as I hopped toward the bed.

Leon whirled around, kneeling on the gray carpet before I could object, holding my knee between his fingers, eyes intent on my jeans as if waiting for blood to seep through the fabric.

I tried to slide back, but his hands held fast.

"It's not as bad as it looked," he said, letting go of my knee, and I wasn't certain he was talking about my knee.

He sat back onto his sneakers, hands resting on his thighs, and waited for my breathing to slow, his coffee brown gaze unusually insecure as it searched my face for signs I was ready to talk.

I wasn't. How had he just popped up out of thin air? How, for God's sake?

Then the scene from the nursing home replayed in my mind, Leon disappearing with Gran's soul in his mouth, his lungs, or whatever separate organ he might possess. I shuddered involuntarily and slithered further away from him, folding my legs on the bed, out of his reach. Not that it would make any difference. If he had just hopped from his house right into my room, he could probably overpower me even if I ran to the other end of the world.

"How—" I gulped down a couple more breaths before I managed to steady my voice. "How did you do that?" I wasn't sure if I meant his travel mode or what I had witnessed in Gran's room. Either way, I asked.

The tension crumbled from Leon's face like a mask at the sound of my voice—or the indication that I was ready to talk.

"I am glad you are asking the easy question first." His lips split into a weak smile. Not weak. Uncertain.

He studied me for a moment as if debating whether I could handle the answer. "You know you *can* kick me out," he said, darkness entering his expression at the offer.

"And what good would that do?" I found myself asking in return, holding his gaze, my voice still not up to the standards I had mastered over the past year when shakiness had been dominating my every word in the first weeks after the accident. It was as if no time had passed as Leon straightened and gestured at the edge of the bed.

I shrugged, the same way I had a year ago. And Leon sat down in the exact same way he had after the accident, forearms resting on his thighs, fingers interlaced between his knees, looking at the floor. Only this time, there was a comfortable distance between us, his warmth too far away to be comforting ... and far away enough to keep my panic at bay.

His weight shifted the mattress enough that I unfolded my legs, setting my own feet down onto the carpet.

"I'm sorry for your loss," he said, not looking up, face hidden by white-blond strands.

For a moment, I eyed him from the side, anxious to meet his gaze, but then I turned away. This wasn't the Leon I knew. This was some strange version of my Leon, soul-sucking and invisible ... wait, *was* he invisible right now? If Mom walked in, would she be able to see him?

"Thank you," I said for lack of a better response and absently rubbed my knee where a bruise was probably already developing under my pants.

My gaze fell on the alarm clock on the nightstand. 7:38. My chest tightened.

"Why are you here?" I finally asked when I had given up on knowing how much time had passed.

Leon straightened beside me, his movements as familiar as my own, and yet strange. "I promised I would explain."

Our gazes finally met as I turned to face him. Coffee brown, vivid eyes stared back at me with sorrow and wisdom I had never noticed before. My breathing slowed as I held his stare, the depths of his eyes like an anchor ... and yet...

"Then explain," I murmured, unable to look away.

It was Leon who broke the gaze, freeing me of the intensity of his eyes, of the years of memories of growing up together ... and the image of him inhaling the silver star of Gran's soul.

"You weren't meant to be there," he said, staring at his hands now, at the floor, at the wall, the ceiling. Anything seemed to make him more comfortable than my measuring gaze, the questions burning there. "I was meant to pick her up last night, but she held out longer ... long enough for you to wake, for you to come to the nursing home so you could hear her final words. So that you would *see* me..." His voice trailed away as if realizing what he was saying didn't make any sense to me.

He got to his feet like the Leon I remembered, but somehow each of his movements was more deliberate, not as carefree. For a minute, he paced the small space between the door and the dresser, frowning each time he met my gaze.

"You knew Gran was dying?" I prompted before I added the other suspicion, the one that made ice crawl up and down my spine. "Or you killed her?" My words were less than a whisper. Not Leon. Not my Leon, who had been my rock since childhood. But then, did I truly know who *my* Leon was? After today—

He stopped in his tracks, horror on his face as if he was just realizing this was the obvious conclusion to his words. "Of course, I didn't kill her, Laney," he purred and continued pacing. "I wasn't even there when she died the way I should have been ..." His brows furrowed more deeply as he studied the uninteresting gray of the floor.

As for me, I had no idea what to make of his words, what to believe, what to even think. So I sat and watched him unravel what he had to say. Better not jump to conclusions too fast.

What would have helped was to know which questions to ask in order to get some answers that made sense to me ... and the nerves to not run screaming from the room at the sight of what was obviously impossible.

"What were you doing there? What did you do to her?" One question at a time would have been better, but I couldn't hold them in.

The corners of Leon's mouth twitched at the urgency in my voice. He knew me too well to conceal how I was feeling; the fear, the curiosity, the grief that threatened to swallow me whole.

"I was there to take your grandmother to heaven." His words hung in the air between us as he stopped right before me, leaning down a bit, the way he had over Gran's bed when I had entered the room this morning. Reflexively, I shrank back, unsure if he was planning to do the same to me, ridiculous as it may sound.

"Heaven," I prompted, hearing the mockery in my own voice. If there were such a thing as heaven—

"Yes, heaven," Leon said, leaning closer until he was bracing his hands on either side of my legs on the bed. His eyes were the Italian roast type of intense once more, making my breath catch—not just from fear. But there was something more to Leon than I had noticed until now. Something dangerous, something incomprehensible, something divine... "And *you*, Laney, saw me." He was close now. So close that I could feel his breath on my face. "You weren't supposed to, and yet, you *saw* me. And you saw *her*." He didn't move as I wriggled out from between his braced arms, putting the entire bed between us before I dared look at him again. There was no reason for denying it. We both knew it was true.

For a moment, he appeared like he was going to leap across the covers and attack me, harm me, do something to silence me. Only ... he didn't. He remained where he was, his eyes on mine ... and they softened.

"I didn't think it would ever happen," he whispered and finally sank to his haunches, his arms resting on the bed.

"What would ever happen?" I asked, the changed expression on his face making him look more like my friend than ever, and yet ... different. There was a hint of frustration pinching his brows, and his smile was only half the standard I was used to from *my* Leon.

I loosed a breath as I studied him, the boy I had grown up with, and not. The creature who had taken my grandmother to heaven—if I could believe him. But ... what reason was there not to? I had seen him when he was invisible to my mother. I had seen Gran's soul. I had seen it tighten into a star and wander into his mouth. I had seen him vanish. The only gap was what had happened after. Had he truly taken her to heaven? Did heaven really exist?

With shaky fingers, I pulled myself up, crawling a bit closer to him on the bed just to be able to look into his eyes. "Who are you, Leon Milliari?" It was the only question left to ask. "And no evasions," I added. "The truth."

10. Laney

Leon rested his forehead on his arms and sighed, making me wonder if he was going to evade my question or if he was simply summoning the right words to his lips.

"I'm a Lightbringer, Laney." He lifted his head as he spoke, not allowing any emotion into his voice, any hope that I would understand—or accept—what he was saying.

I wondered how long I could play with the end of my braid until it would become obvious I had no clue what he was talking about. Judging by the way his features tightened, he already knew and was waiting for me to demand more information. That was so much the Leon I knew that it was almost a reason to smile—always careful, patient, waiting for me to be ready. He had not once pushed for me to take him to visit Gran. And now that I had seen him depart with her soul contained within him, I wondered, if that was the reason why. If he had known that one day—I could hardly think the words—he would be the one to be there when she died.

"What is that?" I asked, unable to bring myself to fake enthusiasm. I didn't want to know, really—and yet, I did. Because it was crucial to know what had happened to Gran. Where her soul had gone. Or I would go crazy at some point, imagining her somewhere in the wind, in the sky, in the stream behind the forest. It couldn't happen. I couldn't turn any crazier than I already was. I had seen the *dead*, for God's sake. I had seen them a year ago and again today. Only, today, I had seen Leon with new eyes, too.

He sighed, resorting to sitting on the edge of the bed again, leaving a good distance between us; hardly enough to avoid him if I intended to. I didn't.

"I am a messenger angel, a collector of souls, a deliverer of the pure to the bright side of afterlife." Leon held my gaze, his eyes pained with my long silence as I stared at him, trying to see it. Searching for something that gave away he was telling the truth, that it wasn't all a bad dream.

"Angels don't exist," I breathed, my gaze darting to his broad shoulders where I was expecting some sort of wings to emerge ... and found only his plain white shirt making a nice contrast with his golden tan neck.

"Are you sure?" was all he said and slid a bit closer, bringing one knee up on the bed and angling his body sideways as if to willingly expose his back a bit more.

I leaned forward, curious, now that he offered the view ... but there was nothing indicating wings in the slightest.

"I can take off my shirt," he suggested, and it was only then that I noticed there was dry humor in his words.

"There are no wings," I concluded. And he shook his head, lips twitching a bit despite the still pained look in his eyes.

"No wings, but I am one of them, nonetheless." He laced his fingers together in his lap. "With or without wings."

"And you take souls to heaven," I repeated what he had said about Gran.

Leon nodded, a muscle feathering in his jaw as he studied my face, my eyes, my clasped-together hands. "That's all I do with them." He took a deep breath as if bracing himself for what he was going to say. "I arrive when their mortal shells die and collect them to carry them to safety."

He gave me a look that wasn't that of the Leon I knew but of some mythical creature who wasn't supposed to exist ... who knew that they weren't supposed to exist. At least, not in my rational world where life functioned because of the laws of physics and the rules that applied to everyone.

"I am still the same Leon," he said, holding one hand out to me as if he were going to touch me, but he dropped it between us on the blanket as I shook my head.

"You're not," I whispered, averting my gaze from those eyes that belong to the one who had helped me through so many days when I hadn't had the strength to do it on my own, from his hand which had innocently held mine over and over again until...

Until I had walked into Gran's room and found him there. Him and the other boy.

"Was the other one a Lightbringer, too?" It was hard to pronounce the word without letting my lips twist with the turmoil of emotions that welled in my chest.

Leon shifted, one hand running through his hair as he thought about how to answer.

"Was he?" I prompted.

He eyed me as if I was going to break if he told me one more thing.

Maybe he was right.

I pushed anyway. "Was he a Lightbringer, Leon?"

He shook his head, and for a moment, I thought he believed he was going to get away with that tiny response. But then, he pursed his lips and nodded to himself. "He is the exact opposite of what I am."

Great. Another riddle. I frowned at the *angel*—it hurt my head to think about it.

"He takes them to hell." Leon rushed out the words as if hoping I wouldn't catch them if he only spoke fast enough.

But I heard him very well. "Hell?" A hysterical giggle escaped my lips. "You are trying to tell me that hell actually exists?"

He gave me a look that apparently was supposed to be answer enough.

"Hell, Leon. Seriously. Heaven and Hell."

He kept staring ... until the giggle ebbed ... and I realized that he was dead serious. That what he had told me was a secret, not a joke. It was a plain truth that I should have acknowledged the day I had seen the dead rise from the mangled cars. And I had never given it a thought. I had never taken a moment to let myself consider what it meant, what happened to us when we died.

"He is a Shadowbringer."

The storm-gray gaze, the amused smirk, the pale face of the other boy flashed through my mind at Leon's words. The way he had leaned against the wall at the nursing home, how he had stared from between the aisles at Santoni's. The shadows that had veiled the air before he had turned up there.

"A Shadowbringer," I repeated, letting the word settle.

"Shadowbringers take souls to the eternal shadows of hell while Lightbringers take them to heaven." Leon seemed pleased that I hadn't run screaming from the room—or kicked him out.

I was honestly considering it as my mind threatened to explode, but Leon's gaze held me in place.

"You are taking this much better than I expected," he murmured, and I wasn't sure if he had meant to speak the words.

"Much better how?" I asked anyway. Now that we were finally talking, did it matter any longer to pretend to be able to keep it together? A tear slipped from my eye. "There was someone there trying to take Gran to hell." It was the logical conclusion. If they had both been there, the Lightbringer and the Shadowbringer, then they must have bargained for Gran's soul.

You owe me, the Shadowbringer had said to Leon before he had walked out.

Leon lifted a hand to wipe the tear away, but I cringed out of reach.

Hurt flickered across his face at my reaction, but he said nothing.

"He said you owed him before he walked out," I prompted. "What did he mean?"

Leon gnawed his lower lip. I had never seen him do that. Not even when we had snuck out of school early to go sit by the stream and talk about all those things none of our classmates cared about. Except for Jo, maybe. But somehow, Leon never included her in those little adventures. They were only for the two of us, he had said once as if telling me a secret.

"What did he mean?" I repeated, the scenarios unfolding in my mind threatening to paralyze me. If Leon had made some kind of bargain with the Shadowbringer for Gran's soul—

Leon's lip was white where he had been chewing it as he opened his mouth to speak. "Your grandmother refused to die until she knew there was a chance to see you, and then she refused to leave her body until you were actually there." His words sounded as absurd as if he were telling me that angels were real—wait, that was exactly what he had told me earlier. I swallowed hard to get my throat freed up in case I finally felt like it was right to yell at him. "*He* was there when I came to pick her up, and she was still fighting death. I don't know if he had anything to do with the delay, but I checked in every hour for her and—" He stopped mid-sentence, noticing my open-mouthed stare. "I can stop, Laney, if it is too much for you to comprehend," he offered. "I can go home and give you space to process what I shared. And we'll meet tomorrow and talk again ... if you feel like it," he added.

Again, the offer to give me time, to wait for me to be ready. But would I ever be ready to hear the rest? Did it make a difference if he told me everything now?

I shook my head. "How much worse can it get?"

Leon's chuckle filled the air. Not the carefree sound I grew up with but close enough that, for a moment, I could fool myself that he would tell me all this had been a joke.

"The Shadowbringer was there to bargain for your grandmother's soul. He was ready to do it when your mother came in, and he would have, even with her there, hadn't you walked in"—he gestured into the air as if what was following was obvious—"and seen us. Both of us."

I remembered the expression of shock on the other boy's face.

"I didn't even notice you could see me in my non-corporeal form until I saw the Shadowbringer stare at you. And then—" He stopped himself, dropping his hands again. "Well, you were there for the rest."

I had been there for the rest as he said. I had seen the two of them linger over Gran's body and wait for her soul to peel off her body. Until the other boy had retreated and observed with amusement as if he was watching a particularly entertaining show. "Why did he stop?" I wanted to know. "Why did he leave her to you and not bargain at all?"

With all the things Leon had told me, all the events that I could hardly wrap my head around, nothing had scared me the same way as the fright that mirrored in his eyes as he said, "Because he found something much more valuable to bargain for."

The blood froze in my veins. "And what is that?"

Leon gave me a long, measuring look, as if deciding whether or not I could take the news, before he wiped both hands over his face in exasperation. "You."

11. LANEY

I didn't know whether to laugh or cry.

"Why?" Surprisingly, my question sounded dry. Not at all as panicked as I felt inside.

Leon surveilled me with concern as I paced from the window to the bed and back to the dresser.

"Why would the Shadowbringer be interested in me?"

It didn't help that Leon didn't jump an answer at me but seemed to be searching for the right words to say.

"Oh, just spit it out." I finally stopped at the dresser and leaned against it, biting the nails on one hand as I waited for him to sort his thoughts.

"I don't know if you've noticed, Laney, but not everyone can see us." He paused, letting me grasp the meaning of his words.

"Mom didn't see you," I followed the direction he was leading me—or thought I did, "at the nursing home. She has no clue you were there."

He nodded, features relaxing a bit as he realized he wouldn't need to explain every little detail.

"But your grandmother did." His fingers drummed on his knee as he spoke. "She knew exactly what I am the day you brought me to the nursing home."

In my mind, Gran's face as she had told me to stay away from Leon flashed by. She had known. And she hadn't told me. Hurt flickered in my gut.

"Your family is special, Laney. You have the blood of Lightbringers in your veins as does your mother, and as did your grandmother."

I sucked in a breath, tempted to ask if he was certain, but what was the point in trying to deny that something *was* different. That I *did* have the ability to see souls and Lightbringers ... or Shadowbringers. I shuddered.

"But Mom couldn't see you," I objected anyway. Maybe he was mistaken after all. Maybe this was all just one big coincidence. "Mom doesn't know."

"She doesn't," Leon verified. "She has the blood, but the ability jumps one generation or more sometimes."

I eyed him, anxious to see how serious his face was, and was surprised to see his features had softened. There was true compassion in his eyes now that he was speaking freely, no longer keeping this secret—this burden—from me.

"Your grandmother wasn't a Lightbringer, but the ability to see us, and to see souls, manifested in her. And you"—he gave me a look that made me feel bare—"might be the next Lightbringer. We have been anxiously waiting for one to emerge. You might be it."

I slid down to the floor and hugged my knees for lack of anything better to do, anything to say. I couldn't be one of them. I couldn't. Simply couldn't—

"It's all right, Laney." Leon got to his feet and joined me by the dresser, resting his arm against my shoulder. I didn't cringe this time. "This is a lot for you to process."

I slowly breathed in and out, remembering faces flickering before my inner eye as I went through my last years. Leon, how he had grown into the man he was today; Mom, Gran, both kind and smart and loving. Then, the gray eyes of the Shadowbringer, his pale face, bluish-black hair.

"What does he want from me?" I asked instead of succumbing to panic.

Leon understood who I meant. "There is a brief window of time when a new Lightbringer manifests, during which their sight and light can be stolen." He eyed me from the side, gaze weighing heavily on me as he explained.

"What do you mean, *steal sight and light*?" I asked, not daring more than a whisper.

"Losing your *sight* means you can no longer find the souls who need your help. And losing your *light* means they take your soul right to hell as a trophy." He paused as if unsure what he was saying was clear.

I didn't dare move for fear his words would turn into reality if I as much as breathed.

Leon leaned away from me just enough to be able to look into my eyes, his gaze dark and serious as he said, "I can't let that happen. I cannot let you be taken away to hell."

For some reason, his words did little to reassure me.

"As a trophy," I repeated, trying to suppress the surge of panic. "Does he need to kill me to do that?" I couldn't believe I was speaking the words.

To my relief, Leon shook his head. And then it settled in that what he was saying might be much, much worse than death could ever be.

Leon noted the fear in my eyes, for he reached out with one arm and wrapped it around my shoulders, pulling me toward his familiar, warm chest where I rested my cheek and let my tears flow.

A messenger angel was what he was. If Leon was telling the truth, he was the next closest thing to heaven I would meet on earth. Except for—well, me.

If that was the truth, too, I was on my way to becoming just like him. A Lightbringer. A messenger angel.

I shuddered, and Leon's arm tucked me in more tightly.

"The Milliari family has been watching over your family for a long time," he said into my hair as salty wet soaked from my eyes into his shirt. I let him speak, unable to respond. "My grandfather was the one to look after your grandmother. Remember how she said she knew a man who looked just like me when she was younger." He waited for my quiet nod before he continued, "Well, that was my grandfather. Mom always says I look just like him. Down to the way my hair won't straighten in the back. They even named me after him. Leon."

He obviously found some humor in his words, for he chuckled to himself, the sound a low rumble in his chest.

"Dad looked after your mom ... not as intensely as I am watching over you as hers is the generation that skipped the abilities. But there is a reason our families have been close all those years."

As I listened—besides having learned that there were Lightbringers and that I might turn into one unless a Shadowbringer made me a trophy—a new kind of fear overcame me. The fear that Leon wasn't what he had been letting me believe he was. My friend.

"So that's why you keep putting up with me," I whispered into his chest, and a rumbling laugh shook through his body, making me tear out of his arms and glance at the door, anxious my mother might be able to hear him and come up to check the room.

"That's one of the many reasons," he answered plainly, a smile still apparent in his voice.

Mom didn't come to check on me that night, so after a long, long conversation, which left me wondering if anything I had believed was true, I headed downstairs to find Mom fast asleep on the couch, still in the same clothes from this morning. I picked up a blanket from the cupboard and wrapped it around her as she blinked her eyes open.

"Is it morning already?" she mumbled, half-asleep, mascara smudged on her lids and down her cheeks.

I shook my head. "Sleep, Mom." I kissed the top of her head and watched her eyes slide shut once more, grief and pain wiped away by the bliss of sleep's oblivion.

"I love you, Mom," I whispered before I slouched back up the stairs and into the bathroom, running through the quickest routine to get ready for bed.

When I returned, Leon was standing by the open window, facing the meadow behind the house. I studied him from the threshold; his tall shape, broad shoulders, the shock of white-blond hair dancing around his head in the September breeze. His muscled back and neck was something I had rarely paid attention to. It was, for a fact, more than one would expect from a seventeen-year-old boy in high school. But his carefree nature, his jokes, Leon as I had gotten to know him during my childhood, made it easy to forget he had grown into a man. I swallowed the sensations that came with the acknowledgment of what was obvious—besides the other things like he was a freaking angel. A messenger angel, whatever that meant in the hierarchy of angels ... if there even was a hierarchy.

"She is lucky not to know of this world," he said, without turning, and closed the window.

I could see the reflection of his face in the glass now, the elegant features as he met my gaze as if through a mirror.

I nodded. If, after today, there was one thing I was sure of, it was that no one should be drawn into this world if they can help it. Mom was safer not knowing a thing about souls and Lightbringers or ... Shadowbringers. My chest tightened at the thought that someone would be hunting me for my own soul. Even if it was just for a brief window of time—whatever that meant.

Leon would have to explain in more detail. Soon. But not tonight.

I caught myself yawning as he strode over, his gait slow, tired, almost as if my yawning had released him from his own tension.

"You don't mind if I stay tonight, do you?" he asked and flopped onto the floor beside my bed, waiting for me to settle.

I did. In my clothes. Closing my eyes, I slept until the early, graying morning.

Mom didn't wonder when Leon rang the bell before breakfast, his honest condolences on his lips as he hugged her. I, on the other hand, wondered when exactly, during the night, he had left. If he had left at all or just disappeared from my room the way he'd shown up the night before, only to reappear on our doorstep.

He left for school just in time to make it to the first class and returned in the afternoon, bringing my homework assignment as if nothing had ever happened—at least not when it came to that hidden world he had shared with me.

I didn't ask what was to happen now. If there was anything else I should know. If he had a plan—

The weekend passed before the funeral, going by in a blur of sorrow and worry, and even if I didn't leave the house except for grocery shopping while Mom was taking care of funeral arrangements, Leon was as devoted to keeping me company as ever. Maybe even more so now that he had shared his reasons.

He was in a black suit as he entered my bedroom, holding out a hand to beckon me into his embrace. What a contrast. His white-blond hair and the dark, elegant fabric. I let him squeeze me tightly against him, no more tears within my body to shed, before we walked down the stairs together.

"Ready?" Mom asked ... herself as much as me, I supposed ... and led the way to the car.

We rode in silence, neither of us able to find words for what was coming.

As we pulled into the parking lot, I noticed we weren't the first to come pay our respects to Gran even if we were an hour early. And as the hour passed, the graveyard filled with people, friends, acquaintances of Gran's whose faces I had never seen in my life. Mom nodded at some in silence. Some came over to shake our hands and express their condolences. It was hard to keep up the façade of the grieving granddaughter when I knew that the body in the plain, wooden coffin was no longer part of the wonderful person my grandmother had been. When I had seen her soul escape from its shell and slip into the messenger angel who had taken her to heaven. So, I laced my fingers together and tried to copy Mom's moves as best I could while Leon stood a bit away from us with his mother, who gave me a compassionate smile when I met her gaze once. Was she one of them, too? A Lightbringer? Did she know about what her son was? What her father had been before his timely death?

It was hard to focus on anything but how surreal the funeral had become. Not a ritual for the dead but for the living, to cope with their loss. And with Leon telling me that Gran had been able to see souls and Lightbringers who took those souls to heaven, just the way he did, the way I might one day—I swallowed at the thought—I no longer knew where that put me. Would I one day be part of that loss people felt? Would I take the people they loved so much to a better place? Would that bring me comfort? Or would it make me feel like death itself?

I tuned out the people, the voice of the pastor, the music that might have amused me under different circumstances, and mainly noticed the white roses everyone held in their hands. Mom had chosen them even if Gran would have probably loved to have hortensias on her grave. I hadn't objected, too preoccupied with the new secret Leon and I shared. The one that was already building inside my chest as he kept not bringing it up again ... as if everything that needed to be said had been said.

When eventually the coffin was lowered into the earth, I felt empty. Relieved, almost. As if a burden had been taken off my shoulders. But it wasn't a burden that had been lifted. Leon had placed his hand on my shoulder in silent comfort, his touch as familiar and alien as the new version of him I had yet to figure out.

"You know she is at peace, right?" he whispered into my ear, and I nodded, my eyes flickering over the grave faces, following the wooden box with the remains of my Gran.

There, on the other side of the grave, right where the earth opened and swallowed the coffin, stood a young man, his face pale and features unearthly beautiful. Unlike the rest of the crowd, he wasn't watching the coffin disappear. His eyes, gray as the storm brewing above us, were staring right back at me.

12. LANEY

The halls of Glyndon High were as gray as the morning haze that had settled over town. For the first time since I could think, Leon hadn't joined me at the small table in the corner of the cafeteria where we sometimes sat before classes to avoid the masses coming in.

I flung my bag onto the empty chair and stared out the window, waiting for time to pass until the first class of the day would bind my attention and I would stop thinking about Gran's death, the funeral, and Leon's role in all of it. Then, there was still the mystery of that other boy—the dark one. The Shadowbringer. The way he had looked at me—

Not just when he had waited for Gran's soul but at Santoni's, at the funeral.

My stomach felt full of stones as I shoved the thought aside. He couldn't have known about me. If he had known about me ... if I had known about what my heritage meant, that I hadn't been the first in my family to see souls and those creatures of light and shadows who helped souls transition into the afterlife, I might have refrained from going there. I could have protected myself, stayed away had Gran told me about what she was ... what it meant ... had Leon told me.

A sudden cold ran through me at the thought of how people I had trusted, who I had known my whole life, had lied to me ... and protected me at the same time.

Outside, groups of students trickled through the yard, their collars pulled up against the cool moisture of early fall. Avery and her minions were wearing matching scarfs—soft red and cream that made me think of Christmas. They filed in the door to the biology building, chattering animatedly as they kept glancing back over their shoulders. I didn't bother checking where they looked, for Jo slid into a chair beside me, a tired smile on her face and a cheery "good morning" on her lips.

"You look like the weather," she told me without giving me a moment to put on a brave face.

"I feel like the weather." A glance at my gray shirt, black pants, and boots was enough to tell me she was right. They weren't exactly my mourning clothes. My closet was full of gray and black, so except for those few who knew what had happened, nobody could suspect someone had died in my family.

I gave Jo a look that was supposed to be cheerful but couldn't find it in me as I recognized the tired paleness on her face.

"You alright?" I asked, shoving aside my own sorrow.

Jo nodded. "Didn't sleep well, that's all." She gestured at the building at the other end of the yard, as much enthusiasm on her face as I felt at the thought of joining Avery and her minions for biology, but I got to my feet regardless, ready to suck it up. *Just another day*. That was what it was. Even without Leon by my side functioning as my shield against Avery's evil eye, I would survive.

He hadn't left my side for the past weeks since the funeral except for the nights where—after that initial night following Gran's death—he had instructed me to ping him the second something felt wrong. I didn't really understand what he meant by *something felt wrong*. Everything felt wrong, knowing what he had shared with me, having seen what I had seen. So I didn't disturb his nights even when, most of them, I didn't sleep as soundly as I used to.

As I picked up my bag, talking to Jo, who had already started walking, one of the figures moving in the fog slowed and stopped right in front of the window.

I caught the dark shape from the corner of my eye as I was about to turn and follow Jo into the hallway when I noticed the familiar face and the hard, gray eyes staring right at me.

My fingers clasped my bag tightly to my chest in reflex as I took in the features that couldn't possibly be from this earth.

And he ... he stared back at me through the window, the Shadowbringer, his pale features and sleek, dark hair reminding me of a black and white movie, the same questions filling his gaze as he tilted his head, black strands shifting on his forehead. He pursed his lips.

"You coming?" Jo called from the door, oblivious that I had just seen a ghost.

I nodded absently, her voice little more than an echo as the boy raised a long-fingered hand and waved it once in greeting.

My head jerked sideways in response, checking to see if there was someone else behind me he meant, but there was no one.

When I turned back to the window, the boy had disappeared.

My heart, however, was racing at the confirmation that I hadn't imagined him there at the nursing home. Or at the graveyard or the grocery store. And that Leon was right, that the Shadowbringer would come for me.

Loosing a stuck breath, I turned and stalked from the cafeteria, hands sweaty and pulse racing.

Where *was* Leon today? I had no idea what to actually do, how to prevent the Shadowbringer from getting me. Leon hadn't yet shared the specifics of how I could protect myself. Just that as long as I was with him, the Shadowbringer had no power over me—whatever that meant.

So I focused on breathing in and out slowly, eyes darting toward the doors to the yard as soon as I entered the hallway, putting almost as much effort into appearing calm.

Nothing. No sign of the Shadowbringer. Just the usual stream of bored-faced students as they made their way to classes, their books under their arms.

Maybe I was seeing things after all. Maybe what had happened at the nursing home was haunting me during my days the same way it did in my dreams.

I found Jo by the lockers, waiting for me to catch up before she started walking again.

"Everything okay?" She handed me a book she had borrowed from the stack in her arms as we turned into the corridor that led us to the biology labs.

I nodded and shouldered the door open, ready to endure Avery and her despising glares—anything to distract myself from the gray eyes that had stared at me through the window—when Leon joined us, one hand reaching over my head to hold the door.

"Where were you?" I whispered as he squeezed into the classroom with me.

I hated that it sounded like an accusation. Leon wasn't my bodyguard. He had a life of his own. Even when his family seemed to have been watching over mine for decades or longer.

He didn't answer, letting Jo pass before he followed into the room and slumped into the chair beside me.

When I glanced over at Jo, who had sat down in her usual spot by the window as far as possible from Avery, she gave me a look that reminded me of what she had said about Leon monopolizing me. I gave her an apologetic smile and wished that, for once, there was nothing to worry about but Avery Macmillan, who with her gossip, her glares, and mocking had made herself the undoubted queen of high school.

When I returned my gaze to Leon, he frowned.

"Unimportant," he muttered under his breath. "What's important is that I am here now."

I gave him a look that was supposed to make him squirm in his seat.

All I got was a soft chuckle and a light nudge from his elbow before he turned to the front and pinned his attention on the teacher, who was explaining the importance of certain cells in the human body. Unsurprisingly, my focus didn't suffice for memorizing anything the man said.

I spent the hour pondering whether I should invite Leon to stay the night—just in case the Shadowbringer returned—

and then dismissed the idea at the thought of what that invitation could mean for either of us.

As if Leon was listening to my thoughts, he turned and raised an eyebrow. I shook my head—more to myself—and glanced at Jo, who was taking notes, her face paler than usual.

When the bell finally sounded through the room like a tortured, metal cat, I got out of my chair and joined my friend by the window.

"I was thinking—" I said, my eyes on Leon, who was cocking his head at my abandonment and seemed to be debating whether or not he was supposed to join us.

When I didn't continue, Jo said, "I am glad you were, honestly." She grinned. "It does help."

I detached my gaze from Leon's coffee eyes and faced her, taking a deep breath to shake the shock from this morning. "I was thinking maybe we should have a movie night."

She nodded eagerly. "We haven't done that in forever."

True. And it would help me get my mind off of things.

"Tonight?" she asked, gathering her books before we started walking.

Again, I nodded. "We could stream a film or watch a series until we fall asleep," I suggested. "I'm sure Mom won't mind."

I was certain she wouldn't. She had been telling me that it was okay to continue living my life after Gran's death. That death wasn't the end of everything ... just a new beginning. A different sort of life. Those were the moments when I wondered if Mom, after all, *did* know about the secret world that Leon lived in. The world that Gran had been a part of. The world that *I* now feared on a daily basis—minutely, to be honest.

"Great!" Jo hooked her arm into mine as we crossed the threshold, her steps less bouncy than usual even if her voice was convincing.

As we crossed the yard, I realized the temperature had dropped further, making me pull my collar more tightly around my neck. Beside me, Jo did the same.

"Isn't this sweet," Avery's voice filtered through the lingering fog. I didn't turn to look at her but kept walking toward the English classroom, Jo doing the same. "You make a great couple, the two of you." Her tone was almost poisonously sugary.

Jo shot me a look that meant not to react to Avery's words ... or to the laughter of her minions.

When neither of us reacted, the Queen of Glyndon High sped past us in a graceful gait and planted herself in my path, her pink lips pouting. "And there I thought you were already taken," she said with fake concern. "Or ... or is it that ..." She glanced at Jo again then around the yard, looking for something. "Or is it that Leon finally got bored with you?"

Her words stabbed me in the gut. I knew her teasing. Knew her mocking. She had nothing over me but the fact that Glyndon High's most handsome boy spent every spare minute with me ... and that it seemed to be an impossibility in her shallow mind.

Still, her words hurt. They catered to that tiny voice in my head that had been attempting to verbalize to me the fear that Leon wasn't with me out of free will but because it was his task as a Milliari and a Lightbringer.

I shook my head at myself.

Avery seemed to understand it as an answer to her question.

"So where is he?" she prompted as if to prove I was lying.

I shook my head again. This time at her.

"None of your business, is it?" I bit. "It's not as if he would ever deign to spend a minute with you."

I could see all of the color that wasn't makeup leave her face. Beside me, Jo chuckled and tugged on my arm.

Never, since my first day at Glyndon High, had I spoken up against Avery. Never had I found the words to make her shut up. Today, for the first time, I had rendered her speechless with a response so simple that I could have thought of it earlier.

And by the look on her face, I knew it would cost me.

13. Laney

Leon didn't join me for lunch that day, or for the walk home from school.

Maybe Avery was right after all. Maybe Leon had lost interest now that I wasn't the same friend any longer but an object to be protected from a Shadowbringer ready to steal my soul. However that worked.

At least, I wouldn't be alone tonight even if having Jo over might put her in more danger than was good for anyone to be in.

Mom was still at work when the doorbell rang hours later, and Jo greeted me with a box of sushi and a tray of pastries. "Ready?" She beamed, the paleness from earlier all gone.

I waved her into the house, picking up dishes from the kitchen on the way to the living room.

When I joined Jo on the couch, she was resting her head against the purple cushions and closed her eyes.

"It's the weather," she said weakly and gestured in the air as if that was supposed to explain something.

I didn't respond other than getting back to my feet to grab a glass of water for her.

Jo took it gratefully and smiled after a deep drink. "Thank you."

She set down the glass and picked up the remote control. It didn't take long for us to decide on a rerun of Vampire Diaries, and we were back in the pattern of rooting for the two brothers while we kept wondering why Elena didn't take more control in her own life.

And it didn't take me long to realize that I myself wasn't exactly doing anything to improve my situation. Even if I hadn't been attacked, there was a Shadowbringer out there, ready to take my soul, and my protector had vanished without explanation.

Shame overcame me while I was still marveling at the supernatural creatures in the show. As charming and intriguing as they were onscreen, seeing something paranormal happen in real life was a quite different thing. It scared the hell out of me. I bit my tongue at the thought. Then fear might be something good if that meant hell couldn't take root in me.

While I was still in thoughts, Jo's comments on the vampires' haircuts ebbed, and eventually, her head sagged against my shoulder, her breathing deep and even.

Gently, I slid my hands under her neck and laid her down on the couch, grabbing a blanket from the backrest to tuck her in. Then, I got to my feet and put away the leftovers from dinner, leaned against the kitchen counter, and closed my eyes for a minute.

The buzzing of my phone tore me out of my moment of peace.

"*I've got everything under control,*" Leon's text appeared on the screen. Plus the smug emoji.

For a second, I smiled at the screen, but then I realized that his words meant that there was a situation to be controlled and that he might be in danger because of me.

"*What is going on?*" I demanded, my fingers flying over the keyboard.

"*Brightening some shadowy corners,*" he responded within seconds.

His words, however, made me none the wiser.

"*Where are you?*" I finally dared ask, and tension grabbed me as the display turned dark and didn't light up from a new message.

I pulled open the fridge and plopped a leftover sushi roll into my mouth to pass the time until he would reply.

"*You ordered my favorite,*" he texted, and I reeled around, facing the window and staring out into the darkness.

His face was staring back at me from the driveway.

My hand flipped to my throat in reflex at the sight of him. He lifted one hand to wave and, with the other, fumbled with his phone.

Mine buzzed in my hand.

"*May I come in?*" Outside, he lifted both shoulders in question.

It took me a moment to breathe normally before I was able to nod.

A soft knock on the door sounded almost the same second Leon started walking—and blurred away from the spot.

My heart stuttered. How was this even possible?

As I made my way from the kitchen, goosebumps rose on my skin in time with a shiver, a draft of chill air arriving long before I opened the door.

"Hi—" Leon's smile dropped as he studied my face, looking as if I were a ghost.

"What's wrong?" I used to be able to read Leon's face, his eyes, the tone of his soft voice. Now, everything he said, every look, every twist of his lips was an enigma.

"You..." he whispered as if unaware of the meaning of what he was saying.

And I ... I wasn't certain whether I should be irritated at his words or simply be amazed that I had no idea who my best friend was.

My hand twitched, threatening to shut the door in his face, but his palm was against the wood before I could make a decision and really try. He pursed his lips and took a step closer, studying me with warmth in his eyes.

"You are not in your solid form, Laney," he explained in a murmur, face changing as he let his hand slide over the door right onto my palm. And before I understood what he was saying, what he was doing, he stepped past me, pulling my hands with him off the door and shutting the latter behind him.

"What do you mean, *not in my solid form?*" I prompted, almost forgetting that Jo was still sleeping in the living room.

Leon gestured at the kitchen. "Let's talk there," he suggested and tugged me along, his fingers firm and gentle around mine, evoking a sensation so different from what I was used to.

He leaned against the counter where I had been standing a minute before and observed me from under white-blond strands of hair, his eyes more intense than even the night after Gran's death.

"I don't know if you have realized, Laney"—he lifted a hand, weaving it in the air as if to prove a point—"but you are not corporeal right now. If someone comes inside the kitchen at this moment, they won't see a single soul in here." He chuckled at his joke.

I, however, didn't find it funny at all. "What?" I checked, eyeing down the front of my body, whether I was still there, still visible, or if I had dissolved into something more ethereal—and was relieved to find all my limbs in place. Then I looked at him more closely, taking a step toward him. "How is this possible?"

Leon looked the same as he had in the nursing home, the same as he always did. Only now, when I studied his features, his eyes, his entire body, he seemed to have a subdued glow that normally wasn't there. Before he could answer, I said, "You are *invisible*, too, aren't you?"

He only nodded then lifted his chin as if to tell me this wasn't about him.

"What did you do to end up in your ethereal form?" he wanted to know.

I didn't know if I should laugh or cry as I realized that this was real. That what had happened at the nursing home wasn't a bad dream.

"Take a breath, Laney," he ordered, his tone still gentle, but with so much authority that I simply inhaled deeply and exhaled before I took another step toward him.

"You are becoming one of us ... a Lightbringer," he said what I was sure was supposed to sound like something to look forward to.

Somehow, I couldn't get myself to find enthusiasm. On the contrary. Panic filled me, the room suddenly too small, the air too heavy, as I wondered how I had involuntarily switched into a shape that disguised me from the rest of the world. What if Jo had seen me disappear? What if my mother walked in now? Would she be able to see me? To hear me?

And then ... even worse than that fear ... what if I didn't manage to return to my normal form?

My chest constricted at the thought, and I started coughing uncontrollably, suddenly no longer able to get enough air—or the right kind of air.

"What's happening?" I ground out between coughs, hands at my throat.

"I don't know." Leon was beside me in an instant, one palm rubbing across my back and shoulders while, with his other hand, he steadied me enough to help me into a chair at the table at the center of the room. His voice was calm though his features betrayed his rising panic as he crouched down in front of me, murmuring words of reassurance.

"You'll be fine," he kept repeating, and I could tell by the look on his face that he had no idea whether or not his words were the truth.

There was a tug on the center of my chest that beckoned me to get back to my feet and walk out of the room. It was so overwhelmingly strong that, for a moment, I forgot that I was hardly able to breathe. I struggled into an upright position, ignoring Leon's demand to know what I was doing—I had no idea what it was that I was trying to achieve. All I knew was that something was calling to me, and I had to answer.

As I sent one shaky leg before the other, Leon stayed by my side, his arm around my waist holding half my weight. Every tiny step I dragged myself forward the air came a bit more easily, making laughing fits ebb into shallow gasps ... into labored breaths ... until I crossed the threshold to the living room and the string pulling my chest tighter and forcing me forward loosed as my gaze fell on the sleeping shape of my friend Jo. Her breathing was even, undisturbed by the noise of my struggle for air, of my feet sliding over the wooden floor, Leon's muttered words of relief as my breathing became easier. Of course. For even if she was looking right at us, she wouldn't be able to see us. We were invisible, not corporeal. Not human in the sense she was.

Lightbringers.

"A soul." Leon's words hit me in the gut as if he had struck there with his fist.

And as he said it, I saw it. The silver layer that enveloped Jo, the texture of the star that my grandmother had turned into. A soul.

I took a deep breath, the air flowing easily into my lungs as I kept watching the flickering soul that was the essence of Jo.

"A soul," I repeated, and beside me, Leon nodded. "I guess your Lightbringer nature is breaking through," he said with what sounded like a smile. I couldn't tell. I was too absorbed in the sight before me.

The delicate shine that emanated from Jo's skin, the sensation of the room that had once been a mere living room and had now turned into a well of light and shadows, of pulsing life and hovering death. I could feel it like I could feel the blood in my veins rush faster and faster as if my body was trying to catch up with my mind, my own soul ... I wasn't sure what it was ... maybe my essence.

"You can feel her, can't you?" Leon said and placed a hand on my arm, cautioning somehow.

I nodded. It was a strange allure. Wild, calming, like water and fire all at once. A burning and drowning and being reborn.

And the soul sang to me, beckoning me to come closer, to touch it, to free it.

I took a step forward, the fear of remaining stuck in my ethereal form forgotten at the wondrous sensation.

"I should have known," Leon murmured and followed me toward the couch where I settled down beside Jo, the soul still calling me forward. My chest felt empty as if it were a chamber prepared for something more than my thumping heart and my pumping lungs. There was something ... missing in there.

Leon placed one hand on my shoulder, his touch gentle but firm enough to let me know I wasn't going to succeed if I intended to move any closer to Jo.

"What's wrong?" I asked without taking my eyes off the slightly pulsing silver light.

"Your Lightbringer instincts are awakening," he said with a mixture of awe and fear in his tone. "The soul recognizes you as someone trustworthy, someone good ... someone who will eventually take her to heaven. One day." He cocked his head beside me as he watched Jo's still shape, fascination in his words. "You are becoming one of us even faster than I'd thought."

"That's good, I suppose," I tried. "The sooner I finish my ... transformation ... the sooner I am safe from the Shadowbringer, right?"

"Let's let her rest." He gestured at Jo and pulled me up by the shoulder. "We have things to discuss."

14. LANEY

I didn't object when Leon led me up the stairs, his hand a steady weight on my shoulder. On the contrary, I was grateful to be taken away from the lure of the soul that was hovering within Jo's body.

"Can you breathe?" he asked as he led me into the room, the heat of his palm seeping through my sweater as he guided me through the door to my room.

I nodded. It was surprisingly easy now that I had figured out what the aching in my chest was—

As I let him sit me down on my bed and watch him settle beside me—in close range that would allow him to intercept me if I darted back for the door; and God knew I wanted to—Leon fixed his gaze on mine. "You'd better get used to this," he said with a frown, his face so different from the Leon I used to know, no cheerful smile playing on his lips, no twinkle in his eye.

"To the coughing?" I didn't buy my own humor—neither did Leon.

"You know what I'm talking about," he responded with more force than necessary. His hand slid off my shoulder, leaving the air cold after the warmth of his touch.

I studied him—the ristretto gaze, the sensuous curve of his lips, the tension in his shoulders as he rested his forearms on his knees and laced his fingers together.

Did I ... know what he was talking about? Truly?

"Not sure," I breathed into the space between us, wondering if I looked as different to him as he did to me. There was something to his appearance in this form—the non-corporeal one—that spoke to me on a level my best friend Leon never had. Something mysterious, something divine—

Leon cleared his throat. "I am speaking about you wanting to deliver Jo's soul to heaven," he said as if that wasn't a disturbing thought and the most natural topic to converse about.

"What—" I tore my eyes away from the curve of his neck and let his words settle. "What do you mean I wanted to deliver her soul?"

"You were obviously drawn by her soul, Laney," he said as if that was something he could accuse me of.

But I bit back the protest that normal Laney would demonstrate had normal Leon chastised her about anything.

"You felt her soul, right?"

I nodded, still feeling that tug inside my chest even if I was able to ignore it enough to not jump back to my feet and run down to stare at Jo.

"Right." He shook back his hair and gave me a look that made the room feel very cold.

For a moment, I held his gaze, waiting to discover if I could stare down his ethereal form the same way I could with normal Leon. Then, I thought through the meaning of his words, the fact that he had never finished explaining since that first incident when he had shared about what he was, what *I* supposedly was.

I ground my teeth and turned away. "How does it work exactly?"

Leon sighed through his nose, something he did when he didn't know the answer during a quiz at school. "How does what work?"

There was a richness to his voice which I had never before noticed. "Transporting the souls to heaven?" I helped him to get onto my train of thought. "How do you do it, bring a soul there?"

I had seen him breathe in the star Gran had become, but what happened from there I couldn't even begin to imagine.

At that, Leon chuckled. "Aren't you going to ask me the more important things first?" he asked in return. Whether to distract me from my interest or because he had more important things to share, I couldn't tell.

So I played along, that tug in my chest still singing a hollow song. "And what would that be, Leon Milliari, Lightbringer of the umpteenth generation—" I squinted my eyes, pretending to think. "What generation are you exactly?"

Leon laughed, a hoarse sound that scraped along my body, so different from his usual laughter.

"Seventeenth," he said, his lips curling as he measured the shock on my face.

"Really?" It didn't bother me that I sounded stupid as I asked for confirmation.

"Really." He nodded, a hint of that carefree smile stealing itself back onto his features. "Well, if you count the fact that only every second generation actually becomes a Lightbringer"—he tilted his head as if thinking hard—"that makes it only the ninth." He waved a hand as if to belittle the number. My mouth, however, remained open with wonder.

"So how did you become one?" I asked, sensing that the questions I was asking now were those he was willing to share the answers to.

"When my grandfather died, I awakened," he explained as if that, too was completely normal.

"Awakened?" I prompted and wondered if that was what was happening to me.

He gazed at the ceiling as if to read the answer there. "The essence of the messenger angel was passed on to me."

"What do you mean, passed on?" With every answer, he was answering as much as he was bringing up new questions.

Leon gave me a long look that spoke volumes and yet did nothing to satisfy my curiosity. "Angels are not beings of solid bodies, able to walk the earth, Laney," he explained with a degree of exasperation I had never seen on his face. "They need a carrier to walk the earth. And my family—and yours—was chosen to act as such for the divine."

As his eyes, so dark and bright all at once, locked on mine, a shudder ran through my body, the meaning of his words settling in.

"We are possessed by angels?" I half-shrieked, for lack of a better reaction.

At that, Leon laughed again, this time, some mockery in his voice as he said, "Not possessed but enhanced."

"Are we even ourselves?" I tried to ignore the sudden sensation that I was sharing my body with another being.

"I mean ... are we even acting on our own accord, or are the *angels* making us do things?"

This was worse than I had managed to dream up even in my worst nightmares. Creepy. Not what I had believed angels to be. Like a bad horror movie but not divine ... nothing at all like divine—

Leon's handsome features, however, were proof of the exact opposite. Divine.

"Nothing like that, no," he shook his head. "We aren't God's puppets or the angels' body-suits"—he laughed at his own joke; I didn't—"but think of it rather as having some sort of energy pulsing through you." He struggled with finding the right words, his hands fingering in the air before him as he was explaining. "The essence of the angel weaves into our bodies and makes us able to travel that path between earth and heaven while our human body provides the vehicle for the soul to travel—" He stopped, his eyes wary as he studied my face. "It sounds like bullshit, doesn't it?"

It was so Leon to say that, that I involuntarily chuckled. "It does." But my amusement was short-lived. I remembered when Leon had lost his grandfather years ago. He couldn't have been older than ten or eleven. And as I let his words replay in my mind, everything he had shared with me since that moment in Gran's room, I realized how lucky I was.

"You were only a child when it happened to you," I whispered and as he nodded, the profoundness of that small gesture hit me like a bolt of lightning in the chest. Leon was the smart and patient and sometimes absurdly wise Leon I knew, not because of the childhood we'd had together, not because of his upbringing, but because he had been forced to live his life around death.

"And now it is happening to you," he said instead of wallowing in what had surely left its mark on him—invisible and divine, and yet so dark that I couldn't help but grief for the child I had played with in the sandbox.

I held his gaze for a long minute, reading in the coffee brown depths of his eyes where all the answers seemed to be buried, and found that there, under the layers of familiarity lay a person I didn't really know, an angel of death. Even if his job was to bring souls to heaven, he was an angel of death all the same. Blond strands had shifted onto his forehead, contrasting his sun-kissed skin, and with the unearthly light that had to surely be part of that essence he had been talking about, there was a wild, sinister feel about him that I had never appreciated.

"I had my grandfather to share all this with me," he said, his voice even as if his words weren't at all important, but his gaze told me differently, too intense, too eager to share all this with someone ... with me. "Your gran however never became a true Lightbringer, so she couldn't share with you what every passing generation of the line should—because she never learned for herself."

I looked at the floor to escape his gaze just for a moment, to be able to breathe. "And what is that, Leon?"

He took a deep breath, blinking for a second too long, hiding the depth of his gaze from my inquisitive eyes. "The secret of how to choose the right souls."

15. CAS

Dull was just another of so many words that didn't even remotely describe the farce of following the girl around like a lapdog.

It wasn't that I was one ... just that she had seen me was all but compelling me to seek out her presence.

A Lightbringer. I knew by the pulse of light under her skin that was more than that of the average soul. She was an emerging Lightbringer.

I stalked down the street, my thoughts back at the schoolyard where I had located her. And naturally, the other Lightbringer had been with her. Another Milliari. That family had been haunting this region for too long. My jaw clenched as I turned the corner to her house. I had overheard that she was going to spend the evening with her friend instead of the Lightbringer, so there was a chance that if I simply knocked, she would open the door and ... and that would be that for her.

A clean slice through the bonds that held her soul in her body, and I could take my trophy home. And her body ... well, that would be living on in a less fortunate state than now. But what interest was the mushy brain of a human—if I had a Lightbringer soul to show.

It was rare to come across one of them when they were still manifesting and too weak to protect themselves. The moment she would take her first soul, she would become untouchable for me, and she was developing fast. I could tell by the zing in the room when she had walked into Mrs. Parker's room. Or the funeral where she had found me even in my disguising shadows.

So the window was small until my chance would be gone.

Mrs. Parker had smelled like a Lightbringer even if she hadn't been one. A dormant generation, they called it. The ability to let the messenger angels' essence manifest jumped one generation, but even the ones who were meant to carry the essence, in a lot of cases, never turned into Lightbringers. All they could do was see us—if they looked closely. Not even all the time. Some were so weak they only noticed us right before their death when their souls were already trying to escape their bodies. Mrs. Parker had been one of those. And her granddaughter—

Just another mile of walking. I could see the house ahead by the next crossing, looming like a fortress of light. Around me, in the houses scattered along the landscape, souls were humming like electric lines in the brutal cold of winter. But they all lost their lure compared to that one bright and delicious soul of the girl.

I couldn't even imagine what it would feel like to let her settle in my chest and take her to the one place she could never again escape. Only that it wouldn't be settling because, for that, she'd have to be dead, and what I was about to do to her was so much worse.

The house came closer unnaturally fast as I walked up in my ethereal form even though I could have traveled on my essence. I preferred to scout my surroundings for dangers as I circled my prey.

The other Lightbringer, the Milliari, was one of those dangers. He had been hovering around the girl like a shield since she had walked in on us at the nursing home. I remember having noticed her around him before when he had become a Lightbringer. When the essence of the angel had slipped from his grandfather to him—

There was light on the upper floor of her house, the window an old, poorly insulated wooden frame that would soon become a nuisance for a human when the icy temperatures of winter settled in.

A shape moved behind the glass—a shape that let me growl in disappointment.

The Lightbringer was with her. Again.

Behind his broad shoulders, the girl floated by, her arms over her head as she peeled out of her sweater. I ground my teeth in disappointment. And a mild annoyance that the Lightbringer did a proper job protecting the girl.

As if he'd heard me, his head flipped to the side, and his eyes pierced into the darkness of the night, right through my shadows.

I didn't stay to see if the girl would stop at the sweater or strip down to her bare skin in front of him. It didn't matter. Instead, I wrapped my shadows more tightly around me and traveled back to the hellhole that was my home—literally.

16. Laney

School was just as endless as every other day even with the new thrill of knowing that I might skip into my ethereal form if I didn't watch out.

Leon had shown me how to return to my solid self that night it had happened ... almost a week ago. And he hadn't left my side for the better part of that timespan, making me feel twenty-four-seven babysat. Only during the nights would he disappear with the promise that I had nothing to fear.

I didn't ask where he went, if he slept, how he kept up with school while keeping me safe. And when the Shadowbringer didn't show up again after that brief moment at school, I began to wonder if I was even in any real danger. Or if it was all some made-up fear.

Jo yawned widely in response to Mr. Warner's mention of another homework assignment then waved one hand at me. "I didn't sleep much," she whispered her excuse and I gave her a smile. Neither had I. The thought of that sensation when both Leon and I had been in our ethereal forms was something I couldn't just eliminate from my mind. It came with a tingle in my stomach that I couldn't quite place.

"You look seriously tired," I whispered back.

It was true. There were purple shadows under her eyes, and her skin was pale, almost wan. To be honest, Jo seemed tired all the time lately.

Leon sat across the room, near the Avery-faction where he had a good view on the door and the windows—and on me. I glanced to the side, only to find his coffee-gaze studying me, eyes inquisitive.

I shrugged, ignoring Avery's glare as she noticed the silent exchange between Leon and me.

It was then that at the front of the room the door opened, Mr. Warner falling silent at the entrance of a tall boy with bluish-black hair and eyes as gray as the clouds before a storm.

I felt more than heard Leon's gasp as I noticed the attention of every person in the classroom shift to that compelling gaze of the Shadowbringer who was prowling over to Mr. Warner, a bag slung casually over his shoulder, and handed him a slip.

The teacher nodded, probably seeing nothing more than the teenage boy he pretended to be and not the dangerous stealer of souls he was, and pointed at the back of the room where one empty desk was waiting for the new arrival.

In his chair near Avery, Leon had gone rigid, his face no longer holding those friendly features I was so accustomed to but that of a breathtakingly beautiful avenging angel.

It took me a second or two to tear my gaze away from him and instead direct it to the boy, who was now walking down the aisle toward the empty desk, preparing to pass by my own desk on his way. His eyes were on the back of the room, no sign of recognition on his face. At least, not while I still had the courage to watch him approach. The second he reached the row before mine, I turned away, searching Jo's face for whatever she must be seeing.

But my friend just shrugged and set down her pen on the notebook before her, scribbling something, and beckoned for me to read it.

"Not long before the Avery games begin," her neat handwriting said, and I noted a smirk on her face that was very much unlike Jo.

I hadn't dared study the Shadowbringer's face long enough to tell if he was the kind of boy Avery would pay attention to. After the last encounter and her color-drained face, I was almost sure that she would try to pull any rug from under my feet she could find. She was just biding her time. Leon sitting right next to her had already made her gloat.

But the Shadowbringer was different. He hadn't paid me a second of attention. And it wasn't as if I would mind if she went after him—I was anxious for the girl who tormented half the school. No one deserved to be with the devil's right hand.

For a brave second, I risked a glimpse over my shoulder and found the Shadowbringer's gray eyes resting on my back as if he was imagining to carve my soul out from between flesh and bone.

A shudder spreading through me as if I had been touched between the shoulder blades with an icy finger made me shrink back and focus on Mr. Warner's unintelligible scribble on the blackboard.

"Now that we've all acknowledged your new classmate, Mr. Ferham, we can return to work," Mr. Warner announced, saving me from beginning to wonder if this was a nightmare and the Shadowbringer wasn't really here. No, it was real. And *Mr. Ferham* was as much in his corporeal form as Leon and I. Meaning my soul was in more danger than ever before.

I spent the rest of the hour ignoring the itch to turn in my seat and stare at him, but instead, I searched for Leon's gaze, which was as cold as the Shadowbringer's eyes on my back.

Leon had bundled his hair back into a ponytail, exposing the profile of his face as he kept staring at the front of the room like a robot. What was going on in his mind?

I was curious if only to have something to wonder while the minutes were trickling by too slowly. If there was any real danger, he would already have given me a sign to run, wouldn't he?

Beside me, Jo had rested her arms on our desk, her head on top of it seeming as heavy as a stone. Her eyelids were drooping when the bell finally rang.

"I was just getting comfortable," she complained as she reluctantly lifted herself off her books and gathered her things.

Run, I wanted to tell her as, behind me, the other students were getting to their feet—probably including the Shadowbringer, who was after me and had now chosen to seek me out in bright daylight. But what would I tell her was the reason? Certainly not the truth. The truth, Leon had informed me, was something meant only for those who become Lightbringers. Even my mother didn't know.

I gathered my books, resisting yet again the urge to let my head flip to the side and reassure myself the Shadowbringer was still a good distance away, and was about to get out of my chair when Leon's tall frame appeared beside me.

"Thank God," I whispered, ready to throw myself into his arms as he lifted them slightly as if he were equally ready to wrap them around me.

There were so many questions on my tongue that I had to hold back until we were out of earshot of the crowd. But one was more pressing than the rest of them. "Jo?" I whispered at Leon, hoping that the mention of her name would be enough to make him understand that I feared for her safety.

Leon waited for me to get up before he wrapped his arm around my shoulders in a gesture that was as startling as it was surprisingly comfortable ... safe.

Avery's laugh sounded from somewhere by the door, but I didn't bother to look up. Leon's gaze had locked on mine, demanding my undivided attention as he leaned closer and whispered, "He's after you, not her." And he guided me out the door, his fingers secure around my shoulder letting me forget there even was danger.

The hallway was filled with the buzzing voices of students as Leon led me in a careful slalom toward the cafeteria. Somewhere beside me, Jo chanted that she'd join us later, and some minor part of me that wasn't paralyzed from either the sudden appearance of the Shadowbringer or Leon's gentle arm wanted to smile at her and reassure her I'd be saving her a spot.

Leon didn't give me much opportunity to consider my options as he brought me to a table and sat me down, slipping into a seat right beside me, his arm reluctantly sliding off my shoulders, leaving a streak of heat that was more than I was used to from when he normally so casually touched me.

"What is he doing here?" I finally got out, my voice low and shaky.

Leon's eyes darted across the room while mine focused on his. "He must have realized that you are transforming faster than expected." His gaze eventually locked on mine, relief appearing in his eyes as he didn't find what he had been looking for. "He must have realized that there is no way around me outside of school."

I gave him a long look that could have meant I didn't understand a word or that I agreed. I wasn't sure which one it was. All I felt was confusion.

"There hasn't been a single moment since your grandmother's death that you were truly alone," he admitted with a downward twitch of his lips.

"What do you mean, *not truly alone*?" Now it was my turn to screen the room for the dark figure that meant my descent to hell.

Leon shrugged and grasped for my hand, unbothered by Avery's curious gaze as she noticed the new familiarity between us. A familiarity I was certain seemed like something entirely other than what it was ... even if his touch did feel so very different now since we had touched in our ethereal forms.

A zing ran through my body, starting where Leon's fingertips brushed over my palm.

"I told you the Milliari family has been watching over your family for a long time." His voice was a husky melody in the cheery cloud of lunch chatter, drawing my gaze back to his. "As my grandfather watched over your grandmother, I am watching over you."

He held my gaze, intensity pooling in the coffee brown depths of his eyes, his lashes a star-like frame that seemed to make the rest of the world cease to exist.

"Day and night," he added, a small nod confirming he meant what I thought he meant.

"How—" I wasn't sure what I was supposed to ask. How did he watch over me? How was he protecting me? "I mean ... during the nights and all..."

Again he nodded.

"You don't climb into my room through the window, do you?" I grimaced at the image of the intrusion into my private space, into my vulnerable hours of sleep.

At that, Leon chuckled, brightness entering his gaze at my suggestion. "I am not a stalker, Laney," he told me and leaned closer. "I am protecting you, not flushing out your secrets."

Relief flooded my system. "So how does it work? Are we connected somehow? Or do you simply stand guard outside my house?" As if that weren't equally creepy...

"Something like that," he responded, a hint of my old friend Leon shining through.

I nudged him in the shoulder with my free hand, and he tightened his fingers around mine, instantly washing away that sense of the familiar friend I had been relying on for the past years. No, this Leon was something different. Something *other*. Something divine. I felt my heart flutter as he met my gaze again, a smile still playing around his lips. "You were in no danger until you saw me in my ethereal form, Laney. Seeing the souls a year ago after the accident ... that was just a first sign that you would become like your grandmother, but not an indicator you were transforming into a Lightbringer." He paused, checking around if anyone was listening before he leaned a tad closer and whispered. "It was only when you walked in on the Shadowbringer and me when I realized that there was a chance you'd become like me." His eyes said something more than that. *Equal*, they seemed to speak from their depths.

"I haven't gotten a single assignment since you manifested," he continued, holding my gaze with a focus that was new as if he hadn't allowed himself to truly look at me in a long time. It made my skin tingle. "Except for making sure we don't lose you. So all I do is hover, in my ethereal form, close enough to watch the perimeter of your house while you sleep"—Was there embarrassment in his voice as he shared his secrets?— "and make sure the Shadowbringer doesn't get any ideas."

It took me a while to understand his words. To relate them to the purple shadows under his eyes, to the way he had slung his arm around me and literally pulled me from danger. He was giving up his nights to watch over me—

"You don't sleep," I concluded.

At that, Leon laughed. It was again the sound that reminded me of my friend.

"I do," he admitted, the change in his face telling me that he wondered what other theories I had about him. "Why do you think I keep showing up late for school?" He didn't give me a moment to ponder his question before he answered for himself, "I take half an hour in the morning to crash in the library once you arrive safely. I zone out as best I can during classes. And in the afternoons, when we hang out together, when I am right next to you ... it is almost as if I am dreaming..." He finished the last words as if he was speaking to himself. As if he hadn't meant to say them, his eyes growing a bit more distant as he was staring into his own mind.

"It does make me tired, though," he chuckled again and pulled my hand onto his knee, absently kneading my palm as he scanned the room again ... and froze.

It took a moment to realize the Shadowbringer was sitting at a table across the room, his eyes directed at us, face impassive as he studied us together. The sight of Avery Macmillan beside him made me almost laugh out loud in an attempt to vent my fear. The girl was jabbering animatedly, her minions standing behind her, admiration in their dull eyes as they watched her conquer the new arrival.

"He is here because the school is the only place where I slip up," Leon answered my unanswered question. "Here, we have separate classes. And as I said, sometimes I nap in the library."

I could feel his breath on my cheek as he spoke, his eyes on the Shadowbringer even though he was facing me.

"You said before he doesn't need to kill me for that. So what is it that he needs to do?" I wanted to know. So far all I had learned was that the Shadowbringer wanted my soul as a trophy, but not what that implied. If I needed to die in order to achieve it.

To my relief, Leon shook his head. "No, not to kill you," he confirmed, voice flat. "Something much, much worse."

17. Leon

I could feel Laney's pulse racing through her palm under my fingers. Even if her face didn't betray any emotion, fear was making her heart speed in her chest. Her eyes, pale blue in the neon light of the cafeteria, locked on mine, full of unspoken questions ... and that new facet of her gaze that I had never noticed before. Almost as if she saw me in a different light now that she knew the truth, as if Leon, her best friend, no longer existed.

I had yet to make my mind up about whether or not I liked that change.

"What do you mean, *something much, much worse?*" She stared me down, determined to get an answer. And the look in her eyes brought back memories of the hours between the messenger angel's essence had settled within me and the moment I had taken my first soul. I had been quick. Less than two days. Two days full of fear. There had been no one looking out for me during that initial time frame when I might have fallen victim to the Shadowbringer.

But I had been prepared. My grandfather had spent days and nights telling me about our history, about our mission, about our purpose—and about the Parker-family. Even if Laney was now a Dawson, with her mother marrying that man and moving away and all.

The task to watch over her lineage might have fallen to someone else entirely had she stayed away from Glyndon. But ever since she was back, her safety fell under my purview of tasks. Besides taking all those souls in Glyndon to heaven.

They weren't excessively many with a small town like this— a couple of deaths every so many weeks—I had to face my original purpose less often than my kin in more densely populated regions. But it freed up my time for watching over the emerging line of Lightbringers that Laney descended from.

So I took a deep breath and did my duty to protect her ... by telling her what could possibly be worse than death.

"I told you that they take your light and sight." I waited for her to confirm she remembered our conversation, and when she blinked, I continued, "You have the sight of the angels." It sounded less ridiculous in my mind than when I had to say it out loud. Remembering how I had laughed at my grandfather when he had first told me, I wouldn't be surprised if, at some point, the delicate creature before me would one day simply laugh at me and walk away.

But she remained attentive, serious, staring at me intently as she waited for more information, her eyes so compelling that I had trouble sorting my thoughts. "You can see whatever is between heaven and earth ... or between *hell* and earth for that matter," I added. "That includes souls that are ready for transfer but also us Lightbringers and the dark side of the coin—the Shadowbringers."

I paused, verifying that she was following me, but she was, her attention on me only as if the Shadowbringer didn't even exist.

With a sideways glance, I reassured myself he was still there, brooding in his seat next to the Macmillan girl, who had slipped me dirty notes during class. He raised an eyebrow at me as if in greeting then tilted his head to the side as if asking how much longer I was going to keep up this game.

For me, it wasn't a game.

"And that sight would be taken from you alongside your soul, leaving you as a conscious shell, capable of pain and grief, constantly searching for the one thing that you are lacking—your soul." I didn't look at her when I told her about her potential fate. It wasn't something I liked thinking about, liked envisioning. Laney, broken and agonized for the rest of her mortal life.

I shook my head, unable to face her. "I won't let that happen to you," I promised and pulled her against my shoulder, her shape, warm and breakable against me, filling me with a different sensation; pride.

I was proud to hold her, that she was here with me, that she didn't cringe away from the dangers I represented in her life. No, she tightened her fingers around mine and let me curl my arm around her.

"Once you are fully developed into a Lightbringer, you'll be safe," I told her. "No Shadowbringer can get your soul as a trophy then."

She nodded against my chest, her hair hiding her face, and I couldn't tell if she bought my reassurance.

18. Laney

Reluctance was involved when I uncurled from Leon's chest half an hour later, not having eaten lunch but still having a lot to digest.

Jo joined me in the hallway just as I said goodbye to Leon, who was heading to his classroom with an expression of suppressed worry on his features. Jo watched him walk away, face unreadable and skin mildly green.

"You don't look well," I noted and slowed my stride to match her slouch.

"I don't feel well," she answered with little humor. "I think I need to lie down."

I hooked her arm into mine and pulled slightly. "I'll take you to the nurse."

All Jo did was nod with pale gratitude as I supported her along the corridors, past the lockers, and across the yard to the nurse's office.

Leon had promised me to be within reach if I needed him. That all I needed to do was call his name. However that worked, I wasn't sure. Something with heightened senses, I assumed.

He would travel to me in his ethereal form, and no one would be the wiser—except for the empty spot he would leave in his classroom. That would be an issue.

Later. I would worry about all of that later if I even needed Leon's help. Chances were that in a school like this, I would hardly even notice the Shadowbringer. I could avoid him easily between classes, and he couldn't attack with a teacher and twenty-five kids in the classroom.

The bell rang when we were entering the building at the other end of the yard. Warm air and the scent of paper and coffee greeted us as I led Jo past the dean's office, our footsteps the only ones left. The rest of the students were back in their classrooms. Including Leon. He would be sitting next door from where I was supposed to be.

Beside me, Jo moaned quietly before her weight sagged into me, half-tearing me to the floor as she collapsed. I caught her shoulders and head last, moments before they could hit the beige linoleum.

"Jo," I hissed her name, half-expecting her to vomit all over me, but her face was no longer greenish; it was wan with sweat beading her forehead.

Her breathing was labored, and she rolled her eyes as she blinked them open as if the light hurt.

"I'm okay," she muttered and tried to pick herself up, failing to even lift an arm.

"You're not okay," I objected and knelt down, lowering her head into my lap, my free hand searching for her pulse on her wrist. Her heart was racing.

"I will be in a second." She closed her eyes and took a deep breath.

I was considering my options, whether it was better to just call for help and see if any of the offices down the hall would hear us or if I should leave Jo alone for a minute and go get the nurse, when a soft voice said from behind me, "Allow me."

I shrank aside, my head flipping to the source of the words, and found a pair of storm-gray eyes staring right back at me. My body locked up, not even a sound escaping my lips as he crouched down to reach past me, sliding his long arms under Jo's shoulders and knees, and lifted her in a swift motion, too fast for me to object, to push him aside, to prevent the Shadowbringer from touching my friend.

He was already on his feet and walking down the hallway when I unfroze and darted after him, uncertain if there was a chance in hell that he would put down Jo and leave us alone. That if I pleaded with him to let her go, he would. Or if I would need to give myself up for that.

"Where are you taking her?" I asked before I could finish playing through all the options.

The Shadowbringer didn't even look at me as he said in a flat voice, "The nurse. That's where you wanted to take her, right?" He didn't slow his pace, his long legs making it difficult for me to keep up as I ran along beside him like an outsmarted child. "When I saw your friend go down, I thought you might need some help," he added, this time glancing sideways at me, the gray of his eyes seeming to swirl as his gaze bore into mine.

The glacial cold from before spread through my body. *Enemy*, my system warned me. He was after my soul, and that was the reason he was here. Not to aid me with my helpless friend who had opened her eyes again and was now glancing between the Shadowbringer and me with confusion.

He stopped and gestured at the door, indicating with an impatient look for me to open it for him.

I did—with mixed feelings—then stepped aside and watched him carry Jo into the nurse's office, an apology on his lips, and set her down on the paper-covered bed.

The nurse got to her feet, alarmed by our unannounced entrance, and started fussing over Jo in an instant, asking questions about what had happened, if Jo had fallen, if she had hit her head—

And I ... I answered, mechanical, and kept staring into the storm-gray eyes of the Shadowbringer, whose face I saw from up close for the very first time.

His features were pale and angular, his nose that elegant line of the beauty standard of another era. His brows were two groomed, dark arches, balancing the pale-pink curves of his lips and the sharpness of his cheekbones. His hair, that unnatural bluish-black, was dancing across his forehead as he shoved his hands into his pockets and leaned against the wall beside the bed, his gaze like a play of thunder and lightning as it kept boring into mine.

"She was feeling sick before she fainted," I said to the nurse, who wasn't finished interrogating. "She has been tired a lot, lately." The words sounded distant as though I wasn't speaking them myself even if I felt my lips moving.

The nurse turned away from the bed, leaving the view on a pale but alert Jo, who was smiling up at the Shadowbringer, who, at her attention, released me from his gaze and sat at the edge of the bed, a smile on his lips. "Are you feeling better?" he asked, his voice like onyx, dust-covered drops of morning dew pearling along a cord of velvet. Unearthly, dark, bright, frightening, intriguing, all at once.

It wasn't hard to miss Jo's color returning in the form of a blush as the Shadowbringer unleashed his undivided focus on her. Only, she shouldn't feel the way she did. She should be afraid.

"All right," the nurse waddled past me, an ice-pack in one hand, gesturing with the other for the Shadowbringer to remove himself from the bed.

Personally, seeing him move aside made me feel a lot more at ease. The farther away from Jo, the better.

"I'm going to call your parents to come pick you up," the nurse said to Jo before she turned to me and the Shadowbringer, who was now standing right next to me, his elegant posture seeming out of place in the small, pale yellow office. "And you"—she gave us a look that made me wonder if we had done something wrong—"get back to class."

Jo nodded at me from the bed, her color much better as she pressed the ice-pack to her forehead.

However, I was reluctant to leave. Not because of Jo not being in good care but because of the Shadowbringer who had already walked out and was now holding the door for me, waiting for me to join him in the suddenly grim-looking corridor.

"I'll be fine," Jo said, sounding convincing this time, and when the nurse shot me another impatient look, I knew there was no procrastinating. I had to join the enemy in the hallway—and eventually call for Leon.

When I stepped past him, his eyes scraped over me like a hungry wolf, his nostrils flaring as if he was scenting his prey.

He had done everything right, waiting for Leon to leave my side, for me to get into an empty corridor, for Jo to go down, giving him an easy entrance...

Now, all he needed to do was wait until that door was closed behind us, and he could do his worst. He could take my soul and leave me that pained shell that Leon had spoken about.

I knew that my body should lock up in fear again, that my pulse should be racing in my throat, that I should be calling Leon already and run as fast as I could to the next populated office. Maybe I could have found an excuse to stay with Jo a little longer, but the nurse had made it clear she wanted us back in class. Only, she had no idea that neither of us would be returning to class. The Shadowbringer would return to hell where he had come from, and I—

I would remain a crying, agonized bundle, unable to think of why I had even ended up in this hallway, to begin with.

Now that I was thinking it through, fear was setting in, and my palms turned sweaty as the sound of the closing door filled the air behind me.

I didn't turn back, hoping that if I didn't see him, didn't acknowledge him, he might disappear like a nightmare, like the monster under the bed when I'd been a child that Mom had said would go away if I pretended it wasn't there.

Only, this was not the hallucinated fear of a child. This was a Shadowbringer, someone who had come to steal my soul as a trophy.

19. Laney

"I have been thinking," he spoke and fell into step beside me as if my thoughts of him had conjured him from the shadows I so desperately wanted to ban him to.

I didn't look at him for fear his eyes would be as compelling, as hypnotizing as they had been back in the nurse's office. "Great, you're thinking," I mumbled, hoping that some kind of humor, no matter how desperate, would make the ghost beside me less threatening.

"It may amuse you, but I actually *have* been wondering how I could make this happen," he said, unfazed by my attitude.

"Make what happen?" I asked, involuntarily looking up at his face and finding him studying the floor before his feet.

"The whole trophy thing, you know." There was something disturbingly unbothered in his tone as he spoke about taking my soul for sport. It made me turn away from the beautiful angles of his face and look at the dull colors of the school hallway instead.

"What about it?" My words came out like a rehearsed retort, the fear making way for the odd sense of intrigue that had overcome me in the nurse's office.

"You're rather well protected for an emerging Lightbringer." He didn't keep down his voice the way Leon would have as we walked side by side to ... I didn't know where to. So I just continued setting one foot in front of the other, hoping that eventually, I would make it back to the classroom.

"I thought that was the standard procedure," I snapped at him. "To protect us from you guys."

"*Us guys*," he repeated, the words sounding wrong in his soft baritone.

"You know what I mean," I waved one hand before me as if that would explain.

In response, the Shadowbringer stopped, pulling me to a halt with a light touch on my arm.

"No, Ms. Dawson, I don't." His eyes swirled like the clouds in a rainy sky as he stared at me down his nose.

"*Miss Dawson*," I laughed. "Are you joking?"

I should be calling Leon. Now. I should be. Still, the Shadowbringer hadn't lifted a finger against me—yet. So I waited. Hoping that I wouldn't need my friend's help, that I wouldn't need to make him disappear into thin air in the middle of a class and hence, expose him, ruin his life here in Glyndon.

We had discussed the consequences of me calling on him, that he wouldn't be able to explain his sudden vanishing, and therefore it was reserved for emergencies only. And until the Shadowbringer made a move against me, I wouldn't do that to Leon.

"I don't understand," the Shadowbringer said with quiet confusion. "Isn't that your name?"

The laughter that threatened to burst from my lips again died away as I realized he was serious.

"You haven't spent a lot of time around humans, have you?" I replied with sudden understanding. Leon hadn't shared much about the Shadowbringers besides what they did and that they were dangerous. Whether or not they were mortal such as us, I didn't know. Only, from the Shadowbringer's demeanor, I could tell he wasn't the social type.

He cocked his head at my pitying look as I wondered if it was possible that he had gotten in over his head, posing as a high school student. Judging by his timeless face, he could have been a high school student or a college student. The maturity of his body, the muscles cording his arms and chest under his fitted shirt suggested the latter—or none at all.

At least, his clothes appeared to be contemporary—dark jeans and a black shirt that seemed to be of some very soft material— even if nothing else about him allowed me to pin his age.

"Not in the past century," he answered without hesitation, knocking the breath out of my argument.

"That wasn't what—"

"What did you mean then?" he asked, reading the rest of my response from the look on my face.

I shook my head and studied the structure of the wall behind him for the better part of a minute.

The Shadowbringer waited, equally silent, for me to return my focus to him.

When I finally did, his eyebrows rose with curiosity. There was nothing threatening about the way he stood there, measuring my face in silence. Nothing but the knowledge of who and what he was—and what he was going to do to me.

"Lucas ... Cas," he corrected, "Ferham," he eventually said, his voice like midnight and bright stars, and held out his hand. "And you are Mrs. Parker's granddaughter," he added matter-of-factly, leaving nothing for me to do but nod.

I didn't take his hand, staring down at the long, muscled fingers instead. On his middle finger gleamed a silver ring engraved with something that looked like wings and some swirls I couldn't read.

"Laney," I corrected and looked up, meeting his gaze once more. Fear flooded me yet again, as this time, he smiled, flashing a set of straight, white teeth.

"Laney Dawson, emerging Lightbringer," he mused, his lips splitting wider as he studied my horrified gaze.

That was it—his gaze—a trap that made me feel at ease somehow even though my body ought to tense for a fight, to coil and ready itself for a neck-breaking fight or a painful ripping out of my soul—

But none of it came. It was just a smile. Inviting and intriguing ... and very much unlike the creature of nightmares Leon had painted.

"You're still afraid of me," Cas read my face correctly.

"And am I not right to fear you?" My heart thudded in my throat now, exactly where I ought to feel it when panic set in. I prepared to call for Leon.

"That is for you to decide, Laney Dawson," Cas simply said and dropped his still waiting hand to his side before he started walking.

I glanced around the hallway, trying to figure out if someone had interrupted us and I simply hadn't noticed. But the hallway was empty. I was in his power, if he so wanted, with only Leon as a backup—if he would even make it in time—and yet, the Shadowbringer walked away.

As I watched, dumbfounded by how he sauntered down the corridor, the worn beige of the floor almost an insult to his elegant moves, he lifted a hand and waved. "Don't bother to thank me for the assistance with your friend," he said over his shoulder, and the shadows on the side further away from the windows seemed to draw toward him.

Before he turned back, he gave me a look that somehow made me feel like a *thank you* wasn't what he needed when it was some different sort of payment he expected for his help.

When I returned to class, minutes later, the Shadowbringer ... Cas ... was sitting at a desk by the window, his face attentive on the teacher, who demanded to know what had taken me so long. A brief explanation that Jo wasn't well sufficed to turn the focus of the class back to the blackboard and the unintelligible scribbling that I tried to decipher instead of following my impulse to turn my head and stare at the Shadowbringer.

The rest of the hour passed with a knot in my stomach from subsiding fear and authentic confusion. Cas hadn't attacked me as Leon had suggested he would, the first moment he found me alone, but had helped—*helped*—me get Jo to the nurse's office. I wasn't sure if that should make me feel relieved or disturb me.

Avery's giggle frequently interrupted my thoughts, which were hardly any more coherent, now that I was confused, than what they had been from fear when the Shadowbringer had shown up beside me in the hallway.

Every now and then, I allowed my gaze to drift toward the side where I found Avery peeking at Cas from the corner of her eye.

Great. They deserved each other. The wicked high school queen and the boy who took the wicked to hell.

I huffed and leaned back in my chair just when the bell rang, and within moments, Leon appeared in the doorway where students were bolting from the stuffy air of the classroom.

"How about getting out early?" he asked, a terse smile on his lips as he watched me slouch toward him. "You look like you need a break." His eyes scanned me with cautious intensity as if he was looking for cracks in a porcelain cup.

I nodded and let Leon wrap his arm around my shoulders, feeling my heart lightening at the safety of his touch. When he led me from the room, I finally allowed myself what I had been fighting for the past forty-or-so minutes and glanced back over my shoulder.

Cas was still sitting by the window, about to stuff the book he was holding into his bag, his gaze flipping up to mine as if I had called his name.

The knot in my stomach thickened as he didn't even attempt to hide his stare but winked at me before he tucked the book under his arm, got to his feet, and slung the bag over his shoulder.

"Let's go," I murmured to Leon, tearing away from the storm-gray of Cas's eyes, and pulled the Lightbringer at my side forward.

The drive back to my place was quiet. Leon didn't inquire about the hour I had spent apart from him but watched me from the side while I was driving. He got the door for me when I was ready to get out of the car and held his hand out to help me up. I took it without hesitation, his sun-kissed skin familiar and reassuring on mine as he closed his fingers around my palm.

The moment I got into the house, I called Jo. She had made it home safely but still sounded tired. Leon's forehead creased as he listened to the conversation, perched on my desk, fingers flipping through a textbook.

"Is she all right?" he wanted to know once I ended the call, asking—judging by the look on his face—not only about Jo. "What happened?"

I nodded, answering for both Jo and me. I hadn't shared the details about my encounter with the Shadowbringer yet, too grateful for Leon for having come up with the idea to ditch the last class of the day. But now that he asked about Jo, the fear rushed back into my body like a tidal wave that had been held up by my temporary preoccupation.

"She felt nauseous and faint on the way to class," I retold what had happened after he'd left us in the hallway.

I didn't spare him any details about how the Shadowbringer had shown up, that he had carried Jo to the nurse's office, that he had offered his hand in greeting—

"Lucas Ferham," Leon repeated the name I'd given him.

"Better than Lucifer, right?" I tried to joke, but Leon's lips didn't even twitch.

"Why didn't you call for me?" he demanded, something like disappointment shining in his eyes.

"It didn't"—I searched for the right words—"feel like an emergency," I suggested. "I didn't want to expose you."

In response, Leon frowned, his Lips turning pale as he pressed them into a tight line.

"I could have just snuck out of the classroom and found you," he said after what felt like an eternity of silence.

"He didn't attack me," I reminded him. "He was polite, helpful. No sign of the soul-sucking monster I expected." I wasn't even sure what I *had* expected. Anyhow, it was nothing like the boy who had winked at me. Nothing like the fear-instilling intrigue of that pale, beautiful face—and I couldn't deny that he *was* beautiful. Just in a completely frightening and inappropriate way.

A Shadowbringer. A danger. A messenger for hell.

With a sigh, I leaned back on my bed and crossed my ankles.

Leon must have read it as fear, despair, frustration ... whatever he saw, it made him get up from the chair and come to sit beside me, his hand resting beside mine, just an inch away. The frown was gone from his features. "I am glad you didn't get hurt," he said and locked his gaze on mine. "For a moment, when you said he had followed you, I thought he might have succeeded."

20. LANEY

It took a solid week to get used to the Shadowbringer's presence. Leon was on high alert at every step we took at school—and outside of school.

He spent so much time at my house that I was tempted to invite him to stay over whenever he disappeared for the nights—and every night, I thought better than to cross that line that I knew might lead somewhere beyond what we had.

Leon was my friend, my protector, assigned to me. Even if his deep gazes sometimes suggested he saw more in me than an object to protect. I knew I *was* more. Just not in the way that an invitation to stay the night would suggest. I was his friend. Nothing more.

"What are you thinking?" Leon's velvet voice called me from the haze in my mind.

I glanced up at him, playing with the water bottle in my hand and thoroughly ignoring the rest of my lunch.

"Don't your parents wonder where you are all the time?" I asked instead of speaking what was bothering me deep down—that ever since I had spent some hours with Leon in my ethereal form, something had changed for me. I felt him differently, sensed him. It was as if someone had pulled off a layer of disguise from the magical creature he was. From the strong, dedicated man he had become. I no longer saw a boy with dimples and a lost gaze.

I saw strong arms, a sharp-cut face, a sensuous mouth that spoke my name more often than any other person in the world. Even my mother. She was at work most of the time, no longer held back by the guilty conscience of putting Gran in the nursing home and seldom visiting.

Ever since Gran's death, I hardly ever saw her. Only in the mornings when we both rushed from the house. She to work and I to the minefield of Shadowbringer gazes at school.

"They know where I am," Leon said with a smile, "most of the time."

He wiped his hair out of his forehead and grinned. Somewhere in the background, Avery's giggle tore through the dulled buzz of tired conversations. It was fairly safe to say that wherever her voice shrilled, the Shadowbringer couldn't be far.

I sighed through my nose and opened the bottle. "Really? They don't find it curious you leave early in the morning and return late at night ... and that you basically don't even sleep at home." I placed the cap before me, putting a lot of effort into aligning it with the tray and the salt shaker. "I mean ... someone has got to notice your bed is practically unused."

Leon leaned a bit closer as if he was going to share a secret, his cheeks turning slightly pink as he opened his mouth to speak ... and stopped, picking up a slice of pizza from my plate instead.

"What is it?" I prompted when he shrugged and pointed at his full mouth as an excuse not to speak. "It can't be that bad."

"Not bad," Leon responded after audibly swallowing the half-chewed food. "But..."

He gave me a look that made my stomach clench.

"But?"

"I don't know if you'd approve—" He looked positively helpless as he waited for me to let him off the hook.

"Why don't you try me?" I hadn't noticed that I had been leaning forward, too, until Leon shoved his tray aside and rested his forearms on the table, bringing his face another inch closer.

"I told them we are an item." He held my gaze despite the awkwardness that was obviously fluttering between us, intent on seeing through my reaction.

To my surprise, I had none.

I wasn't outraged by his assumption that I would be fine with his explanation. I wasn't disappointed. Or pleased. I just was—

"Now would be the time to tell me I'm an idiot," he said when I didn't respond for a minute.

I blinked, watching the color slowly drain from his face as he realized I didn't understand what he had been saying ... had been trying to say.

"Oh," was the first thing I got out.

Leon pushed back an inch, a grin playing on his lips as he noted the realization in my eyes.

"*Oh*," I repeated and took in his face, the handsome planes and angles that were the most familiar features on the planet.

"You didn't just tell them we are an item," I spoke what I thought he had been trying to say. "You actually *meant* it."

Now it was Leon's turn to fall silent and stare at me.

For a long moment, we eyed each other, me studying him as if I had never seen him before; the strands of white-blond that contrasted so perfectly with his dark eyes, his tan skin, the white shirt he wore, and the beige and brown plaid scarf that was wrapped around his neck.

"No," he said, a hint of defiance in his tone as he leaned closer again—so close that I could see every fleck of light-brown in his coffee eyes. "But what if I did?" He tilted his head just an inch, narrowing his eyes as he read my face.

He waited for me to say something, so I took a deep breath, not entirely sure what I was going to tell him, when a voice woven of night and stars said from the side, "Tick tock," followed by a chuckle.

Both Leon and I shrank away from each other, Leon getting to his feet as if ready to fight.

But the Shadowbringer was already by the door, trailing after Avery and her minions. His eyes were on me, ignoring Leon's branding look.

When he was out of sight, I realized that the cafeteria was almost empty. We had been so deep in conversation, in thoughts, in fears and hopes, that we had both missed the bell.

Leon's posture relaxed a bit as he watched the Shadowbringer disappear, but as he turned to face me, his features were still tight. "You don't need to answer, Laney," he said. "It is just the best way to explain to my family why I basically live at your place ... even if I don't ... and technically speaking, everyone thinks it anyway." He gestured at the empty room. "So I let them believe it. Might be the easiest way to keep that Shadowbringer away, too," he added, offering his arm, waiting for me to close the untouched water bottle, get to my feet, and slip to his side.

We strode down the hallway to English together, his arm suddenly heavy on my shoulders. His words hadn't shocked me, but they seemed to have made something more apparent: Leon didn't see us as more than just friends.

And somehow, that bothered me.

After school, Leon didn't take me home, but he drove us to the nearby forest. His words, his pink cheeks of embarrassment still clung to my mind. But the Shadowbringer's voice also stuck there like a dart that had pinned itself into my mind.

I shook myself at the biting wind that greeted us at the edge of the forest where we got out of the car.

"Where are we going again?" I reached up to pull the collar of my jacket more tightly around my neck.

"Surprise," Leon said with a smile and walked around the car, his backpack slung over one shoulder, to join me by the trees.

"I don't like surprises." It wasn't entirely true. I'd used to like surprises, but ever since my life had become filled with paranormal creatures, I tended to feel saturated with surprises—and that surprises were rarely good ones anymore.

"We're going to my grandfather's cabin," he said with a grin. "He left it to me when he died." He led the way into the shadows between the fir trees. "And it is where all his notes are stored." He glanced at me over his shoulder, beckoning for me to follow. "Maybe we'll find something about that Shadowbringer there."

I followed him down the leaf-strewn path that was squeezed between a mixture of evergreens and trees that were blooming with all of the colors of the east coast fall.

"I spent a major part of my childhood here," he explained as he ducked under branches, setting one surprisingly silent foot after the other. "My grandfather made sure I learned about Lightbringers at the perfect time—before he found his timely end."

The sour tone in his voice gave away that that memory was still bothering him, that the loss of his grandfather was something he might never get over. I didn't have to see his face to know.

"You're lucky someone took the time to fill you in about all that"—I searched for words—"supernatural stuff."

A low chuckle was Leon's response.

I battled my way across roots through the growing twilight. "Had I known what was awaiting me, I would have besieged Gran to tell me," I murmured, not sure if he would laugh again. If his laugh had even been humorous.

"And what do you think she would have told you?" he asked and turned away from the path, into the thicket, vanishing between evergreens.

My heart sped in my chest at his disappearance.

"Leon?" I muttered into the suddenly chilly forest.

His head appeared between branches as did his hand. "What are you waiting for?"

He waited for me to lay my hand in his and then tugged me into the trees where I almost bumped into his shoulder.

Almost. But I stabilized myself in time to stop and keep upright beside him, my attention solely on the small stone cabin that was nestled against a rock-wall as if seeking shelter from the wind that was cutting through the tiny clearing.

"This is—"

"Unexpected," he finished for me.

I nodded.

A couple of steps away, the building, belonging more in a fairytale than the real world, stood with a carved, wooden door and carved window blinds, a tiny chimney atop age-worn rooftrees.

"Totally." I marveled at the building and didn't wait for Leon to lead the way before I took a closer look. "This has to be ancient." I took a closer look at the iron door handle and lock. They were rusty as if they hadn't been used in years.

"Grandpa Leon inherited it from his grandmother and she from hers," he said with a shrug and pulled a set of equally ancient-looking keys from his pockets. "Most Lightbringer families have some retreat where their history and knowledge are hidden." He stepped up to the door, and the lock squealed as he turned the key. With one hand, he pushed the door open, gesturing for me to enter.

A retreat. That was exactly what I needed. Not the bright corridors of school or the sad face of my mother. Even Jo … I couldn't pull her any deeper into this. The simple fact that the Shadowbringer had gotten involved when taking her to the nurse was too much. He was after me, and I couldn't have her in danger's path. So I had resorted to long phone calls with her instead of hanging out at school.

She had missed a couple of days after the incident, and I dearly hoped Lucas Ferham quickly forgot how much I cared about my friend. Not that he had spoken a word to either her or me until earlier today when he had reminded Leon and me so eloquently that time was running out—my time.

When I didn't move, Leon ducked through the low door and pulled something else from his pocket on the way in.

I followed just in time to see a flame flicker to life in his hand. He replicated the fire on candles, which were sitting on every other surface in the cozy, dusty place.

"No one has been here in a while," he apologized as he wiped a layer of dust off the table before a narrow fireplace. "I didn't think I'd ever need to return." From the look on his face, I could tell that the memories he had made here weren't exclusively good ones.

I closed the door behind us as quietly as I could manage, wondering if anyone besides the Milliari family had ever set foot in this place. It surely did look untouched by anything but time.

The window blinds blocked out the gray daylight, leaving us with the warm orange hues of the fire. However, the flames were too small to heat the room, and after wandering through the forest in the cold October weather, I was shivering.

Leon noticed—of course, he did—and dropped his backpack on a chair before he pulled his scarf from his neck, folding it around my shoulders with a smile. "Here." He added his arms atop the soft material and pulled me against his chest. "The Shadowbringer would be disappointed if you froze to death before he gets a chance to grab your soul." There was little humor in his voice despite the sweet smile on his lips.

Speaking of the Shadowbringer... "He did have a chance, and he didn't take my soul," I pointed out, wondering why my words sounded as if I was defending him. "Why do you think that is?"

Leon detached himself from me, holding me at arm's length, and studied me with weary eyes. "I wish I knew," he admitted with defeat in his voice. "I thought he'd strike the second he got the chance, but instead"—he shook his head in frustration—"instead, he let you believe he was actually helping you." He let go of me with a sigh, leaving me to wrap my own arms around my chest to replace the warmth he'd taken with him. "There is something off about it."

"That's why we're here," I reminded him, "right? To figure out what the hell-angel wants."

Leon lifted an eyebrow. "Hell-angel?"

"Isn't that what he is?" I followed him as he made his way to the fireplace, put together some kindling, and started a fire.

"Hell, definitely," he said as he stared into the flaring flames. "But, an angel..."

"Isn't he like you?" I presented what I thought I had pieced together. "A messenger angel but taking souls to hell instead of heaven."

Leon lifted his gaze to mine. "He's very much different from us," he said, reminding me that he wasn't the only one with angel essence but that I would be like him soon enough.

"How?" I wanted to know, holding his gaze as the fire grew and crackled, brightening his features and letting shadows dance across the planes of his face.

"For one, he's immortal," Leon threw at me with an unreadable look.

Even though Cas had indicated it, it hit me like a bolt of lightning. "Immortal." I stared into Leon's dark eyes, into the depths of knowledge that I yet had to learn. "Like never-dying immortal?"

"How many other types of immortal are there?"

21. LEON

The orange glow of the hearth-fire warmed Laney's face, chasing the shadows away—at least, the ones that were apparent on her skin. The ones that hid behind her crystal-clear eyes were an entirely different story.

I sat back in the wooden chair I had pulled up to the fire, not even bothering to open the window blinds. Some things were best left hidden—things such as the contents of this cabin.

"I think I found something," she whispered from her own chair where she sat bundled up in my scarf and jacket, still looking like she was freezing. For a moment, I had wondered if she was sick, shivering beside the fire. But then I remembered how I had felt coming here for the first time. How I had literally felt the power resonating within the walls of the cabin—the power of generations.

It was then that I'd known Grandpa had been telling the truth; that there was more than what was apparent to the eye in this world.

I held out my hand and let Laney lay the book into mine, making sure her fingers brushed against my skin.

Her touch didn't fail to make me feel the way it always did. Alive.

Her eyes locked on mine for a brief second, lips twitching involuntarily as I let her take in my face. I knew it was a matter of patience—not my best trait—until she would realize that none of it was an act. That none of our embraces, of our hand-holding, was something I took lightly. She had ceased being a mere friend a long time ago. Sadly, she had never realized just how much I saw when I looked at her, when I looked into the electric blue of her eyes where heaven and hell seemed to collide.

When she tore away from my gaze, I lifted the book I held and pretended to study it, unable to truly read the meaning of the words when she was so close. Not that I needed to read the page before me. I had memorized most of the contents of all the rows of books and journals years ago when I had gone through my own transformation and locked myself away here for a good number of days—until I'd been ready to take my first soul.

Grandpa had explained it all to me, the whole process of inhaling a soul, how it would settle in my chest, right where the angel's essence was woven into me, and how I would be able to use that same essence like a map to take the soul home.

"What do you think?" Laney asked with the same whisper as before, almost like she was anxious she would wake up some slumbering evil. If she only knew how right she was. How close good and evil were to each other. Like love and hate, woven of the same texture that kept the world together.

I took in the page I had been blankly staring at and recognized the drawing of a figure wrapped in shadows. "A Shadowbringer," I noted. "The mechanics of their dark workings."

Laney nodded, hair sliding over her shoulders as she turned back to the fire as if reading answers there. "It says they bargain for souls," she told me what I already knew. "That Lightbringers will need to go up against them for the rest of eternity to try to save the ones worth saving."

There was something like reproach in her voice now that she had given up on whispering, and the melody of her alto carried like a sweet song through the scent of dust and fire.

"Until the end of the earth," I confirmed.

But that wasn't what bothered her. It was something completely different. Something I should have anticipated but was too ignorant to do.

"How do you know a soul is worth saving?" she asked, glancing at me with a look like molten ice.

Her question hit me right in the chest. Of course, she would wonder that. I had wondered when I was little. How does someone decide who was good and who was evil, who was redeemable and who was beyond saving?

"It's a gut feeling," I answered truthfully. For that was what it was. "Something you develop over time." I watched her as she tried to read from my face whether I was being serious. "Of course, there is that calling that occurs whenever discovering someone with a soul worth fighting for."

She tilted her head, probably wondering what I meant by that *calling*. So I gave her a small smile and explained, "The essence of the angel feels when a soul is about to leave a body—when someone is struggling with death—and we can answer the call, pulled by the knowledge of the angel."

Laney's face twisted. "Isn't that like ... I don't know ... having a parasite?"

I stifled a laugh. "Worse," I joked, a smile still stealing itself onto my lips as her expression turned into horrified. "Can you feel it at all yet?" I was curious. While my grandfather had manifested in his early teens and made me a Lightbringer through his death so early in life that I was still a child, Laney's grandmother had never manifested. So it was possible that she wasn't even like me. That she would never become like me and would remain trapped with the sight of the angels and nothing she could do about it. See souls leave, see Shadowbringers bargain for the souls of her loved ones—

"Nope." I couldn't pinpoint if that was relief or disappointment in her voice—or something entirely different. However, the face of the girl I had watched growing up, who I had been protecting by instinct almost as much as by choice, turned into that glowing texture that it only had when she was in her ethereal form. She had switched without noticing—again.

So I did, too—and within a second, the rush of sensations that came with being out of the solidity of the human form hit me. Everything was brighter, more intense, stronger. Full of the essence of things. I could see the light of Laney's soul shining behind her eyes, could feel her goodness, through and through, like a song that was singing to me.

She noticed then, as I lowered the book into my lap, that we both had switched, and her pupils widened as she took in my ethereal form. A gust of air huffed from her lips, her posture relaxing out of defying the cold and the power that filled the room, and she turned in her chair, facing me in full.

My body responded instantly, mirroring her, turning toward her until our knees touched.

And at that touch, something zinged through me. An electric current that at the same time made me fly and grounded me.

22. Laney

I had forgotten the book in Leon's hands. What had we been talking about?

All I saw was that light in him, felt the overwhelming intensity of him in the tiny cabin. The entire space seemed to hum with force—no, with power. A sensation I couldn't place; even stronger than when I had first switched into my ethereal form.

"How did that just happen?" I asked, my eyes taking in every angle and aspect of Leon's face, the depth of his eyes, dark and bright at the same time, the stillness with which he sat, his lips open as if he was tasting the atmosphere rather than seeing his surroundings.

I hadn't switched since that one time when Jo had slept in my living room. And I had thought I might find a way to control it before I accidentally exposed myself in public by vanishing into thin air.

"Some strong emotion, maybe," he suggested. As he stared into my eyes, I could imagine what strong emotion he might have felt. But he was right. Strong. Fear from the world of the Shadowbringer. Wonder about how things worked in this new life that I seemed to be damned to.

And then ... the miraculous creature that Leon was. The strong, angelic being.

For a long moment, we examined each other's faces as if we were trying to read in the layer of light and the secrets that were hidden there. Then, with a twitch of his lips, Leon leaned forward and reached out with a hand, brushing aside my hair, his fingers lingering by my cheek when he had tucked the strands behind my shoulder.

"You are so beautiful," he whispered as if now he was anxious to keep those words between us and us only.

My stomach did that thing that felt as if thousands of little wings were winding through my insides, and heat flooded my cheeks. I blinked and turned to the side, my eyes examining the flames rather than acknowledging the obvious beauty of the Lightbringer before me.

"Don't hide," he murmured, his fingertips brushing along my cheekbone, down my jaw until they dropped into his scarf. He wrapped his hand around it and gently pulled me forward by the soft fabric. "Don't ignore that things have changed between us."

His words ran through me like searing heat and glacial cold all at once. He was right. Things had changed. Too much to pretend they hadn't. Too much to act as if his embrace wasn't the safest place in the world, as if his fingers around mine weren't like a lifeline—I looked up, and his gaze met me with branding intensity—or to ignore how much my body was aching to close that gap between us.

"I am still Laney," I whispered, our breaths mingling, so close was his face, his hand still tangled in his scarf, securing me into his lips' reach.

"And I am still Leon." His eyes grazed down to my mouth, thick lashes hiding the dark depths of them, and I wondered if he felt it, too, the need to seal our lips together. "Still the same Leon. Only, now you know who he is," he whispered against my mouth, not more than an inch from releasing us from those chains of our friendship and allowing me to experience the man behind the best friend for once.

The door banged open with a crash, bringing in a flood of cold evening air and making both Leon and me shrink apart.

Leon was on his feet first, taking a protective stance in front of me while I was still struggling to keep myself upright. A growl escaped the man, so tame, so gentle a second ago, and I realized what had happened with a gasp when the storm-gray eyes of the Shadowbringer greeted me from the threshold.

"Bad timing?" He cocked his head and took a step into the room.

"You have no idea," Leon glowered at the boy who had intruded on our private moment, his arms reaching back as if to check I was still there, safely within his reach.

It took a second for the shock to leave my system and for a mixture between fear and annoyance to replace it with the bubbling rush of adrenaline. The Shadowbringer had to have followed us into the forest. And now, he had come to take my soul.

"I have been known to show up when it is of the least convenience for your kind." He lifted his chin at Leon, or at me, or both of us—I couldn't tell—resentment in his handsome face.

"You can go back to hell for all I care." Leon took a step toward the Shadowbringer, the layer of light on him shining more brightly as he moved in the direction of the enemy.

"Well, wouldn't that be convenient for you?" The Shadowbringer chuckled darkly, his voice pure night, no stars and no brightness showing this time as he bent sideways to have a better view of me and said, "It would be most convenient for *me* if you just listened to your grandmother for once."

I stared at him, clueless as to what he might be meaning.

All he did was hold my gaze, making me wonder if I *should* know what he was talking about, and added. "Mrs. Parker was a wise woman. Her advice should not be taken lightly."

"You shouldn't walk around, handing out advice either," Leon warned the Shadowbringer. "In fact, you shouldn't be walking around here at all. How *did* you find us?"

The Shadowbringer chuckled again. "As if your kind has ever been any good at hiding your tracks." He sauntered into the cabin, hands in his pockets as if he didn't have a care in the world, huffed out a set of candles on the cupboard, and coughed at the cloud of dust that rose in the air before him; then he leaned against the wood and raised his eyebrows at us. "You should be cleaning more often in here. It's like a paradise for dust mites."

"You shouldn't be talking about paradise as if you had any clue what that meant," Leon retorted.

In response, the Shadowbringer just chuckled and pulled one hand from his pocket, waving off Leon's comment. "All I wanted to do was make sure Laney here remembers Gran's precious advice. That's all." He pushed away from the cupboard and prowled back to the door as if nothing had happened. But before he crossed the threshold, he paused and glanced at me over his shoulder. "Nice scarf," he said to Leon. "Didn't you have anything better to offer her?" And then to me, "If you ever feel cold, Laney, call for me. There is plenty of heat where I came from."

Dumbfounded, I stood and watched the Shadowbringer march out the door, and as quickly as he had shown up, he disappeared.

"What was that," I ground out just before Leon rushed to the door and banged it shut with the push of one hand. It rattled on its hinges but didn't break.

"This"—he gestured into the air—"was your new classmate interrupting the first time I worked up the courage to actually kiss you." He eyed me from behind blond strands, fury the only emotion left on his beautiful Lightbringer face. He was still in his ethereal form as was I. I couldn't, however, tell if Cas had been corporeal or not.

As he held my gaze, his words settled in, and the moment before the Shadowbringer had walked in flooded me like a mystical memory. Leon had actually been about to kiss me. My skin tingled, and his gaze, no matter how furious, felt like a gentle touch as I understood what he had been saying.

But before I could say anything, react, tell him I was glad that was all the Shadowbringer had done, Leon turned to pick up his backpack and grabbed my hand.

"It's time you learn to travel on angel essence," was all he said, no softness in his eyes, no glowing excitement, no warmth. Just the dark depths that promised an efficient solution to the problem the Shadowbringer was becoming. "We need to get back to civilization where that bloodhound of the devil cannot just barge in like a maniac."

My head bobbed automatically. Even if this new, soldier-like side of Leon was as unpredictable as the electric current his touch now made circulate in my body, I trusted him to know what needed to be done.

"You need to feel it," he said and placed one hand on his heart.

I didn't need to ask what he meant, for in my chest, something had started pulsing like a second heart—not the thudding, wild beat of the organ that ensured life but a resonating that made me feel alive on a different level. The essence of the angel.

Leon saw the question in my eyes and nodded. "Reach for it with your mind. Embrace it," he instructed. "Become one with it."

I tried and tried, but the sensations ebbed whenever I felt I might get a hold of it.

Beside me, Leon became nervous. "You're pushing too hard," he commented. "You need to be gentle. Cradle it. It's the essence of a divine being through which we are able to do what we do. Invite it to assist you."

As he spoke, I did feel the sensation spread. It vibrated along my chest and through my limbs into my mind until I felt light and bodiless.

"Good," Leon's voice was a distant trickle of words that was steering me. His hand, however, seemed to weave right into that new, shapeless being I had become. "Now, fly back to the car."

He didn't wait for me to panic at his demand but tugged on my arm, making me lift off into the air and flit through the trees as if their thick branches and solid trunks weren't obstacles at all. I didn't feel any more of them than a light breeze. And then, I was flying. Moving through the air beside Leon, zooming forward to where I could make out the edge of the forest. There was nothing that could hold me back. Nothing.

The words Cas had spoken hit me much later when I was alone in my room, back in my corporeal form, blanket pulled up to my nose, and listening to the sounds of the wind.

Leon was out there somewhere. I hadn't invited him to stay the night. Not after what had happened—almost happened—at the cabin. I wasn't ready to face what this shift in our relationship meant ... or would mean if we got to that point of the almost kiss again.

Also, I couldn't stop thinking about Gran's advice. There had been two times she had given me advice in those final days of hers; my chest ached at the thought of how I had last seen her, dissolving into a silver star and vanishing into Leon's mouth.

Stay away from him, Laney. That was the first warning, and *Be careful who you give your heart to.*

She had warned me about Leon first and then—

The second warning still didn't make any sense to me. Had she warned me about Leon because she could see him and didn't understand what he was? That he was taking souls to heaven ... he was one of the good guys.

Had she even known the difference between the Shadowbringers and the Lightbringers?

I was no longer sure how much else she had been hiding from me.

The rhythmical footsteps climbing the stairs that could only be my mother approaching, followed by a soft knock on the door.

As I called for her to come in, Mom popped her head through the door. "I just wanted to let you know I'm home, honey." She examined me in the dim light of the small lamp on my nightstand and smiled. "I know I've been working day and night," she said with the face that only a mother with a guilty conscience could show, "but I promise we'll do something together on the weekend, all right?"

I propped myself up on my elbows and returned her smile. Normal. This was normal. Mom sneaking in late, worrying about the weekends, making plans, dropping them last minute. It was comfortable. Not like the sudden crossfire of heaven and hell I had gotten in-between.

"That would be great, Mom," I said and felt my heart warm as all guilt vanished from her features, leaving a broad smile on her tired face.

"I love you, Laney. Sleep well."

"Love you, too, Mom." I watched her retreat from the room, and the familiar sounds of the shower and her footsteps shuffling back and forth through the rooms carried me into a light sleep that randomly showed me Gran's face and Leon's and Cas's. And it wasn't a nightmare.

23. LANEY

The weekend came fast and with all the relief of not being exposed to Lucas Ferham's unreadable stares for two short days. It also came with a twenty-four-seven plan of Leon's on how to stay safe from the Shadowbringer. It involved him hanging out at my place, him walking me to Santoni's, him all but sleeping on the floor beside my bed.

He wasn't happy when I shut the door in his face on Saturday morning after explaining that some mother-daughter time was in order. But he was a good soldier and swallowed my rejection—on different levels.

Neither of us had brought up that almost-kiss again. He hadn't pushed for anything but to stay around me and make sure I was safe. And I—well, I hadn't brought up that my grandmother had warned me about him the first time she had met him.

I had spent every unoccupied second, wondering what exactly Gran had known that wasn't apparent to my eyes—

Then, this whole Lightbringer and Shadowbringer thing hadn't been apparent to my eyes for seventeen years before it was shoved right into my face at my Gran's deathbed.

I ground my teeth and stirred my hot chocolate.

"You don't think we could have invited him to come along?" Mom wondered again. She had observed my fierce denial of needing Leon's presence for breakfast and had come to her own conclusions. Ones that, unfortunately, were very similar to what Leon had let his own parents believe.

"Honestly, Mom, I'd rather hang out with you today. I see Leon's smoldering gaze every day."

Mom didn't truly buy it when I smiled. I could tell by the way she pulled on the short strands of her hair, nervous for some reason, while the late morning sun flooding the space behind her made the dirty dishes on the counter sparkle.

"You know you can tell me anything, Laney."

Of course, I knew. And I *did* tell her everything ... everything that didn't involve knowledge of heaven and hell and the pretty boys who delivered souls to either destination. Or that I one day would be one of those messengers who sucked souls in with a breath and took them to heaven. That an angel-parasite was living inside of me—I shuddered. The concept of the angel essence was still something I couldn't fully wrap my head around even with the books Leon had brought for me from his cabin. I'd read about how the essence of the angels was mainly light, and that was what created the glow in the non-corporeal form. Also, with Lightbringers being mortal and needing to learn about their abilities when they emerged, it cost Team Heaven a lot of time that Team Hell didn't waste with their smaller group of immortal Shadowbringers.

With a sigh through my nose, I eyed my mother and said, "There is a lot going on at school, Leon being just one of those things that are making my days more draining." It was the truth, and Mom recognized it as such.

She lifted a plate from the table and held it out for me to pick up a raspberry Danish. I didn't hesitate.

"He's such a good kid," she said, watching me bite into the pastry and chew.

She had no idea just how good. So good he had been chosen to deliver souls to heaven. To bargain with the Shadowbringers for those who stood a chance of going to heaven. Too good—

Too good for me.

"He is also my best friend," I pointed out, knowing that this argument was no longer valid. That ship had sailed.

"When I see the two of you look at each other, I see something different," she noted with a wistful look.

I had nothing to say to that. So I lifted my cup and took a sip, waiting for the chocolate to do its magic and lift me up, and glanced out the window.

Leon was there, leaning against a tree—in his ethereal form, of course—a smile painted on his face. He waved, acknowledging that I had noticed him, and pushed himself up into the air within a fraction of a second until he sat on a branch. I noticed the glow even now that I was in my common, inconspicuous form. My stomach gave a jolt that shouldn't be there.

"It's okay when feelings change, Laney," Mom continued her thoughts on Leon and me. "It is common that friendship becomes love and—"

"I don't think I love Leon, Mom," I stopped her. No, I couldn't allow this conversation. Not now that Leon was out there, potentially listening to every word we were speaking.

From the way his face changed at my words, I had an idea he had heard—

Again, my stomach jolted, and I knew it wasn't the big sip of hot chocolate. The feeling of Leon's breath on my face, of his lips an inch from mine ... I had to look away from the window in order to hide the heat that was rising in my cheeks.

"Oh," was all Mom said in response before she picked up a Danish and bit into it. She chewed thoughtfully and swallowed then said, "I ran into Jo and her Dad at the drugstore the other day." She poured herself a glass of juice and leaned back in her chair. "Something about her looks different." She seemed to be searching for words. "Tired, somehow."

I thought of the day I had taken Jo to the nurse's office—and the Shadowbringer who had invaded my efforts. And was close to rolling my eyes. "She hasn't been feeling well a lot lately," I agreed. "She says she's fine, though."

Mom gave me a pensive look. "Not everyone who says they're fine actually *is* fine."

Involuntarily, my mind flipped to the earlier months of the year when I had been still stuck in the aftereffects of the accident Leon and I had witnessed. How many times had I said I was fine? And how many times had it been true?

"I'll talk to her on Monday," I promised. "And don't worry about the Leon situation," I added. "We're good. The same as always."

Mom smiled, her nose crinkling as it only did when she was overdoing a fake-smile. Then she pursed her lips, pondering for a long moment. "Just know that it is all right when feelings change. It happened with your father and me." She paused, waiting for my reaction as she talked about Dad, who she usually didn't bring up. "It's okay to fall in love with your best friend." She smiled—a real smile this time. "And it's okay to fall out of love again, too."

There was nothing I could think of to say. Even had there been something, I wouldn't have been able to speak, for a sensation like a bolt of lightning ran through my chest, and it cost me all of my focus to keep my face straight.

What was going on?

Somewhere in the background, Mom's phone buzzed. From the corner of my eye, I saw her get up and dive into her bag.

It took about a second for Leon to show up beside me, still in his ethereal form, probably walking through walls and everything. It didn't shock me half as much as it should have when he placed a hand on my shoulder and bent so his lips were at my ear. "Breathe, Laney," he whispered without the least sign of worry that Mom could spot him showing in the calm flow of his breath.

It was tempting to turn and look at him, to try and read from his face what was going on, but Mom—thank God she had gotten to her feet and was pulling a glass from the cupboard above the sink, humming some song we had listened to in the car on the way back from Santoni's.

"You can feel it, right?" Leon asked, the quiet calm before a storm in his words.

There was no need for me to deny or confirm. He wouldn't have bolted into the room otherwise.

I wanted to ask what it was that I felt, if it was a bad sign that my chest felt as if it was breaking apart, but that would have needed spoken words ... words that I would never let cross my lips while next to Mom. I eyed her slender figure as she filled up the glass with orange juice and turned with a smile.

"I know I promised we'd do something together—" she hesitated as she took in my face, the expression that had to remind her of a constipated toddler rather than her teenage daughter.

"Tell her it's okay if she needs to work," Leon guided me like a lifeline, his hand on my shoulder warm and light and evoking that exciting electric current I usually just felt in my ethereal form. In reflex, my eyes darted to my hands to make sure everything was still corporeal.

I sighed through my nose.

"It's okay if you need to work, Mom," I said and forced myself to smile. It was honestly the expression of relief I felt crossing my features, but the pain in my chest made it easier to hide just how glad I was I wouldn't be expected to go on a shopping spree with her. Or play board games. Even if that was what I enjoyed most on our mother-daughter weekends.

"Really?" Mom didn't look convinced.

"Nod," Leon instructed, his thumb running over my shoulder in calming strokes, and I relaxed a bit. My chest expanded more easily at his reassuring touch, and my head bobbed obediently.

"It's fine, Mom," I improvised. "I have homework to do and whatnot."

Whatnot was what I hoped Leon would explain to me the second I was out of Mom's reach.

So when Mom drained her glass of juice, I lifted my cup and gulped down the hot chocolate, grimacing at the rush of sweetness in my mouth. "I'll be in my room," I let her know as I braced myself against the table and got up, Leon lifting most of my weight as he wrapped his hands around my waist and pulled me upright.

Mom was refilling her glass when I set my shaky steps toward the door and reached the doorframe before she turned. "Maybe I'll call Leon to come over." I managed a wink, which was meant for Mom as much as for Leon, who would have a chance to show up in his visible form and pick me up to do *whatnot*, and Mom would be none the wiser.

"Should I help clean this up?" I gestured at the table just to behave as normal as possible.

She shook her head. "You go call Leon." A smile brightened her temporarily concerned expression. "I'm sure he'll be delighted I am no longer claiming you for myself all day."

At that, Leon chuckled beside me. "You have no idea, Mrs. Dawson," he murmured, and I was glad my mother couldn't see or hear him.

When she turned her attention on the table once more, Leon gently guided me up the stairs, letting me lean against him as if he were as solid as in his corporeal form. I didn't think to ask him if I had switched, too. I didn't have the muse to check with a glance at my hands. All I did was breathe through that pain that felt like a crack was running through my chest, breaking it open with sharp force.

24. Laney

"I am not sure whether *don't panic* is the right way to put it," Leon said in his most gentle voice, "but please don't panic."

"Panic about what?" I blankly stared at him, now certain that I had flipped into the non-corporeal version of myself. "That thing that is prying my chest open?"

The pain hadn't ceased. It had gotten worse. Almost like someone was tearing an anchor from the inside out through my ribs.

"That"—Leon acknowledged the plain panic in my face with a frown and sat down next to me where I was perched on the edge of the bed like a bird about to take flight—"and the reason for why you are feeling the way you are."

He had my attention. "Whatever it is, spit it out." By now, anything had to be better than groping through the darkness of oblivion.

"You are feeling a soul call—" He stopped himself as he noticed the realization on my face.

"Like with Jo?" To my horror, Mom was the only other soul in this house at the moment, and if her soul suddenly drew me like Jo's that night—

What would I do? Could I simply rip it from her? Were Lightbringers even capable of killing? A shudder ran up and down my spine like spider legs.

"No—" Leon shook his head, exasperated, and I wished he would simply say what he was thinking instead of waiting for me to figure it out.

"Tell me," I demanded and flopped back into the blankets, fixing my gaze on the cream color of the ceiling and the dust particles dancing in the late morning light. Frustration sounded heavy in my voice, dulling the pain for a bit.

"You are feeling the call of a soul that needs to be transferred," he finally said, his eyes squinting as he looked down at me, biting his lower lip for a moment as if hesitant to finish the thought. "Someone is dying, Laney, and you are feeling that there will be work to be done."

I froze right there on the teal sheets and counted the irritatingly regular beats of my heart while Leon examined me, face first, then my tight shoulders, my arms flattened to my sides, and my hands clutching the cotton beneath me. "Breathe," he repeated. It was the only thing that made a difference. Focus on breathing.

"So you're saying," I stuttered between hasty gulps of air, "that this is my future?" I pointed a stiff finger at my chest. "I will be hurting like this for the rest of my life whenever a soul needs *saving*?"

To my surprise, Leon cringed at my words.

"We're not saving anyone, Laney," he said quietly. "We are taking the souls where they belong."

I panted and clamped my hand around his forearm to pull myself upright again.

"It will fade when you follow the direction of the tug," he added and lifted a hand to gesture out the north-west window, and as I watched him, I knew it was true—that was the direction that anchor in my chest was trying to break through my ribs and sail toward.

It was then that I noticed the frown hadn't left Leon's face. It was a slight crease between his arched brows that I had noticed that day he had taken me to the bookstore; the day before Gran had died.

"You are feeling the same thing," I concluded. He had to be. It was the same face. The rare frown on his usually so smooth and cheerful face.

His chin dipped in response. "What did you think?"

Now it was I who cringed. He had been living for too many years with this burden, without sharing it. His pain ... he had been hiding it since he had been little more than a child. How did he stand it so calmly, so gracefully? I hadn't even lived through one calling soul, and I was already despairing.

"What do we do now?" I asked into the taut space between us where suddenly, nothing mattered but that I had so dearly underestimated the smiling boy who had been protecting me all my life. He wasn't just divine; he was brave and strong. Stronger than I could ever be.

He turned away as if he had read something in my eyes he'd rather not. "I know what I need to do." He sighed and studied the floor rather than facing me again. "But it is up to you whether or not you're ready to answer that call."

I loosed a breath, unsure of what was the right thing to do, of what he expected, of whether my decision would affect the chances of someone going to heaven.

"The pain will fade the second someone takes the soul home," he added, and by his phrasing, I could tell that he didn't mean heaven only—there was a Shadowbringer ready to take the soul to the fiery pits of hell.

And suddenly, it was very clear what I needed to do ... even if it turned my stomach just to think about it. "I'll come," I whispered. "But you need to tell me what to expect first. And you can't leave me alone wherever we're going. I don't want to get stuck with a soul I can't deliver or lost somewhere in paradise."

Leon's head flipped to the side, and his gaze locked on mine, eyes a liquid tone of caramel rather than the usual dark brown as if relief had brightened him from inside. "Here's what you need to know." He ran a hand through his hair, shoving back the strands that kept coming loose. "Travel with me on the angel essence; let the tug guide you. When we arrive wherever the soul calls us, all you need to do is watch and learn. You don't need to inhale the soul; you don't need to take it to heaven." He gave me a serious nod. "I can do that."

I wasn't sure if I found his words reassuring at all. "And what do I do?"

At that, his frown deepened. "You observe how to deal with a Shadowbringer when he comes to claim what's ours."

Cas.

My stomach tightened for no apparent reason other than that if I followed the call of the soul, I would be facing the

Shadowbringer who wanted my own soul as a trophy. And I wasn't sure if I was ready. Especially not after what had happened at the cabin.

If you ever feel cold, Laney, call for me. There is plenty of heat where I came from.

I shook my head at the memory of Cas's voice, of his bored gaze as he had stopped on the threshold. I still hadn't worked up the courage to talk to Leon about what had happened at the cabin—not the Shadowbringer but that he had admitted he'd been about to kiss me.

And that I hadn't been at all intending to avoid it.

If it hadn't been for Cas, Leon and I might actually be what everyone already thought we were.

To my surprise, that thought felt about as natural as I could allow myself to believe.

I studied his face, his high cheekbones, and his large, dark-framed eyes, the tan of his skin, and the stark contrast of his white-blond hair. He was stunning even with the crease that angled his eyebrows together more narrowly than usual.

"Let me handle the bargaining," Leon tore me from my thoughts. "Just promise you won't let the Shadowbringer upset you."

"If he is there," I wondered aloud, trying to memorize everything Leon told me, to listen intently rather than stare at his face, "won't he try to steal *my* soul?"

To my surprise, Leon shook his head. "Not while he's on duty. Securing a soul is the most sacred job in the world—even for the Shadowbringers. He won't try anything until after the bargaining is over. Besides, I will be there the whole time. He can very well try—"

Leon bit his lip as if he was cutting off his words.

My chest ached, the pain more bearable now that I grasped the meaning of it and understood what I might actually be capable of doing to stop it. It was a relief to know I would be safe even when Cas and his disturbing stares would haunt me days after—I was already sure they would.

"Also, the sooner you get acquainted with the procedure, the better. Once you have transferred the first soul yourself, you'll be safe from him forever," Leon added in an afterthought. A quite important afterthought, but it didn't matter, for my mind was already circling the one issue that I had been unable to wrap my head around.

"What does that bargaining look like?" I wanted to know. If that was truly the way things went, if someone negotiated on my behalf whether I could go to heaven or should go to hell, what did my life, my actions, my choices mean? If, in the end, all that mattered was how well the light side was prepared to bargain with the dark side.

"It's fairly easy," Leon said with an unchanged expression. "Lightbringers get called to every soul who is worthy of going to heaven, even if they have done wrong, while Shadowbringers are called to every soul who deserves a place in hell." He gestured in the air between us, shaping spaces, forms that made no sense to me. "If someone was only good in life, and it is clear they belong in heaven, a Shadowbringer may show up but never claim the soul. It is the same the other way around." He paused to check whether or not I was still following him and found me listening attentively. His voice helped tune out the ache in my chest. "The vast mass of people however are neither—entirely good or entirely bad that is. They are something in between with plenty of sins and plenty of good deeds redeeming them. We feel—both the Lightbringers and the Shadowbringers—that there is a reason why they should be in either of the realms of the afterlife, and we feel the urge to secure them for our side. So we bargain, we negotiate, we try to convince the other side that the souls belong to ours."

I listened to Leon, my imagination running wild, my thoughts already ahead in a hospital where someone was bleeding out, Cas and Leon conversing beside the gurney, flipping coins for the soul. No, that couldn't be it. It would mean there was nothing worth fighting for in our human life, once we had gone wrong. That there was no chance to be sure we would ever be *safe* from going to hell. Not that hell even was a concept I had truly believed in a couple of months ago.

"How do you know," I asked, unable to hold myself back. "How do you know who to fight for and who to give up?"

He stared back into my eyes, a flicker of emotion crossing his features. "It is hard to explain. But you'll understand once you are there. Once you see it happening. It's like some part of us knows where that person stands on a scale between either side. It's that one moment, only when they leave their bodies, that we know." He shrugged. "A gift of the angel, I suppose. Like traveling on its essence or shifting into our ethereal form."

Suddenly, my own life flickered before my eyes. I had done plenty of things that I wasn't proud of. Nothing that would give me a criminal record, but I was sure that when I died, a Lightbringer wouldn't be the only one waiting to take my soul. There would be a Shadowbringer for sure.

As if Leon read my thoughts from my eyes, he leaned forward and brushed his fingers across my cheek. "I will be there to fight for you when your time has come, Laney. No matter where you stand on that scale." His gaze was fierce, but his hand was so gentle it made me shiver over the aching tug in my chest. "Even if hell were your only option. I would fight until the very end."

25. LANEY

When we arrived at the scene, my stomach turned. This wasn't for the faint-hearted. Leon's hand was still there on mine as we materialized in the crossing where a red van had been squished by a truck. The truck driver was being loaded into an ambulance while the driver of the van was being zipped up in a black body bag.

So, this was it. The first dying I had *heard*. I didn't even know if it was a man or a woman—all I could tell was that the person's life had abruptly ended.

"Any second now," Leon said and pulled me closer toward the gurney where they were loading the deceased.

The pain in my chest had faded the moment we had taken off to follow the soul's call. Now that I was less than three steps away from the target, I could feel the thrumming of the life—not the physical life of the human body but of the soul that was struggling to hatch—like a beat to the cacophony of shouts and orders among the firemen and paramedics, the words of speculation among the spectators who had gathered by the edge of the town.

Had I walked here from my home, it might have taken me twenty minutes or less, but traveling on angel essence, it had taken a blink of an eye.

"There," Leon commented, guiding me along as we followed the gurney to an ambulance. "Can you feel it?" He didn't wait for me to respond but let his head flip to the side with a frown. "I was wondering if this time you were going to grace us with your absence," Leon said sourly, and I didn't need to turn and look to know who he was talking to.

"There, there," Cas said by way of greeting. "And then I thought you'd remember that you owe me a favor."

Leon ground his teeth.

I remembered the Shadowbringer's words as he had left Gran's room at the nursing home.

"Have you come to call it in?" was all Leon said before Cas stepped into view, taking the opposite side of the gurney to gloat at us before he reached for the body bag as if he was going to open it.

I sucked in a breath, and Cas gave me a grin that made me wonder if that was what he had been taught in hell or if he had been born with it ... given he had been born at all. How could anyone keep up with the specifics of that species?

"Not freezing today?" he asked me, shoving his free hand into his pocket, and leaned against the ambulance next to a paramedic who was writing a report.

I ignored him as best I could, reminding myself of what Leon had promised—that I would be safe with him; that the Shadowbringer wouldn't try anything until the soul was secured.

"Oooh—" Cas grimaced, reading from the clipboard. "Broken neck and an open fracture of both thighs. The poor bastard bled out before help could even arrive." He winked at me, watching me fight the nausea that threatened to make me double over, and braced one foot against the car. "So you are ready to transfer a soul?" he asked me with a voice full of stars and night, drowning out the rest of the world for a brief moment with a deep gaze into my eyes.

I shuddered, searching for a smart response. Something that would leave him in the dark about how miserable I was as the three of us were waiting for the soul to emerge from the bag—if that even was how it worked.

I was about to tell the Shadowbringer that he could go back to that hot place he so loved, and leave the soul to Leon, when a bright, silvery light rose from the body bag. I halted, mouth open, words lost, as I observed a man's shape float up and hover.

"I lay claim to his soul," Leon said harshly. He had let go of my hand for the benefit of stepping closer to the gurney.

Cas eyed Leon with a bored face. "You realize that he belongs in my domain as much as in yours," he drawled before he glanced at the paramedic, who had put down the report and was now opening the doors to load the body into the back of the ambulance, oblivious to our presence—or the significance of what was happening to the lost patient.

As Cas spoke, I tried to sense it, where exactly that man stood on the scale between good and evil. If he was meant for heaven or hell. Yet there was little I felt but the squeamishness in my stomach that had replaced the nausea ever since I had turned my back on the wrecked vehicles, the red stains on the street, and all the thoughts and memories that came with them.

"Heaven," Leon said, his tone businesslike despite the daggers he'd shot at the Shadowbringer from his eyes.

"I don't know what that man did to want him in your domain so badly," Cas retorted, "but I am willing to let you take him, if"—he turned to me, his eyes the gray of thunderclouds—"she does it."

Several things happened at once. My heart picked up speed, fluttering along in my chest like a tortured butterfly. My knees started shaking as if someone had knocked into them with an iron bar. Leon shook his head beside me, making me feel even more useless than I already did—his sidekick while he saved the soul.

Not to forget the wide smile Cas gave me as he noticed the horror that rushed through me. I couldn't. Even if I wanted to, I just couldn't say the words. That I would do it.

It would save not only the soul, but it would save me from being hunted by the Shadowbringer. As soon as I'd taken my first soul to heaven, I'd be safe.

Was it irony that it was the Shadowbringer who suggested I rush into it and do it right now?

"You think you're smart, don't you?" Leon hissed, ignoring how I went to pieces beside him, his anger a controlled mask on his features now, but I knew him too well, not to see the white-hot rage beneath it. "You know the rules. Play by them." Oh, Leon would punch the mattress when he got home, imagining it was the Shadowbringer's face.

"Rules—" Cas shook his head before he winked at me again. "Are you up for it?"

"Halfway," Leon interrupted before I could give an answer. "He is on the scale halfway between heaven and hell." He folded his arms across his chest, eyeing the soul as it contracted into a silver star the way Gran had.

And there, it hit me. I knew that Leon was right. I just knew. Like my lungs knew how to breathe or my heart how to beat. I knew that the soul amidst us messengers of heaven and hell was on the exact centerline between our domains. He belonged to each of us equally.

"Give him a chance to purge himself of all his regrets," Cas suggested, his voice smooth, unaffected by Leon's rigidness. "Let him take a couple of decades in hell before I send him over."

Leon growled.

"All right." Cas shrugged. "Years then."

"You can do that?" I blurted out into the middle of their bargaining, causing both their heads to snap to me. "You can send them to hell now and pick them up later?"

While Leon frowned, Cas fashioned an expression somewhere between humorous and wistful. "It is called purgatory, love." He turned to Leon. "So, do you concur that our friend here could do with a couple of years before he joins you in your boring, fluffy realm?"

He didn't even stop to gloat at my shock. Neither did Leon, who was so busy proposing an exact number of months that he didn't seem to realize that he had never told me that the bargaining wasn't about where the soul would be taken but about how long they had to remain in purgatory. And that purgatory wasn't a place somewhere in between. It was right there, in the realm of eternal punishment.

The nausea returned, and I stumbled back, unable to draw a deep breath. The gurney had been loaded into the ambulance, and the thud of the doors falling shut behind it didn't disturb the Lightbringer and the Shadowbringer who were both eager to place the soul in the right level of hell for its life choices. I didn't hear the end of the bargain, the conclusion they came to, as I retreated step after step until I stood in the meadow on the corner where the two streets met and watched from a distance the way Cas leaned forward, mouth open, and the silver star floated between his lips.

Hell it was, then. If only temporarily. Hell.

"You didn't think of telling me, did you?" I bit at Leon as we returned home only minutes later.

He had grabbed my hand after he had sealed the bargain with Cas, and we had traveled back to my bedroom. Less than twenty minutes had passed before my mother's footsteps stopped at the head of the stairs as she called, "I'll be back before dinner," and was already on her way again when I answered that I'd be home for sure.

Whether or not she'd heard me, I couldn't tell. I couldn't even tell right now in what form I was. However, by the way I all but sensed Leon's form in the room, I guessed it was non-corporeal. Which meant my words had been as silent to my mother as Leon, Cas, and I had been to the paramedic. And invisible, of course. That was something that I still had to get used to.

It might come in handy if I ever thought about playing a trick on Avery to get back at her for being extra-horrible.

My thoughts stuttered to a halt at the thought of what I had learned just minutes ago. Purgatory was a thing. It wasn't heaven and hell, and one simple decision that would be made about my soul one day, but I would be sent to redeem myself—and it didn't make my heart feel any lighter to think of that as a chance. It was still purgatory, run and maintained by the agents of hell, it seemed.

"I didn't think it was important," Leon defended himself.

"Not important?" I stared at him incredulously and wished I could switch into my corporeal form just to know the windows would shake in their frames when I yelled at him. "You thought that this little detail was something I should find out while the Shadowbringer is there to witness?"

Not that it was important whether or not Cas knew how much it had shaken me to learn that there was a chance I might end up in purgatory; it bothered me that he had seen that Leon hadn't told me about it. That he didn't trust me enough, apparently, to tell me. Or that he thought I wasn't ready.

"As I said, as soon as there is doubt that a soul belongs in one of the two domains entirely, there is bargaining."

"Yes, but you didn't tell me what exactly was being negotiated." I drummed my fingers on the dresser and studied Leon with a feeling of betrayal.

"Now you know," was all Leon said. "You did well for a first mission," he added and gave me a soft gaze.

I didn't feel like returning it. I didn't feel like forgiving him ... yet.

And then, I realized that not forgiving him might already buy me a ticket to hell. If only for a couple of weeks.

26. Cas

It was a darker day than I had expected. Quite honestly, with decades over decades, every day appeared darker than the last. There was no end to it. And nothing that would fill my time with some excitement other than those few hours I spent at school. The last time I had been to school had been shortly before I had been turned into what I was now. The memories were vague and painful, and they all ended in the same scene—

My head flipped to the side in reflex at the sound of the girl's footfalls. Soft and light and bouncy. She was framed—as always—by two young women who seemed superior in wits and inferior in self-esteem. Avery, however, didn't seem to care. They supported her stage. It was all they were good for.

"So you've been scarce," Avery said in a honeyed tone, her hand braced on her hip right above where her low cut pants showed off her slender waist. I looked away, wondering if those many decades ago I would have felt a degree or two warmer at the sight.

"My apologies, Miss Avery," I said and cocked my head, giving each of the girls beside her a tight-lipped smile.

"See?" Avery turned to the one on her left, who actually had eyes the color of firs and skin like fresh cream. "That's how everyone should be addressing me."

The girl gave a nervous nod.

I tuned out the other voices, the footsteps that were shuffling to classes in the mid-morning. There was nothing much for me to do than wait. It seemed to be the story of my—what was it exactly if it wasn't a life?

"I am here now, aren't I?" I pointed out with the version of my voice that I normally used to shape the shadows.

Avery frowned for a brief moment before she managed to straighten her face as she took in my tone—the lack of enthusiasm at her attention.

"And just in time to witness my exit." She turned, tossing her reddish hair over her shoulder, and swaggered toward the classroom, leaving the fir-green-eyed girl to shrug at me in what seemed to be an apology.

"Never mind," I whispered at her as if I were sharing a secret, and she smiled, her full lips like fresh berries and her nose crinkling with authentic amusement.

"Are you coming, Al?" the Queen of High School called from the threshold, and Al staggered after her as if stung by a bee.

Those mortals ... so busy with their social games, their status, their popularity. If they knew where this took them. If they knew that seeking my attention was almost like knocking on the gates of hell.

With a sigh, I turned on my heels and followed the gaggle of girls to take my seat at the back of the room.

Laney walked in with the Lightbringer just before the teacher and hurried to her place near the quiet one whom I had carried to the nurse's office. The Lightbringer, however, gave me a burning gaze that might have branded me had I not been indestructible.

I waited for him to sit and turn to the front of the room before I returned to studying Laney's dark brown hair. It was braided today, unlike all the other days when she left if loose and I could find wavy patterns in its structure. Regardless, the braid exposed the column of her neck where a lace-trimmed, black shirt contrasted with her pale skin. The pattern reminded me of the fashion the women wore when I was little.

I flipped the book open and pretended to browse through the text as the teacher instructed while my focus remained on my target.

She was sitting rigidly in her chair as if she felt my gaze. As if she knew what it meant, too. The next class she would be spending apart from her protector, and I would finally get to talk to her again. It was necessary that she understood. I needed to—

The tug in my chest came as unwelcome as it came sudden, making me suck in a breath. But I wasn't the only one who felt it. Laney was shifting uncomfortably, sweat collecting at the nape of her neck where she rubbed her hand over her skin. The Lightbringer felt it as much as I did—only, she wasn't as skilled at hiding it.

A soul to bargain for if they felt it, too. Not just a one-way trip to hell for someone who had messed up their life.

The sensation was light, not yet urgent enough for me to leap out of my chair and skip into my non-corporeal form the second I was hidden from sight, but it was annoying enough to make me want to move around rather than sit and play teenager for the next forty-or-so minutes.

And if it was that difficult for me, how did the girl stand it?

She had almost collapsed the last time the Lightbringer had brought her to collect a soul. For a second, I had thought that he was serious. That she would take the soul and manifest as a Lightbringer right then and there. But by the state she'd been in—her greenish, sweat-sheathed skin, her flinching and cringing—I had known that if I taunted the Lightbringer to have her take the soul, he'd not allow it. She wasn't ready. Which meant more time for me to get what I wanted.

I leaned back in my chair and crossed my arms over my chest, wondering if it would be worth it to simply bolt from the room and give up on the high school drama. I wasn't made for it, anyway. I didn't know how to act like them, to speak like them, to care like them. And it didn't matter.

There was only one thing I knew, and that was giving souls a ride to hell. And that Laney's soul would upgrade my existence.

27. LANEY

Leon shot me a look that appeared to mean that I should stay put.

We hadn't spoken much since the other day when he had brought me along to collect a soul, and he hadn't apologized for leaving me in the dark about purgatory.

Nevertheless, he had spent his time making sure I was protected and cared for. Whether or not I liked it didn't matter. It was necessary. The Shadowbringer had been circling closer and closer every day at school, waiting for me at corners, a sly grin on his face, hands in his pockets, and storm-gray eyes scanning me with expectation. As if I was his personal experiment about to happen.

Now, as I dared to glimpse at him, Cas gave me the same grin and leaned back in his chair. From the look in his eyes, I couldn't make out whether or not he felt the tug … the pain, really.

So I hoped that this time, Leon and I would go alone and that I would manage to remain in my corporeal form long enough to make it out of the classroom once Leon gave the sign. He had promised he would do that even if I had called him all the names I could think of ... and instantly regretted it with an image of Cas waiting there at the end of my life, forcing my soul into hell for a good period of time.

I had made it halfway through the hour when Jo bent closer and asked if I was all right. I nodded and remembered that I had been wanting to ask her the same thing since the conversation with Mom. There was something more going on with Jo than just being constantly tired.

By the time the bell rang, I was sweaty and sure I could no longer sit still without screaming. There was a soul calling for my attention, and if I didn't answer the call, a Shadowbringer might come and claim it.

Leon met me by the door, his gaze anxiously darting to the back of the room, every now and then, to where Cas kept lounging in his chair as if he didn't have a care in the world. He didn't even look up at me when I searched his face for a sign of whether he would be getting in our way when collecting the soul. Instead, he called Avery's name the same way he had called mine, "Miss Avery."

Avery flashed a smile at the world before she turned, mid-step, to the Shadowbringer, her waves dancing on her shoulders.

Cas waited until she was fully facing him before he cut me a glance and said to Avery, "How about sitting with me for lunch today?" His eyes wandered to Avery's face, assessing as she was obviously displaying something on her features I couldn't see, presented with the view on her red mass of hair. Cas's smile of satisfaction had to be answer enough. So I rolled my eyes just as his gaze sought mine again, and then hurried to Leon, who was now tapping his foot against the linoleum.

"I don't even want to think what he wants to achieve by having lunch with her," he commented and held his arm open for me to slide under as we walked out.

I shrugged and felt his fingers closing around my shoulder in that familiar and newly exciting way that I denied myself to feel while I was still angry with him. However, the sensation was there. More by the day, and with my body struggling to change into its ethereal form, even more so. I felt him over the aching tug in my chest as if he were touching my bare skin.

Much to my dismay, I shivered at the thought.

"You cold?" he wanted to know, sensitive to my needs more than I could have ever imagined anyone capable of. But as a Lightbringer, it seemed he felt me on a different level— just as I felt him.

I shrugged again, a response I had perfected, and asked instead, "When can we go?"

The tug was becoming more pronounced now that we were in motion, and I could almost feel that the time had come. My Lightbringer senses seemed to improve as time was passing and as I was getting more exposure to the invisible world of the messengers of heaven and hell—and as I was slowly becoming one of them.

Too slowly. For the Shadowbringer was still after me. As long as I hadn't advanced to collecting souls myself, I would be in danger of his cruel game.

"Let's find a quiet corner to shift, and then we can be off." Leon walked me along the hallway, down toward the stairs that led to the gym. "It's almost time." He eyed me from the side, recognition in his face as I nodded. "You can feel that, too," he concluded. "You know that it is time ... well, your Lightbringer-self knows."

"That's good, right?" I hoped. "That means I am getting closer to transferring my first soul."

"Anything that increases the likelihood you'll be out of danger soon is good," was Leon's response as he pointed at a corner under the stairs and let go of me to glance over his shoulder and check if we had been followed before he hurried into the shadows.

The corridor was empty.

I followed suit, the tug in my chest almost unbearable now, and watched Leon switch into his ethereal form. "You remember how we got there last time?" He gave me an inquisitive look that made me feel like his apprentice rather than his friend, but I bobbed my head, eager to get to the soul and see this through so there would be peace and quiet in my chest.

"Good." His lips spread into a smile. "Then I'll see you *there*," he said with a significant look. "Wherever *there* is." And he was gone.

That was the beauty of it, Leon had explained. We never knew who was going to die or when exactly it would happen, or where; just that when someone's time had come, we'd feel that pull, and as long as we were willing to answer it, it would lead us right to the deathbed of a ready soul.

Leon trusted in my ability to make it by myself, or he wouldn't leave me behind like this. Also, he had to trust that I would be gone before the Shadowbringer could even think of coming after me. The odds were that Cas hadn't even felt that tug and Leon and I would be there and back before anyone could notice. And then, I would walk into that one class I dreaded all week—the one where Leon and I were separated.

The tug burned under my ribs as I concentrated on it. The direction was clear. I would take off right through the walls and head north from the school. The final destination was unclear but couldn't be too far away. At least, that was what Leon had explained one of the afternoons when he had tried to make conversation and I had refused to talk about anything other than Lightbringer details. I wouldn't allow him to hide important facts such as purgatory from me again.

I took a deep breath and was ready to switch—

Nothing happened. Not even the slightest change in my perception, in the way my body felt ... usually lighter in my ethereal form.

I was about to try again when a soft voice asked, "And you were trying what, exactly?"

I jerked around, my breath getting stuck as I stumbled into the side of the stairs and ended up kneeling on the floor, rubbing the shoulder I'd hit.

I found the Shadowbringer leaning against the opposite wall, ankles crossed and one hand in his pocket while he was gesturing at me with the other. "Not that I don't enjoy seeing you kneel, but you'll be late for class." He said it like it was a secret, tone hushed into a starlit murmur.

At first, I couldn't move, finding myself cornered by the enemy. Plus, he had the element of surprise on his side. "*You'll be late for class,*" I bit at him and pushed myself upright.

Leon, I thought, but even if I cried out his name right now, there wouldn't be an answer. Leon was out of reach, busy collecting that lucky soul that didn't have a Shadowbringer coming to bargain for it.

"Oh, I am not intending on going to class today," he informed me with a wicked smile ... the sort that made your blood freeze.

Meanwhile, the tug in my chest had started pulsing like a second heartbeat. It was time. I knew it. And I wasn't *there*.

"Neither am I," I told Cas and closed my eyes, letting the sensation lead me and conjured the sensation of shifting into my non-corporeal form—

I couldn't. It was as if a wall of shadows had surrounded me, trapping me in my human body.

When I glared at Cas, he winked at me, that simple gesture enough to confirm it was him keeping me from switching.

"Let go," I demanded and earned another grin that reminded me of a grimace rather than humor.

"Not a chance in hell."

"Easy for you to say," I gritted out, bracing myself against the shadows as if I could keep them out by merely wrapping my arms around myself. They were cold and uncomfortable on my skin ... like November haze. "You are hell's servant."

At that, he barked a laugh. "That's what he told you I am?"

Of course, he didn't explain what he meant by that. That would have been too easy. So I rubbed my arms and dared to try taking a step forward.

To my surprise, I stepped through the shadows in my physical form as easily as wading through morning fog. However, they furled and coiled around me, adjusting themselves to my shape so I couldn't free myself and shift to follow Leon.

"Does it hurt?" Cas asked, a mockery of sympathy on his features as he used that night colored velvet voice.

I balled my hands into fists and dropped them to my sides, letting the cold wash through me like a breaking wave. "Oh, wouldn't you like to know?" I wouldn't give him the satisfaction of admitting I was in pain. That he was keeping me from a mission and that Leon would harvest that soul for the side of the good if Cas didn't show up.

I still couldn't tell if he felt the tug the same way I did. Maybe, if I bought some time, Leon would be back in time to stop the Shadowbringer from taking my soul. Leon sure was smart enough to hurry through the mission and return instead of waiting for me to show up. And he'd know by the absence of Cas that the latter had to be at school with me.

"So what does it look like down there, in hell?" I hissed at him, hoping my gaze was burning him. "Flames and all?" It was a pathetic attempt to distract him ... to occupy him with a game of my own until help came in the shape of my Leon. A shudder ran through me at the thought that that was what he truly was. My Leon. Purgatory or not.

Cas chuckled and pushed away from the wall, taking a step toward me as he seemed to ponder my question. His black slacks and gray shirt were the replicas of the color of his hair and eyes, and that ring on his finger gleamed in the low light of the corridor.

"Instead of answering your question, I have a better offer to make," he told me as he brushed his fingers over the edge of the shadows he commanded, making them shiver and twirl under his touch.

"An offer," I repeated. A bargain. Of course. That was what they did, Lightbringers and Shadowbringers. They bargained. So he sought to strike a bargain with me.

"If you dearly would like to know about hell," he said, his lips curling at one side, "How about I show you."

28. LANEY

It was impossible that no one would notice us down here. It was only a matter of time, and the second another being was within sight, Cas couldn't harm me. He couldn't dematerialize or take my soul—however that worked—here and now with people close enough that if I screamed for my life, no one would hear me. And Leon would be back. At least, that was what I told myself when I forced a bored expression onto my features.

"I think I'll pass," I informed him sourly and folded my arms over my chest, pondering my chances, wondering what he would do if I simply started walking.

Would he attack? End me for my daring? Or would he simply restrain me?

A glance at his beautiful face told me that it didn't matter what I tried; his mind was set. He was going to take my soul. So that meant that if everything was already lost, I could bet everything on one card and try.

"Nice chatting with you, demon," I said and inclined my head in a mock display of manners before I spun to the side and started walking.

One step ... two ... three ... I made it all but five steps before his voice sounded right by my ear, making me half-trip over my own feet as I leapt away.

"The pleasure was all mine, Miss Laney."

Somehow, he managed to rush a shiver over my neck—not the panicky type but one of ambivalent excitement.

His arm caught me right as I was close to hitting the side of the stairs again, and he still held a quiet grin as he set me back on my feet. His hand didn't linger where he had hooked it around my waist but darted back into his pocket, his grin turning into an expression of utter boredom.

"So, you and the Lightbringer..." He started walking, apparently so confident I wouldn't run that he didn't check over his shoulder to see if I was following.

"What does that have to do with anything?" I neither confirmed nor denied his assumption. Let him think what he may. Anything that kept his mind occupied was good. It would buy me that time—

I realized I was walking when I caught up with Cas and he heeded me a brief glance that seemed to hold the secrets of the universe.

"Where are we going?" I demanded, feeling my body move as if on its own accord. Except, it wasn't. It was I who was setting each step, struggling to accept that I was following the Shadowbringer around like a lost puppy.

"I don't know where *you* are going," he said with cool boredom. "Now that your Lightbringer has secured the soul, there is no need for either of us to go anywhere."

With shock, I realized that the ache in my chest had subsided.

"You felt it?" I blurted out. "You felt it and didn't go after it?"

He gave me a hellish grin. "I couldn't pass on the opportunity to spend some time with you, could I?"

I snorted. He most certainly couldn't. "What type of Shadowbringer are you?" I scolded him for a reason that wasn't exactly obvious to me, but somehow it seemed him neglecting his duties bothered me.

To my surprise, he didn't have a wicked response for me but quickened his pace, no longer seeming in the mood to *play*.

"Make sure to tell your Lightbringer everything when he returns." He turned onto the stairs and was already jogging up when the bell rang, the shadows around me drifting after him, freeing me to try, if I dared, to go after Leon. But where to? The tug had stopped, and I was stranded alone in the side-corridor now that the Shadowbringer had released me.

"Thank God you're all right." Leon ran up to me from the shadow under the stairs and wrung his arms around me the second he reached me. "I was so worried."

My body, still stiff from the encounter with Cas, relaxed under Leon's touch, and I slung my arms around his waist, pulling him close. "I'm all right," I confirmed and rested my cheek against his chest as he crushed me even closer in relief.

"I thought you were coming," he murmured into my hair. "I could feel you starting to shift while I was still zooming out, but—" He withdrew and held me at arms-length by the shoulders, making my arms loosen so only my hands were resting on his hips. "What happened?"

I tried not to focus on the muscles that shifted under my fingers, his skin and mine separated only by one layer of fabric.

"Cas—" I began and his brows knitted together in horror. "No-no-no ... he didn't hurt me," I corrected his assumption. That I was no longer myself. That I was a shell that would be seeking for the rest of her life for the missing part that a Shadowbringer stole.

Leon's eyes screened me from head to toe as if he wasn't entirely convinced. "He let you go?"

"He somehow stopped me from shifting into my ethereal form," I explained. "I couldn't travel."

Leon's frown deepened. "I didn't know he could do that."

"Apparently, he can." I wasn't sure if I was frightened by the encounter or confused. Cas had had his chance and hadn't used it—again. He hadn't ripped my soul from me. He had merely—

What was it exactly that he had done?

"He didn't hurt me," I whispered, trying to solve the riddle in my head.

"So if he didn't take your soul, if he didn't hurt you ... what did he want?" Leon's tone and turned from concerned to suspicious. "Why does he track you down in the darkest corner of the school, keeping you from joining me for our mission just to ... talk to you?" he suggested.

"No idea." I shrugged at him and curled my fingers around his hips, pulling myself tighter to him—to safety. "I'm glad you're back." I meant it. Also, I no longer cared what he had or hadn't kept a secret. He was my Leon.

I was glad to know Leon had delivered the soul that had called us safely to heaven. Whoever it was, it had been their lucky day that Cas had been occupied with me and had refrained from claiming the soul for even a couple of days in his realm.

Leon had dropped me off at the classroom and kissed the top of my head, an apology on his lips, and went to his own classroom. One hour apart, and we'd be together for lunch again.

Cas gave me a wide grin from the back of the room as I entered, murmuring an excuse to the teacher and hurrying to my chair, making it difficult to set one foot before the other without the memory of his shadows enclosing me. I gave him a glare that suggested he should return to hell.

By the window, Jo raised her eyebrows as she noticed the silent exchange.

"Where have you been?" she wanted to know in a whisper as I sat down beside her. "And does Mr. Ferham have anything to do with it?" There was an impish quality to the way she beamed at me.

"Bathroom," I answered briefly, fighting the itch to turn and stick my tongue out at the Shadowbringer. "And *no*."

Jo only nodded, not fully convinced. "You're sitting with me for lunch today." And that was all she had to say to me for the rest of a long, exhausting hour, during which I was torn between Jo's occasional grin, Avery's glares, and that sensation in my stomach that just wouldn't settle— that my encounter with the Shadowbringer hadn't been the last of its kind.

So when the bell rang, I collected all the courage I had been building up over the forty minutes since I'd had the idea, swallowed my nervousness, and stalked down the aisle right to Cas's table.

I placed one hand on the book he was about to close and braced myself for his stare.

He didn't disappoint. In reflex, his eyes locked on mine, surprise wiped away in an instant by a lazy grin.

"You"—I pointed a finger at him before he could open his mouth to speak—"will stay away from me."

It was really all I had to say. All I had hoped I would get out without vomiting my guts onto his desk from nervousness. And the words came out just fine. Even if they hadn't been more than a hiss. So I didn't push my luck and turned around, stalking toward where Jo was waiting by her desk, watching, flabbergasted by my sudden hostility toward the new student.

"Don't ask," was all I said, anxious my knees would give way if I stopped for a moment to explain, and led the way to the door.

Once in the cafeteria, I sorted my lunch on a tray and waited for the line to move so I could pay and sit. Leon and Jo were with me—Leon making good on his promise to be there the second I left the classroom and Jo calling in what she had claimed during the lesson.

"So what did Lucas do to upset you so much?" Jo asked as we made it to our table in the corner.

I didn't even try to search the room for Cas for fear he would take the opportunity and publicly tear me apart. It had been bold of me to assault him like that, but also, it had felt like a good idea at that time when now ... well, now I felt as if it would fall back on my head at some point.

"What did she do?" Leon asked with what could be fake or real alarm.

Jo snickered. "She said something to him. I don't know what, but it looked serious."

I shook my head at Leon, warning him not to do the protective Lightbringer thing in front of everyone, and laid a hand on the tan skin of his forearm where he had rolled up his sleeve halfway.

His eyes darted down to where our skin met and back up to my face, a silent question in them.

I simply shrugged, savoring the warmth beneath my palm.

"He annoyed me the last time I spoke to him," I told Jo truthfully.

Jo raised an eyebrow. "Well, now you certainly annoyed Avery," she concluded and jerked her chin in the direction of the entrance where I automatically looked—

And found Avery glaring at me, her fiery hair reminding me of the flames I supposed Cas used to warm his pretty little home. Her minions weren't beside her as usual. Instead, Lucas Ferham had taken the spot to her right, offering an arm to lead her into the line of students waiting for their lunch. Avery gave me a sneer and looped her hand around his arm, oblivious that she was dancing with the devil.

Devil—

I was wondering if that was what he truly was. Just disguised as something more human. From the books Leon had brought from his cabin, I knew that there were plenty of Shadowbringers, the same as Lightbringers. But maybe that was the whole point...

Maybe there was no such thing as one devil. Maybe those Shadowbringers combined made that devil.

Or was he a demon? Was he not only the one delivering souls but also torturing them? Was that how bad he was beneath that facade of beauty?

"You look like you're going to scream," Leon whispered in my ear, brushing his lips against my hair, letting it pass as a fleeting kiss.

Jo cleared her throat on the other side of the table, and I smoothed over my expression, finding sudden interest in the salad I had accumulated on a plate on my tray.

"Actually—" I remembered I had wanted to talk to Jo about something else entirely. "Could you fetch me a soda, Leon?" I gave him a significant look that I hoped he would understand for what it was; a plea to give me a moment with Jo.

He nodded and got to his feet, dragging his arm from under my hand with what seemed to be reluctance.

I waited until he had turned his back then opened my mouth to speak, but Jo was faster.

"You are an item, aren't you?" she babbled. "The two of you have been so secretive in the past weeks that it is hardly possible to get you alone for a second."

I considered checking for Leon, who had to be standing in line near the Shadowbringer, but thought better of it.

"Come on," Jo pushed. "You hold hands all the time. You always find a way to touch, and ... did he kiss you just then?"

I couldn't help but grin. What should I tell her? That Leon and I were *just* friends? It was as little the truth as it was to say we were a couple. We were somehow even more than that.

"Lines have been blurry lately," I said truthfully and hoped that when it was my turn to ask her what was going on, she would be honest with me.

"More than blurry, I'd say."

We both laughed, and for a second there, I felt normal. Sharing a secret with a friend—a secret that didn't involve death and afterlife and my role in it; but something so very human that it was sometimes difficult to consider it existed for me. Love.

"I like him," I told her, this time allowing myself a glance at the Lightbringer who had dedicated his life to protecting my soul. "More than that. But nothing has happened."

Jo tilted her head, resting her cheek in her palm. "You know most of the girls here would die to go out with him even once," she informed me.

"I know," I sighed and studied her face as she glanced at Leon then at Cas.

"Or him," she added. "He seems to be an interesting character."

"You could say that," I murmured to myself and tried to tune out Avery's laugh that echoed through the room like a lovely bell.

"Of course, Avery is already at work," Jo noted and returned her attention to our table, picking up a slice of bread and dipping it into her soup.

"Who knows?" I hoped I sounded disinterested. "Maybe he is boring."

Jo rolled her eyes—"Right"—and took a bite, looking every bit as tired as she had the past month.

"How are you feeling today?" I changed the topic, hoping I would get an answer out of her before Leon returned.

In response, Jo shrugged and took another bite. "I don't sleep as well as I used to," she admitted.

I could empathize with that as could Leon with his constant guard-duty.

"Anything that could help you? A book, music, white noise, I don't know—" I searched for ideas.

Jo chuckled. "I've tried all of that, actually. It's not that I can't relax … it's…" Jo stopped mid-sentence, her face pensive. "I have no idea if I should be telling you this. It might not even be anything major but—"

I hated when someone started like that. It meant that something was seriously wrong.

"But—" I repeated with a cautious smile, hoping to get her to finish her thought.

"The doctors say it's just anemia and that with some supplements, I should be fine within a month or two.

Okay, that wasn't as bad as I had feared. "Did you get your meds?" I asked, hoping to learn about what her therapy was and how to help her. "Do you need to hold a special diet? Anything I can help with?"

Jo blushed at the attention. "I got my iron pills, and I need to have a high vitamin C diet. That should be it. So if you see an orange on the buffet, grab it for me." She laughed and waved at someone over my shoulder with a sheepish grin.

"I hope you weren't talking about me," Leon said as he held out a can of soda to me and settled back on the bench beside me, placing his arm where it had been before he'd left, throwing me a wide grin.

So I lifted my hand and laid it where it had been before, thrilling at the electric current running through my body as our skin made contact.

"Thank you," I murmured, momentarily unable to think.

Leon winked at me while his free hand picked up his fork, and he started eating.

29. LANEY

Jo's words didn't leave my mind for the next few days. Neither did my own; a constant swirl of implications rummaging through my body and soul.

"You look horrible," Jo pointed out as she pulled on my dress and grimaced.

I glanced at the mirror, for once not in my own home but at Jo's to get ready for Halloween. The holiday had crept up on us on silent feet, and when Leon had invited us to join him for a party, Mom had suggested I go. Yes, Mom. She was tired of having me curl up with a book every other night and falling asleep early the rest of the nights like a middle-aged woman. "Be a teenager," she'd ordered. "Go, have fun. Celebrate with your friends. Dress up in silly costumes."

I wasn't sure that was what teenagers did, for I didn't need Halloween costumes to invite the eerie into my life. I had it first-hand from a Lightbringer and Shadowbringer … and of course, I was part of it somehow as well. Even if I didn't yet count as a full Lightbringer with that first transport still missing.

"That's the whole point of it, right?" I asked Jo. "Looking horrible."

Jo giggled. "Not if Leon Milliari asks you out."

"He didn't ask me out," I insisted. "He invited both of us. As friends."

Jo rolled her eyes.

"Where exactly is that party?" I asked.

Jo picked up a bobby pin and attached my hair in a messy bun to the top of my head. "One of Avery's minions'."

I coughed out the half-inhaled breath. "Why didn't anyone tell me about it?"

"That's why," she said as she gestured at me and the expression that matched my zombie costume. "Because you would have never agreed if you knew. And I so desperately want to go."

"Go without me," I suggested. "You can have Leon." Not that he was mine to offer. Not like that.

Jo chuckled. "You don't actually believe he would go with me if you flaked."

I knew she was right. I knew my mother was right. And Leon was right. But I honestly was ready to wash off the half-done makeup—the blacked stains under my eyes and the parts that looked like torn skin—and spend the rest of the night on the couch. My life was exciting enough as it was. I didn't need to spend it anywhere near Avery other than the unavoidable time at school.

Jo gave me an innocent look. "Come on. It will be fun."

There was authentic excitement in her eyes, her cheeks rosy, the tiredness that usually dulled her expression gone for the moment.

I eyed her for a long moment, weighing my options. Leon had invited us, so I couldn't use him as an excuse. Mom had encouraged me, so she, too, was out of the question. And Jo ... with her childlike enthusiasm, it was hard saying no.

"All right. Then let's get started on your costume."

Jo squealed and pulled off her sweater and pants before she donned the same tight-fitting, rag-like dress that was supposed to be a zombie costume. She lifted her arms before her, imitating a zombie, and crossed the room to the door and back, laughter shaking her.

"Leon will come pick us up in twenty minutes," Jo giggled and settled down before the mirror where she had been painting my face.

Of course, Leon wouldn't be arriving in twenty minutes. He was probably already outside the door, biding his time, on edge about the Shadowbringer and what he might do to me if he got me alone.

The words I had hissed at Cas by his desk had been the last ones we'd spoken. He had taken my advice to heart, it seemed, staring at me from a distance but never coming close the way he had that day when he had captured me with his shadows. What I should make of it, I wasn't sure. But it gave me back some of my life. I didn't wake up every morning, fearing that he would lurk behind corners, trying to isolate me from the others and eventually take my soul.

A different sort of fear had taken its place. The fear that he wouldn't be there. That he would be gone one day along with his annoying glances and the hushed conversations he held with Avery during the breaks; that I would wake up and he would be gone from the range where Leon could sensibly control the situation and protect me. And that eventually, he would hunt me down in my sleep and rip out my soul ... and I wouldn't even realize what had happened. Only that I would become the insane, haunted, broken person Leon had so vividly described.

It took us until the last second to get ready, and the sound of the doorbell jerked through me like a bolt of lightning.

Leon's voice sounded at the door along with Jo's dad, who interacted with him about not even considering drinking if he was to return Jo and me safely after the party.

Finally, Jo's father called for us and we got to our feet, each of us spinning before the mirror in an ungraceful circle before we stalked down the stairs like the zombies we pretended to be.

Leon laughed by way of greeting, his eyes on my face and my arms, which I used to balance my stiff walk.

"Very natural," he commented and waved at Jo, who was only a step behind me.

Leon had taken the liberty to mock his actual status as a messenger angel and attached a pair of crooked wings to his shoulders. I held back a laugh as I took in his form and the private joke it implied.

"You look great," Jo told him and clapped his shoulder as she headed out the door with a wave at her father, who called after her to have fun.

"Ready?" I asked Leon. He nodded and held out a hand for me, a slight bow refining the gesture.

"For you? Always."

I took it, breaking out of my zombie-character for now, and let Leon pull me to his side.

The drive to Al's house was filled with Jo's excited chattering and music Leon had chosen to play in the background.

When we parked at the end of Al's driveway, there were a whole bunch of cars cluttering the area already. Jo and I reluctantly shrugged out of our coats, and Leon adjusted his wings as he got out of the car. He stretched his arm around me on the way to the door and I laid my arm around Jo.

So together, we entered the night where anything was possible.

The whole school seemed to be there, dancing and helping themselves to the weird dishes on the counter. It took us a moment to find a spot in the open kitchen where all three of us could sit together, but when we finally found that place, Jo and Leon claimed the chairs at the long table and I waded through the crowd to the fridge and grabbed something for us to drink, determined to spend as little time away from Leon and Jo as necessary, when someone stumbled into my back.

I caught myself against the counter, dropping one of the bottles in my hand, and cursed.

"Who invited *you*?" Avery sneered at me from the height of what had to be six-inch heels.

Surprisingly, neither her minions nor Cas were at her side.

"Leon," I retorted, immediately regretting that it sounded like an excuse.

Avery snorted, "Who else?" and turned on those heels that looked more like instruments of torture rather than shoes.

"Nice costume," she said over her shoulder. "Almost like you're not wearing makeup at all."

With a frown, I watched her stalk away, her hips swaying in a furry skirt with a tail attached to it and her hair falling over a lace shirt, ears atop her head. I cocked my head and wondered if she could even sit down in that outfit without tearing it apart. Then, I grabbed a dishcloth from beside the sink and got on my knees to mop up the spilled drink.

"Need any help with that?" Of course, Cas was there, and he had found me like a needle in a haystack.

His voice, addressing me for the first time in weeks, sent a thrill through my system.

A steadying breath later, I turned, dripping dishcloth in hand, and looked up to where I expected the Shadowbringer to be standing, gloating at me.

He was crouching before me, a towel in his hand, dark eyebrows raised in perfect arches as he studied my face and dress.

"So you look different," he commented, a grin splitting his lips.

"You can save your breath," I told him and, "I know I look like a zombie. That's the whole point of it."

At that, Cas laughed, a harsh sound that broke through the music, making me wonder if he would ever have laughed like that had the background noise not swallowed up most of it.

"Quite attractive for an undead," he commented as he leaned forward, bringing his face close enough for me to bite his nose if I was quick. He hovered there for a brief moment before he reached around me—sending a flash of fear through my system—and started wiping up the mess I'd made.

The air left my lungs in a gust as I realized he wasn't going to hurt me.

"I could say the same," I muttered to myself, flabbergasted that the immortal servant of hell was wiping the floor like an ordinary mortal.

I returned my focus to the floor, bringing my dishcloth down into the puddle of fluid, and started mopping alongside the Shadowbringer. There was something surreal about the way his long fingers slid over the tiles. Like a diamond in grease. I had a hard time not staring.

Only when there was nothing more to clean did I dare look at him again, my fingers trembling as I lifted the dishcloth. "Thanks ... I guess."

He shrugged and got to his feet, flinging the dripping towel into the sink, and disappeared into the crowd without a look back.

When I made it back to the table, carrying three bottles once more, Leon greeted me with a look of worry.

"I was about to send a rescue mission after you," Jo said with a grin.

From the look in Leon's eyes, I was sure that he would have gladly led that mission.

"I was on a little rescue mission of my own," I set down the bottles and flopped onto the chair next to his.

Jo raised an eyebrow.

"I dropped a bottle and cleaned up after myself like a good person," I explained.

Leon chuckled, probably because he heard the subtext of worrying about being good.

I twisted the cap off the bottle and took a gulp of the purple soda that had to be a special Halloween edition, shuddering at the artificial grape taste. "Anything interesting going on?"

My eyes scanned the moving crowd in the living room, a collection of sailors and knights, superheroes and robots, nurses and vampires, and to my surprise ... another pair of wings.

I cocked my head to get a better view of the pair of fairy wings moving near the windows and almost laughed out loud when I realized it was the Shadowbringer who was moving in time with a pair of cat ears.

My laugh turned sour in my throat.

It didn't take long until one of our classmates joined us, bottle in hand, and asked Jo to dance.

She blushed and hid a giggle as she got to her feet, leaving Leon and me to ourselves.

"Honestly, Leon"—I nudged his arm—"what are we doing here?"

He gave me a look that seemed to be suggesting whether that wasn't obvious.

"We don't do parties. We don't do social events. That's not our thing," I pointed out. "We do soul-saving and hiding from the evil side."

I didn't fail to hear the darkness in my tone.

Leon gave me a smile. "We are—" He paused and leaned closer so his chin hovered over my shoulder. "I am on a mission to save your soul"—his breath tickled my ear—"by getting you to enjoy yourself a bit. No one your age should be forced to give up her life because a Shadowbringer is hunting them."

I shivered involuntarily—not at his words. "I am not giving up anything, Leon," I reminded him. "You know that I have never been one to go out much."

He nodded. "Maybe it's time you started." He reached behind my neck with one hand, his fingers grazing along my hairline, bringing back that sensation of excitement and the electric current that seemed to flow between us now. "With me."

A smile tugged on my lips. "Like a date?" I asked for clarification.

Leon only nodded and brought his hand down along my spine to my waist. "Dance with me," he asked, and before I was able to say a word, I was on my feet, Leon beside me, leading me into the dancing crowd.

30. Laney

The hard beat of the music carried me over the make-shift dance floor between couches and other put-aside furniture, Leon's gaze was intent as he watched me move, he himself always one step away from me, circling around like a lion. I was wondering if I should switch back into zombie-mode and stalk awkwardly through the crowd just to have some of that fun Leon had mentioned, but his attention ... the hunger in his eyes as he took in my rolling hips and swaying body ... somehow that instilled excitement in me.

"Have I told you that you're beautiful tonight?" he breathed into my ear as he caught me around the waist and pulled me against him. "Exquisite."

"Even with the zombie face?" I asked with a wink.

"Especially with the zombie face," he retorted. His fingers curled at my waist, finding purchase on my dress.

We both laughed.

"You don't look so bad yourself," I returned the compliment, wondering if he had noticed that he wasn't the only one with wings.

Nearby, Jo was dancing with the same boy who had asked her at the table, their arms around each other. I hadn't known she liked someone. Then again ... I had been so busy with myself these past months that I had hardly noticed anything. They looked good together.

I was about to comment to Leon when the painful tug made itself known in my chest. My hand flung to my sternum in reflex, and Leon scrutinized my face with concern. There hadn't been many deaths in the area in the past weeks. Leon had taken me along on all of them and he had negotiated well. Some of the souls he'd taken to heaven directly, and for some, he had gotten a very short time of purgatory.

By now, seeing him and Cas bargain for souls had become so familiar that I didn't even flinch at the thought of going with Leon when it was time to collect a soul.

But tonight was different. Tonight would be the first time I would do the transfer.

My knees felt like pudding at the thought.

There wasn't entry to heaven for anyone but a soul. Heaven couldn't even be found without carrying a worthy soul. Not even for a Lightbringer.

So tonight, when I had inhaled my first soul, I would be not only seeing the gates of heaven for the first time; I would also be free of the Shadowbringer.

That was something to look forward to, I supposed.

For some reason, my enthusiasm remained minimal.

Leon gave me an exasperated look that seemed to say, "Now? Really?!"

I all but laughed at his expression, because for once, it mirrored exactly how I felt.

I didn't want this to end. Didn't want to lose the warmth of Leon's hands on my waist, his fingers clinging to my clothes, his body moving against mine in rhythmical waves, swaying me along with him—

But the pain in my chest was hard to ignore. The tug was strong enough to know it wouldn't take more than ten minutes before the soul was ready, and we had to follow it.

So I did the only sensible thing and detached myself from Leon's arms, growling at myself, God, the universe, over this moment being ruined, and let Leon know that I needed a bathroom before we left. Not that I really needed one. I just needed a moment to sort my thoughts.

He promised to be waiting at the bottom of the stairs for my return and brushed a kiss on my cheek before he gave me a wide smile. "After tonight, you'll be free," he reminded both of us with sparkling eyes.

I didn't respond for lack of words and headed up the wide staircase, diving around a snogging couple, and searched the upstairs area for the right door. Was I relieved that I would be free? That I would no longer need to fear the Shadowbringer? Was I glad to finally be the one to bring the soul to heaven? If it was the Lightbringer side that would be able to claim the soul—

Would Cas disappear from school? Would he disappear from the corridors and the corners and the wrong moments? Would that make me happy?

It would certainly make me safe. So I should be grateful for the opportunity, that finally Leon felt I was ready ... that *I* felt I was ready to face my true nature.

The first two doors I tried were locked. The third one led into what seemed to be a small office with bookshelves lining each wall beside a heavy wooden desk. Behind it, the outline of a man moved in a carved chair, shuffling papers in the half-light.

"I'm sorry," I muttered, feeling caught, "I was looking for the bathroom."

I was going to shut the door when the person in the chair stopped me by merely speaking my name.

"Miss Laney," he said, his voice darker than the night, loaded with specks of silver and woven with liquid diamond. It almost hurt to hear him say it.

As I stilled on the threshold, Cas got to his feet, and I noticed the fairy wings on his silhouette.

"Why don't you come join me?" He pushed his hands into his pockets and turned his back to me to lean against the desk. "The stars seem to be alive tonight."

I couldn't move for what felt like an infinite number of heartbeats, but then ... then my hand pulled on the door handle, shutting out the noise in the hallway, separating the colorful world of the living from this room where the creature holding my fate in his hands seemed to be commanding the shadows.

I took a step, then another, while Cas remained still like a statue. Had I not seen him there before me, his fairy wings the only thing holding some color, the room could have been empty. That's how silent he was, how frozen in time.

With horror, I realized that I shouldn't be following that voice that had called to me. That I shouldn't be here at all where I was unprotected, separated from Leon, where Leon would probably not even hear me if I screamed his name. What was I doing?

"I have been staring at those same stars for so many decades that I no longer know if I love them or hate them," he mused into the swirls of darkness that seemed to billow around him.

Shadowbringer, I reminded myself. *Messenger of hell.* And yet, I took another step ... until I stood on the other side of the desk, within arms' reach should he decide to turn and grab me.

"They have become the only fixed element in my existence. Unchangeable stars. The architecture, the people, fashion ... even languages change ... but the stars..." He sighed and then fell silent again.

I stood there like an idiot, unsure why I was even there, watching him as he surveilled the stars and wondering if his silence would break again.

"I have waited"—he turned his head to the side so I could study his profile against the moonlight—"I don't know how many years for something to happen ... something to change ... and—" He paused, closing his eyes, his lashes a thick, black half-moon on his cheek, his straight nose a sharp line against the curve of the hair that fell into his face. "And it never does ... it never did," he corrected, his eyes snapping open as he turned all of a sudden, facing me, hands braced on the desk. "Then *you* came along."

My heart kicked into a gallop as his eyes found mine, full of cruel delight, full of eagerness. Shadows flexed from him like wings of their own, wrapping him up until all I could see was his face and his neck, pale against the darkness that seemed to originate within him.

"Now you are here, and I can finally bring home the soul of a Lightbringer."

I wanted to scream—tried—but no sound came out, not even a croak. It was as if I had frozen into place, hypnotized by the voice, by the shadows of the creature before me.

He took a step toward me around the desk, letting one finger slide over the edge of the wood.

"I thought I would be able to do this smarter ... that I would have more time to get you to trust me." His grin was nothing short of wicked. "That you would eventually realize that you are drawn to me." He paused right before me, his shadows furling about both of us, drowning out everything but him. His voice. His eyes, two orbs that seemed to be made of solid smoke. "You *are* drawn to me, Laney, aren't you?" It wasn't really a question.

While he kept my gaze locked to his, in my mind, I was struggling to break free, to find power over my legs again so I could run. Or over my own voice, so I could cry for help.

But every time I thought his spell loosened a bit, it latched onto me more tightly.

"I was going to wait until you were ready," he told me, his face now so close that his features swam before me. "Until you came to me. But that would require more time. And we don't have more time. *I* don't have more time." His tome turned pensive, and I felt my breath rush into my lungs more freely. "Even if technically I have all the time in the world ... isn't that sad?" His hand shot out of the shadows and curled around my neck, too fast for me to see. But when his fingers touched me, they were gentle, thumb brushing down my throat in a caress. With light pressure, he pulled my face up to his and hovered there for a moment. "Goodbye, Miss Laney. You were such a delight. It's a shame to see you disappear, but"—he brought his lips so close to mine that I could feel his breath—"I need your soul more than I need your company."

With those words, he closed the gap between us, and a searing pain rushed from where his mouth enclosed mine and reached down into the depths of my chest.

The scream that had been stuck inside my lungs finally broke free, and as I released it into Cas's mouth, he sprung back in shock, shadows gone and eyes wide as he beheld me, panting by the desk, my fists raised before my chest. "I thought I told you to stay away from me," I hissed and let the knuckles of my right hand connect with his jaw. I didn't know if it would do anything or if he was invincible, too, but, God, I had to try.

"Leon!" I screamed while I was shaking out my hand, almost certain that if I looked more closely, I would find blood on my fingers. But I didn't dare turn away from the Shadowbringer who was staring at me as if one of his beloved stars had just dropped onto his head.

"You are not getting my soul," I hissed at him, feeling that tug in my chest more and more strongly. "There is somewhere I have to be, so do us both a favor and don't follow. I don't know what Leon will do if I tell him what you just tried to do."

The truth was I didn't know what he had exactly been trying to do. Had he tried to *kiss* me? Or had that been part of his little plan—to kiss my soul out of me? It had most certainly felt as if the touch of his lips had burned something within my chest.

Or was I already ... soulless?

When Leon burst through the door a second later, my thoughts got drowned out by his shout of fury as he launched himself at the Shadowbringer. The noise of struggling bodies smashing into something followed by the sound of cracking wood filled the room, chasing all the stillness of the Shadowbringer's musing away.

I couldn't tell if they were still fighting, for the tug in my chest had become so overwhelming that I could no longer ignore it, and I hissed Leon's name into the half-light.

He was instantly at my side, his teeth bared as if he was more of an animal, running on instincts.

"It's time," I told him, and he nodded.

"This isn't over," he told Cas as he straightened out his clothes—and his wings—and together, we shifted into our ethereal forms and took off to save the calling soul.

31. LANEY

I soared through time and space, drawn by the tug in my chest, by the calling of the soul. Leon was right behind me, his voice carrying to me as he was still cursing about the Shadowbringer.

As I set down my feet at our final destination, having zoomed through clouds, trees, and walls alike, my body—even the ethereal one—was still shaking.

"Thanks," I murmured at Leon as he landed beside me. "I don't know if I would have made it out without you."

Leon scrutinized my face for a brief moment but said nothing. His attention followed the direction of the soul. There was only a door separating us from our target here, in what seemed to be a hospital.

Leon eyed the door then gazed back at me, conflict running through his features.

"What did he do to you?" he asked.

I took a steadying breath before I allowed myself to dive back into the moment when Cas had touched his lips to mine

... the sensation ... the pain that had surged through me. "I don't know exactly why he did what he did ... but ... he kissed me ... I think."

Leon's eyes widened, the coffee brown of his irises appearing to gleam with ire. "He did what?"

By the look on his face, repeating what I had said would only make things worse, so I added, keeping my voice even, "It hurt—a lot. Like someone was ripping something from my chest." I paused at the memory and the echo of pain that came with it. "And then, I hit him in the face."

For a moment, I thought Leon was going to laugh, but his face smoothed over, ire and amusement both disappearing behind a wall of concern.

"You still look like you," he said, scanning my face. "At least, from what I can tell with all that makeup on."

"I still feel like me," I responded to the unspoken question; the question that was obvious in his eyes—if Cas had managed to take my soul. "Is that how they do it? They *kiss* the Lightbringer to suck out their soul?"

Leon grimaced at my words and pointed at the door that was separating us from our job—me, from my job, to be precise. This time, Leon would be the one to stand by.

"Let's talk about it when we're done here." He started walking. "Somehow, I have the feeling the Shadowbringer won't disturb us this time."

Whatever he meant with his statement, I didn't ask. Instead, I followed him through the door, gliding through the layers of metal, wood, and paint as if I were a ghost—not a ghost. A Lightbringer, filled with angel essence. I blinked my eyes to focus as I hatched from the barrier before I stopped beside Leon and took in the scene.

The hospital room was smaller than expected. A single bed—in it, a woman in a white-and-green nightgown, tucked under the blankets—against a pale yellow wall, the curtains at the windows were drawn to shut out the lights from the parking lot before the window. As I took in my surroundings, my first thought was of the nursing home and ... Gran.

Since my grandmother's death, those late hours of my days had become the time when Leon allowed me to ask questions about what he was. What I was becoming. Except that there were things he had no answers to, like how to get to heaven, or what the Shadowbringer would do with my soul once he had torn it from me. I ground my teeth and focused on the matters at hand.

I could do this. I could.

There were other people in the room as we walked in. A lady in a red, long-sleeved dress was adjusting her hat as she stood up from a chair she had pulled up to the bed.

"See you tomorrow, Marge," the lady said then turned and left after they exchanged a smile, that of the woman in the bed a lot weaker.

Of course, neither of them could see us. We had traveled in our Lightbringer essence, our corporeal bodies temporarily dissolved into energy—another thing Leon had described to me during our afternoons and evenings together.

He looked the same to me as always. Only the slight radiating of light fanning out around him allowed me to tell that he still was using his essence. As for myself ... I saw the light on me too when I looked down at my body; not as strong though. I was only a pale shade of bright shadows compared to what Leon seemed to be.

"It should be soon," he whispered, one hand on my shoulder, a comforting weight that held me in place even in this form where my body seemed to behave like a flame in the wind ... especially under his touch.

"What is she dying of?" I asked, wondering if knowing would make it any less difficult to watch her end. Even if I had accompanied Leon several times by now as he had done his duty, my stomach still turned at the thought of what he was—what we both would be after tonight.

I could do this.

"Pancreatic cancer," he responded, and when he noticed my surprise that he knew, he nodded at the metal board at the foot end of the bed where papers with indecipherable scribbles were attached. "At least that's what the chart says."

There was an IV hanging by the head end, releasing slow drops that dripped into the woman's veins. I noticed the tube disappear under the blankets where she had now bundled up her arms.

"Painkillers," Leon explained. "The type you only get in palliative care."

My stomach tightened. The woman knew she was dying. She had been spending—a glance at the chart told me—six weeks here in the hospital, waiting for either a miracle or a peaceful death.

I studied her lined face from where I was standing by the foot end, hands resting on the metal of the bed. Her eyes were searching the ceiling for something—an answer to unspoken questions maybe, or the gentle wing of an angel of death. I could see the pain in the gaunt structure of her face, in her glazed eyes. Her breathing was shallow as if she was powering herself through her own fear, as if she was besieging heaven to open for her—

If only she knew I was here for her; that there was a good chance heaven was where she would be going tonight ... if the Shadowbringer didn't show up. And then, if she could see me now, in my zombie costume, heaven would probably not be the conclusion she would come to. For some reason, the image of Cas with his fairy wings sprang to my mind, and I swallowed hard.

A glance at Leon told me he wasn't watching the woman as I did, but his focus was on me; on how I did with my assignment.

It was the first time I would breathe in someone's soul and help them get to their destination. Leon would be there to assist me if things went wrong. But he had explained to me on our flight from the party that this was my soul to take, so he wouldn't interfere unless I absolutely needed him.

I cleared my throat, hoping the phantom dryness in my mouth would disappear. This woman before me was about to die within the next few minutes, the tug in my chest told me as much. There was nothing anyone could do about it.

But I could do something for her the second she was done dying. I was her ticket into a peaceful afterlife. Her suffering would end today, and the brightness of eternity was waiting.

The rasping sound of her slowing breathing filled the room, calling for my attention.

It had begun.

The woman was hardly breathing, her chest heaving slowly as her body struggled to keep going. But her lungs weren't the only organ giving out. I could tell, even if I wasn't a doctor, that her body was shutting down. Her body, but not her soul. Her soul would be ready soon.

My sweaty fingers slipped on the metal as I watched the woman's struggle, reminding myself over and over again that the painkillers were doing their part in making this as easy for the woman as possible.

Even though there was no monitor beeping, the door bounced open, and a nurse entered through the pine green door, a knowing look on her face. She headed right for the bed, taking the woman's hand in hers and squeezing it gently.

"I'm here," she said, a smile on her lips. "You are not alone."

The woman looked like she wanted to say something, but her body was no longer cooperating. Her eyes had fixed on the nurse in an expression of plea and gratitude, the only response now possible with her failing strength.

For a moment, moisture crept into my eyes as I watched the decline of the body, her ribs cramping as her chest heaved one shallow breath after the other—

Then fear flooded all of me.

I couldn't do this. Even if I had done it before, I was no longer sure if I could stand and watch a stranger die. I couldn't ... couldn't bring myself to watch her death struggle. Couldn't bear the thought of another person dying. A good person, it seemed, or Cas would have shown up, a smirk on his annoyingly handsome face, and offered a reduced sentence of only a couple decades in purgatory for the woman. I could almost see it before me as if he were there. As if he was gloating at my struggle.

My hands let go of the metal and flung to my throat as my breathing fell into rhythm with the woman's. I didn't even know her name, and it didn't matter—it wouldn't in a moment when her soul would leave her shell. So I didn't glance down at the patient chart to learn it. I needed to get out.

I was half-turning to the door, considering bolting to avoid this moment where it would be my responsibility and mine alone to take that soul where it belonged—anything to not have to see her die, to not be a witness to her suffering; her last and final suffering. My heart beat frantically in my chest, trying to escape while I was still able to hold myself in place.

"Calm down," Leon's voice was a golden thread breaking through my panic, reassuring me that this wasn't a nightmare. "You can do this."

"What if I can't find my way to heaven," I wondered, my voice almost suffocated by my rising panic. "What if I find it and never find my way home—?"

"You will find your way and back," he reassured me in a satin tone that was so soft that it felt like a brush of his fingers against my fear-filled heart.

My gaze met his in a quick glance, and one look into his dark eyes reminded me that, same as the woman, I wasn't alone. He was here with me. And if I managed to master myself, I could do some actual good using my Lightbringer heritage to help this poor soul transition.

I nodded, sensing strands from the bun on top of my head coming loose and bouncing over my shoulder as I studied the way Leon hovered by the dying body, a crease on his forehead, half-hidden by pale-blonde hair through which he glanced up at me. He ignored the nurse altogether as if she wasn't there. Nothing mattered but the soul, who would be free within a matter of moments. He brushed his fingers over the woman's forehead, his eyes back on her, watching her breathing even out.

"Do you see how her chest is settling?" He gestured at the sternum, which was no longer pushed outward by the force of her expanding lungs. "She will be ready soon."

The clinical tone he used helped a little as he guided me through this task ... what lay ahead of the actual task.

"How long does it take to get used to this." I squinted my eyes as I glanced at the woman's lips, which were turning blue, and her skin ashen in stark contrast to the purple pillow someone had shoved behind her shoulders a while ago.

"Does anyone ever get used to death?" He gave me a coffee-brown look that told me exactly how much he had been struggling in the beginning—maybe still did. The rest of his face, however, didn't let on if there was any emotional turmoil involved for him as he was waiting for the soul to peel from the body.

"There," I pointed as I noticed the outline of the woman blurring and slowly rising as if someone had made a translucent, silver copy of her. She hovered for a second and then contracted into that small star that I had seen first with Gran and with all the souls I had observed since.

In my chest, the tug, and the pain that came with it, ceased. Instead, I noticed a lightness. Like a feather, so free and unburdened.

"She's pure goodness," I realized as I felt where on the scale between heaven and hell the woman stood.

To my relief, Leon nodded. "A child of heaven," he confirmed and beckoned me to come closer to the bed. Closer to my target.

My knees felt like pudding as I set one foot before the other until I was close enough to do what I had been observing so many times.

"Inhale, and let her settle," he instructed, voice like a melody at the back of my mind. "Your body knows what to do, and the angel is waiting."

There was no shudder at the thought that I was hosting the essence of a heavenly being, only awe. I leaned forward, lips open, and sucked in a deep breath, watching the soul disappear from sight as it rushed into my mouth, down my throat, and wandered into a part of me I had never felt before—like an extra chamber in my chest made for that purpose alone. It resonated within me, making warmth spread through my body. A tug occurred at the center of my heart. A tug telling me that I knew where it would lead me. And for the first time, things made sense.

I glanced at Leon, who was watching me with gleaming eyes, and smiled.

"Take her home, Laney."

32. LANEY

I was no longer on earth. I was sure of it. But I wasn't in outer space either. I was everywhere and nowhere. Energy ran through me in bursts that were electrifying and exhausting at the same time, and within me, the soul was leaping in joy as it felt what was nearing.

I felt it, too. The infinite power that was thrumming in the air ... not air ... it was no place where a human body could exist...

My ethereal form slowed as the power beckoned me forward like a honey trap. Only, it wasn't a trap. It was the ultimate reward for the soul I was carrying. The all-fulfilling sweetness of nectar and ambrosia. Paradise.

And yet ... I couldn't see it. I couldn't taste it or touch it. All I knew was that it was there, and that, while the soul would hatch from my lips at the end of our journey, I wouldn't be allowed to even glimpse what lay beyond the gates.

As I floated on, the thrumming became stronger, and I realized what it was; the power that protected heaven from any uninvited guest. It was the gate of heaven. Not in the same sense as the door I had imagined but like a barrier that separated dimensions. There were no words in my vocabulary that could describe it, and every word in my vocabulary combined might not be enough.

So I didn't try. I floated on amazed, bewildered as I marveled at the sensation of the closeness of heaven—of completion. A tear slipped from my eye at the unstoppable, all-including force that streamed through time and space, through what could be eons and no time at all, the world, the universe, or merely a handful of sand. Nothing and everything.

"We're here," I said more to myself, unsure if the soul would hear me. If she even needed to hear me or if she felt it as the tug in my chest abruptly ended and I came to a halt. "You're home."

Something stirred next to my heart, and for a brief moment, a sensation like the one when Cas had brought his lips to mine ripped through my torso. A burning pain that made me unsure whether it was purely physical. My non-corporeal hands flapped to my chest just as I felt the need to cough from the pressure that built up inside my lungs. No air. Nothing. Not the need to breathe in my ethereal form. Something different—

The soul, silver and star-like, shot from my lips and whirled away so fast I wondered if I had messed up, if I had done something wrong. But a moment later—if time existed here—a dash of light wrapped around the star as if to cradle it, and the soul erupted into a bright glow, simmering before me as if to say goodbye. I bowed my head, unable to find any other appropriate way of returning the greeting. When I lifted my head again, the light was gone.

I plummeted from the place, my body suddenly heavy, my chest empty. I zoomed out of reach of the thrumming power, of the gates of heaven, drawn by something else that was calling. Something that reminded me that I wasn't to stay where I knew I would want for nothing. I remembered that I was alive. That I had a body. That I had a mother, whom I loved. That I had Jo and Leon and ... that one day if I was lucky, I would be taken to those gates, in the shape of a star, and stay there—

The wooden floor of my room hit my feet, and I was back. The world was suddenly dull, colorless, empty. I thought of that moment I had been allowed to feel the bliss of heaven ... and I cried.

I didn't stop weeping when Leon's hand touched my shoulder. I didn't stop when he pulled me into his arms, against the warmth of his chest. I didn't stop when he murmured words to me that I had never heard from his lips before. Prayers. I didn't stop when he sang a lullaby that I remembered from my childhood. There was nothing that could make those tears cease. For there was nothing on this earth that compared to what I had felt there, at the gates of heaven.

"It will pass," Leon breathed onto my hair. "It gets easier."

His words hit my empty chest like a spear, and I cried not only for myself but for him, who had been pushed into this

Lightbringer existence when he was little more than a child. And he'd had no one to help him, no one to dry his tears.

"I'm so sorry, Laney," he whispered. "So, so sorry." His palms slid over my back, rubbing along my ribs where once, everything had been okay, and now—

I wasn't sure what was there now. A hole. An open slot, ready for the next soul to take a ride. Or just my own, miserable life. I couldn't name it. And it didn't matter. Something was missing.

It was in the early hours of the morning when my tears ceased—not because the grief was over but because there were no more tears left in my system to cry.

Leon lifted one of his arms and peeked down at me, his eyes full of warmth, full of understanding.

"You are so strong, Laney," he whispered, his breath a warm breeze on my face, drying my cheeks as I lifted my head from his chest. "Incredibly strong."

I didn't feel strong. But I nodded for his sake. He had been holding me all those hours, eventually growing silent, when he had run out of words of comfort.

"It will get easier," he repeated … a promise.

I finally found it in me to sit up and lean against the headboard of the bed instead of resting in Leon's arms like a bundle of misery.

"You could have told me, you know," I said and held Leon's gaze where pain and shame and worry collided in an expression that had no name.

"That's the one thing that no one could have told you," he replied, his voice like a song of atonement. "It is not the same for everyone; that's the only thing I know. My grandfather always said it is like losing a piece of yourself. The notes don't speak about it."

He was right. In none of the notes he'd given me had I found anything about ... well ... this. I wrapped my arms around myself and took a deep breath, hoping to fill the void.

"I haven't met many Lightbringers, but the ones I've met are all different. Some of them don't feel that pain we felt at our first return from a mission." He slid up beside me to the headboard and kissed the top of my head. "I was hoping that you wouldn't need to suffer like this. That you'd be like the others who are simply coming and going as they transfer souls."

I studied his face before I cuddled against him once more, his warmth the only thing that made me feel better.

"Why do you think I wasn't pushing you about collecting your first soul? Why do you think I kept you on the sidelines for so long?"

I nodded against his shoulder. Had I known this would happen, I would have run. I wouldn't have inhaled that soul and taken it to it's final, eternal home, but would have hidden somewhere, preferring to live with the risk of the Shadowbringer stealing my soul than ever feeling so ... lost.

Leon's arm was the only anchor, his voice soothing as he spoke to me of how things would get easier with time. That with every mission, I would transition back into my normal self faster.

"Trust me," he said with a dark chuckle, "I would know. I've been doing this job long enough to know the procedure."

And as he spoke, I started to forget the emptiness within me. His words started making sense. I actually felt his warmth, the sound of his voice rumbling from deep within his chest; the gentleness of his fingers as they absently brushed over my arm.

When I looked up what seemed like a lifetime later, the sky was graying, the stars Cas had mused about vanishing like memories.

"Thank you, Leon." I turned my gaze away from the end of the night and looked into his eyes instead where a light of its own was brightening like the rising sun.

His arm slid off my shoulders, hand brushing across my neck all the way up to cup my cheek where it rested, a solid reassurance that he was here. That he was real. That there still was one thing on this earth that I craved ... and that was him.

The fire flared in me so fast I couldn't spend a second to think it through, the desperate need to feel him suddenly overwhelming, all-consuming. My skin was tingling where his palm lay against my face, the look in his eyes sending a shiver down my spine, urging me to take a leap of faith and let the flames spread into a wildfire.

I took a deep breath. Once. Twice. And measured his face, the angles and planes of that familiar yet new, exciting face that had once been my best friend.

Adrenaline flooded my system, blood pounding in my ears from nervousness. But I didn't yield. I wanted this. I needed this—

And so I reached behind his neck, knotting my hands in his hair, and pulled him toward me.

His mouth crushed against mine. Not gentle but eager, hungry. As if he had been waiting for this moment for a lifetime. A moan slipped from his lips between kisses, the sound running through me like electricity, making me crave him even more.

I didn't know how long we got lost in that kiss, how many minutes his mouth searched mine, his hands securing my face against his.

It was only when I heard footsteps in the hallway that I halted.

"Mom's up," I ground out between ragged breaths as I peeled myself away from him just enough that his lips were out of reach.

Leon studied me, breath coming in gusts and eyebrows raised in protest as I kept listening for a sign Mom would check to see if I had come home last night. But his mouth twisted in a curve that informed me he didn't really care who might barge in the door. "It's seven in the morning," was the only thing he said as he flopped back onto the pillows, letting go of my face only to grab me by the shoulders and pull me down with him.

I landed on top of him, catching myself with my hands against his chest, and hovered, my face above his, and studied him.

"This"—he swept up loose strands of my hair and wound them around the bun on top of my head—"turned out very differently from what I expected."

I felt heat rise in my cheeks, but it didn't matter. Leon knew me better than anyone else. It was all right for him to see me blush, for the effect his voice, rough and silken all at once, had on me.

"How did you expect *this* to turn out?" I asked in a whisper, finding it difficult to look into his eyes when his lips were right there, soft and warm and flushed—and featuring a broad smile.

"I was prepared for the tears," he admitted, reminding me of that empty spot in my chest. "But I didn't—never in my wildest dreams—expect *this*." He tilted his head up until his breath was on my lips, and hovered there as if waiting for me to close that gap. "I was prepared for your wrath, for your silence, for anything ... but"—he brushed his lips against mine so lightly it felt like a phantom touch—"this."

The sensation of his mouth on mine tuned out the creaking floorboards as my mother returned to her bedroom. It tuned out anything but that new feeling of Leon's nearness.

I indulged in his kisses until exhaustion took me over and I fell asleep in his arms.

When I opened my eyes, bright light greeted me, bringing back memories of the soul dissipating. It brought back the crystal clear specks of light in the night sky that I had gazed at over the Shadowbringer's shoulder. It brought back the pain that his kiss had instilled in my chest and the terror that had followed ... and the aching, empty spot that might never fully heal.

33. Cas

Damn the stars!

It hit me like a bolt of lightning, the pain in my chest, the inevitable proof that all hope was lost.

It had been mere minutes since the Lightbringer had grabbed me by the arms and pressed me against the desk with the words, "If you come near her again, I *will* forget our sides have a truce, and I *will* end you." His words had resonated with me. The truce was the only reason why they and we could work side by side, bargain on behalf of the souls entrusted to us, and keep the laws of the afterlife intact.

I panted, back resting against the leg of the desk where I had sunk the moment Laney had left with the Lightbringer, that look of shock and disgust in her eyes. A scream stuck in my throat, but I couldn't loose it. I knew what this was. I recognized it as it seared through me from head to toe and back—Laney was taking a soul. She was becoming a Lightbringer. And I—

I didn't want to think of the consequences. Couldn't. Not yet—

From the hallway, music washed around me, accompanied by light and the sound of clicking footsteps rushing to my side.

"Lucas?" It was Avery who knelt beside me, struggling to fold her legs beneath her with her heels. "I've been looking everywhere for you."

I smothered a smile.

"Are you okay?" There was honest concern in her voice, no sign of the superficial girl I'd met at school.

I drew my gaze up at her face and found her kohl framed eyes staring down at me.

"Are you drunk?" was her conclusion, and it would be best if I simply nodded at that.

So I did. Who cared if I lied? I was part of hell. And with Laney having sealed her Lightbringer fate—that wouldn't change any time soon. Another forty or fifty years—

"Come, let me help you." Avery grabbed my arm and slung it around her neck. Then, she pushed herself up, dragging me along with her.

I pretended to make an effort and got to my feet, careful not to put too much of my weight on her delicate frame. However, a new surge of pain rolled through me, and my knees buckled, making me grab the edge of the desk for support.

Avery frowned at me. "You could have at least told me where you were going," she complained. "We could have gotten drunk together."

A chuckle escaped me at that, and she gave me an inquisitive look.

"Trust me, you don't want to be part of what's going on here," I told her, making sure I drawled as if I'd overdone it with liquor.

How could this have happened? I lifted my hand to my chest and rubbed along my sternum, hoping the pain would cease and I would be able to walk far enough to get out of sight and shift into my ethereal form so I could escape this human madness.

Laney had manifested as a Lightbringer despite my efforts, despite my careful planning and circling her.

And I had done my best. Had let her get used to my presence. Had enrolled in high school so I could learn more about her, so she could slowly fall under my spell. But I was out of practice with humans—at least with those whose lives weren't over.

So I had chosen someone to get up to speed with the customs of the times. Avery had seemed like a good choice. Popular, pretty, receptive to my lure...

And she came with a benefit. That girl did anything to get the school's attention—positive or negative. I had seen her try to get closer to Laney's Lightbringer, the boy no girl seemed to be able to look past.

Seeing Avery by my side had somehow gotten me Laney's attention. And I had needed her attention. Her attention first. Then her affection. Then her trust. That one day I could have kissed her and taken her soul with it. Not with the kiss but with her falling in love with me.

I had seen it in Laney's eyes ... that there was something there; a tension, something tangible—

If only I'd had a bit more time, I would have been ready to talk to her. To ensnare her with my shadows and make her see—

I shook my head, stumbling alongside Avery into the hallway. The party was still going on, people dancing on the stairs as we made our way down. Laney's friend—the one with the tired eyes—moved on the dance floor, arms around a boy whose name I had never cared to learn.

Several girls looked up as we descended the stairs, their gazes curious, some envious, jealous.

Laney's eyes sometimes followed me around like that when I was with Avery; with a mixture of curiosity and disgust. A sign that maybe she was jealous. That she had already fallen for the trap of shadows that I was.

But it no longer mattered. My task was over. There was nothing more for me here.

34. LANEY

Jo called around noon.

Leon and I had unfolded from the bed with a mixture of awe and awkwardness seemingly to drive both of us from a restful sleep.

"I don't need to stay now that you are a real Lightbringer. You no longer need my protection." He had chuckled at the mess last night's makeup had left on my face and planted a kiss on my cheek before he'd checked his own face in the mirror above the dresser—and laughed.

He'd turned around and given me his broadest, most delighted smile. "I love you, Laney." With those words, he shifted into his ethereal form and took off, leaving me gaping.

Jo's voice was buzzing through the speaker of my phone, wanting to know where I had disappeared to last night. Apparently, Leon had taken the time to return to the party and offer to drive her home after I had zoomed toward heaven. How decent of him.

I murmured a response that I had been tired and tried to smother a surge of incredulity about what had actually happened last night. Not heaven, even though that was a big thing—so big the emptiness in my chest returned at the thought of it—but Leon. Something in my stomach fluttered at the thought of his lips on mine, of his hands ... the tenderness of his touch.

"Are you still there?" Jo's voice chirped from the phone.

I managed to pull myself together. "Just waking up," I said with as much seriousness as I could muster. "Last night was—" What exactly had it been? Long? Taxing? Exhausting? Life-changing? "Different." I settled on something harmless.

"Different how?" Jo prompted, and I could tell from her tone that she expected a full recap of my evening.

But I hadn't been the only one who'd had an interesting night. I remembered the boy Jo had danced with, how they had moved together—as if of one and the same mind.

"I'll tell if you do." I nodded to myself, and Jo didn't even try to hide her excitement as I asked about the boy she'd danced with.

"We've been on one date before the party, and when he didn't ask me out again, I thought..." Her voice trailed away as, in the background, her father was speaking. "Yes, Dad. I took them after I woke up." She cleared her throat and returned to the conversation. "Dad is being a helicopter parent," she explained before something rustled at the other end of the line. "Actually, it would be nice to talk in person," she said, voice less excited than before. "Can I come over? Or is Leon still there?"

I didn't say a word to confirm or deny he had spent the night, instead telling her that I needed to get out of the house for a bit and that I'd grab lunch for both of us on the way over.

"Anything specific you'd like?" I asked, wondering if, considering the fluttering of a million butterflies inside my stomach, I'd be able to eat anything at all.

I made it to the bathroom moments later, for the first time since Jo and I had done our makeup last night, acknowledging what I looked like.

Leon's words echoed through me. *I love you.* He had said those three little words and smiled at my smeared zombie face. The hoard of wings frantically rushed through my body as I stepped into the shower, hoping that, while the water would rinse the sweat and paint off of me, the memory of Leon's touch would remain.

By the time I made it to Jo's, the car smelled of sauerkraut and Russian dressing. Mom hadn't asked questions about last night, whether or not she had noticed I'd had company. Instead, she'd asked me to say hi to Jo and to bring back a Reuben sandwich for later.

Jo's parents were on the way out when I arrived, both of their faces tight even as they smiled while waving at me when I pulled the car into the driveway.

I watched them walk away, pulling my phone out, and called Leon.

"Everything all right?" he asked by way of greeting, alarm in his tone.

I thought twice before I responded, seeking the truth within me. "I just wanted to hear your voice," I told him, hoping that I didn't sound cheesy.

Leon chuckled in response, a sweet sound that brought back memories of last night, and I shivered. "Did you get a chance to clean up?" he asked, tone playful.

"From head to toe," I told him and wondered if he'd thought of me the same way I had of him—

"Good." His voice was smooth like satin. "I'm almost certain that your lips taste even better without paint."

My stomach tightened, and I wondered if it had been the right choice to call him right now when I was about to get out of the car and ring Jo's doorbell. But I played along. "Why don't you come over later and try?" I teased and forced myself to open the door instead of letting myself fall into the sensation Leon's laugh evoked in the pit of my stomach.

"Actually, I wanted to let you know that I am at Jo's for a bit," I told him, cutting off my train of thoughts before they could run wild. "But you're welcome to come meet me at my house in the evening."

"Maybe," was all he said before he wished me a great day.

Jo opened the door after a minute when I rang the doorbell.

"You look undead," she joked and hugged me tightly before I could say a word. "Thanks for coming."

I wrapped my arms around her, the bag of Rubens clutched in one hand, and squeezed her for a moment.

"I hope you're ready for the breakfast of champions."

Jo gave me a curious look as I held out the bag to her.

"We stayed out way too long to have lunch yet," I explained and followed her into the house.

In the kitchen, a pot of lukewarm coffee was sitting on the counter beside a plate of crackers and an untouched cup of tea.

Jo pulled out two plates and a mug and placed them on the table. Then, she took the bag from my hands, placed a sandwich on each plate, and sat down, bracing her hands on the edge of the table.

"Coffee's over there if you like." She pointed at the counter, and I was about to open the cupboard and grab a mug for myself when Jo stopped me, pointing at the one sitting between our meals. "This one's for you," she explained and leaned back in her chair. "God, I shouldn't stay up that late. I feel like an old woman." She laughed though her face was pale and her voice sounded like an echo of the excited Jo from earlier on the phone.

I reached for the coffee pot and poured myself a cup before I sat down again, all the time observing how Jo was acting somewhat strangely. Not strange but ... different somehow.

"You don't want any?" I asked before I set down the coffee pot.

Jo shook her head. "I have my tea over there." She grimaced as she was about to get to her feet and let herself flop back into her chair.

"Bad day?" I asked, wondering if she was hungover.

"Bad life," she responded with a grin and a frown— somehow she managed both in parallel.

I rushed to the counter and got her cup, keeping one concerned eye on her all the time.

"Wanna talk about it?" I offered and placed the cup in front of her.

"I don't," Jo admitted, still with the same facial expression.

"It's okay," I automatically responded. "You don't have to."

"That's not it." She lifted the cup to her lips and gritted her teeth after a small sip. "I should." She set down the cup again and eyed the Ruben as if it held all the answers.

"It's really okay if you don't feel like t—"

"No it's not okay," Jo cut me off, weak anger flaring in her eyes as she turned the plate around with a finger and studied the other side of the sandwich. "I should be telling you. I should be telling the world ... I just don't want to be looked at like that, you know?"

"Looked at like what?" I wanted to know.

At that, Jo looked up. "Like I'm the girl who's dying."

I had probably stopped breathing, for I could no longer find the air to speak in my lungs.

"What did you just say?" I gritted out after what felt like too much time as if she hadn't just said what she had said.

Jo held my gaze, all smiles gone, the purple shadows under her eyes more prominent than ever, and her eyes ... her young eyes ... so endlessly sad.

"You don't have anemia," I concluded as everything—her constant exhaustion, the days she'd been missing from school—it all got an entirely different meaning. "It's something far worse than that, isn't it?"

Jo didn't speak for a long moment while the clock on the counter ticked into the silence like a sledgehammer. When she finally found words, they broke my heart. "Anemia is a result of it, but not the disease," she explained, her voice calm, controlled, quiet. "I was diagnosed with chronic kidney disease a while ago."

It took me a few minutes to understand she didn't actually mean she was dying but that her kidneys had problems filtering and needed help.

"I'm sorry," was the first thing that slipped from my mouth as the shock slowly passed.

"It's not as bad as it sounds," she said with that weird expression that reminded me of a frown and a smile. "I am getting medication that helps, plus ... dialysis."

I didn't know what to say, what to think. So I got to my feet and walked around the table to throw my arms around Jo. As I enclosed her in my embrace, she sobbed. Quietly at first. Then the tears ran freely. Hers and then mine, too. What had she done? How had she done wrong in her short life to be suffering like that? I rubbed my hands over her back.

"I'm so sorry," I repeated. But Jo shook her head against my shoulder, her fingers clinging to my sleeves.

"It's okay," she whispered. "I'm not actually dying ... not yet."

I held her and listened as she told me how she was so tired all the time because her body wasn't functioning the way it was supposed to, how everything cost more energy than she had been used to, how she dreaded the day she'd go to get her next dialysis.

And all I could do was sit with her and hold her. I couldn't tell her that everything was going to be all right, for that would be a lie.

Everything would be different. That was the truth. The same as it had been for Leon all those years ago. The same as it was for me. And yet different. If things went well for her, she'd have a good life even with some restrictions. She would maybe get a kidney transplant that would improve her quality of life immensely. But if things went badly for her ... she'd be on the receiving end of my extra skill sooner rather than later.

"I'll be there for you, no matter what," I told her and hugged her more tightly. In my mind, I added, "until your very last breath. And afterward, I'll take you *home*."

35. Laney

I wished I could have told Jo the words; wished she could know that I would protect her. But I couldn't. No one should know about what I was—a messenger of heaven. But when the time came, I would tell her, regardless, that there was something more coming after this life, that there was something out there that my soul would be craving for the rest of eternity, now that I'd felt it. And that she didn't need to fear as long as I was there to bargain for her soul, for I would never let the Shadowbringer win.

Jo pulled out of my embrace and smiled at me through tears. "I know you will."

I didn't know if I should return her smile or cry with her, my chest split into two halves; one that wanted to be strong for her and cheer her on, the other wanting to cry her tears so she wouldn't need to.

"Let me know if there is anything I can do," I told her, choosing a third option; to be her friend and be there for her in any way I could.

"Actually, there is one thing..." Jo wiped her palms over her face, drying the wet streaks down her cheeks. "Please, don't tell anyone."

I swallowed. I could do it. "Not even Mom?" I checked. Mom had suspected something was wrong. She was too observant for her own good. "Or Leon?"

Jo pursed her lips as if she was weighing her answer. "Your mom, okay. But not Leon." She gave me a stern look that seemed almost comical after the seriousness of our conversation, but I nodded obediently. Even if it would be difficult to keep a secret like that around Leon. I could understand that she wanted as few people to know as possible. Word spread fast in our school, and if people like Avery found out, they'd find a way to make Jo's life a living hell—

For some reason, an image of storm-gray eyes and a searing pain in my chest followed, and I coughed in reflex.

A memory of the party—a dark room, Cas, who had tried to kiss me ... had actually kissed me and tried to take my soul with it—flashed through my mind, making my hand flip to my throat, fingers shaky at the sensation that still echoed in my chest. I had barely escaped him, only to tumble into this new version of myself where little had any meaning—little but the few people I loved.

Hell. He was part of hell. And he had tried to take part of me with him.

"It's just my family who knows, you, and—" Jo cut herself off, and I focused on her, taking a deep, steadying breath.

"And?" I prompted, my voice not even remotely as inconspicuous as I'd hoped.

Luckily, Jo didn't seem to notice. "And that boy from the party." Her delicate features flushed with a healthy shade of pink as she mentioned him.

"The one you thought wouldn't go on a second date—" I didn't need to finish my question because I already felt the pieces snap into place. "He knew after the first date," I concluded.

Jo nodded as her hands wrapped around her cold teacup and studied its contents with embarrassment. I pulled up my chair and sat down right next to Jo, my hand on her forearm, and sighed through my nose. "Did he dump you after the first date because of that?" It was an assumption. Not a nice one. But it also would explain her reluctance to be open about her health challenge.

"That"—she nodded—"and that he basically told me he wasn't sure if he wanted to waste his time on someone who might be dying before we even graduated." There was a profound sadness in her voice that made me want to hurt my knuckles on that boy's square jaw.

"What an awful thing to say," I vented. "You're not dying." She wasn't. At least not any time soon. Medicine had that sort of illness well under control.

"He apologized a couple of days later," she appeased, but it didn't make me feel any less angry with him.

"So, what happened at the party? Why didn't you kick his ass?" I honestly wondered.

Jo just shrugged. "I don't know how ... I guess, I didn't care for a change. I wanted to have fun instead of being careful, the way the doctors suggest ... and my parents ... and basically every article on my disease." She grimaced the way we sometimes did when we talked about a particularly nasty test at school. "You know ... healthy lifestyle."

"Having some fun is healthy," I insisted, knowing very well that I hadn't even wanted to go to that party in the first place because my type of fun was lying safely in bed with my nose in a book. It might have been better—I would have never had that weirdly thrilling and very much dangerous incident with the Shadowbringer. It wouldn't have changed anything about my becoming a full Lightbringer though. That had been set in stone, it seemed, from the moment I had shifted into my ethereal form.

Jo chuckled at me, her face tomato-red now. "Trust me, I *had* fun."

And at that, we both burst out in laughter.

We spent the rest of the day, watching trick films and drinking tea. I converted to her choice of food just to make it easier on Jo so that she didn't feel like she was missing out on anything. And just to indulge my friend, I told her about the kiss with Leon ... and watched her eyes light up with excitement.

It was almost dark when I climbed into my car, ready yet suddenly unable to bring myself to drive home. Mom might be there, waiting with questions about last night, which I wasn't ready to answer.

I stared at the light in Jo's window for a long time, pondering how life had changed literally overnight. Jo had said she'd spend the evening in the bathtub with music and a cup of tea. A safe sort of evening activity that her doctors would approve of.

And as I kept thinking, I started driving ... aimlessly. I simply took a turn here and another there, having nowhere particular in mind. It was just that for the first time in a while, I felt safe. I didn't wonder if Leon would be out there, watching over me, if he was ruining himself with sleepless nights solely to protect me from the Shadowbringer.

In front of some of the houses, Halloween decorations were meant to scare the trick-or-treaters from last night. What few cars were on the street didn't seem to be in a particular hurry. Just a normal Sunday with the town asleep after a night of dreamed up horrors—

While mine had been real. Cas had tried to take my soul. I had barely escaped. Had I not been able to unfreeze from whatever spell he'd put on me and given him a right hook, I would now be a hollow shell of a person, feeling empty, feeling ... lost—

I hit the brake, not even bothering to check if there was a car behind me, and listened to the screech of the tires as the vehicle skidded to a halt in the middle of a crossing.

Empty. Lost. Like something was missing.

Had he succeeded? Was that the reason why I had broken down in Leon's arms after my trip to heaven? Was I ... soulless?

The thought crept through me like black tendrils of smoke, spreading a cold within me that made me shudder.

Soulless.

It was possible—

"You should continue driving," Cas's night-woven voice said from the passenger seat, and I cringed aside, hitting my arm on the door.

Cas, however, chuckled at me from the other side of the car. "Chances are high someone will hit you if you don't move," he reminded me, those storm-gray eyes seeming to swirl as he leaned over just enough to make me want to reach for the door handle and bolt. "And trust me, you don't want to die with a Shadowbringer sitting right there to collect."

His words were laced with a threat, with a promise of revenge, with anything and everything that made me go utterly cold.

He rubbed his chin over a mild bruise blossoming where I had struck him. "Yes, hell doesn't forget," he warned and leaned back in the seat he had claimed uninvited.

In the rearview mirror, headlights of a car glinted, and I reluctantly took Cas's advice and pushed down on the gas pedal, making the car half-jump as I accelerated.

Again, Cas seemed to find this utterly amusing. He had folded his arms across his chest, his black clothes letting him melt into the shadows that seemed to be swirling around him ... and a grin sat on his lips, spreading them wide like a grimace.

"Get out," I commanded, keeping myself from panicking. He no longer was a threat. Not the way he had been at least. He no longer could take my soul ... and leave me alive to suffer, that is. But could he kill me? Would he go to those lengths just to take revenge on me?

The car was stable again as I took the turn that led back to the main road.

"Are you even allowed to take a soul without waiting for a Lightbringer to bargain?" I asked as he didn't show any intention to disappear to where he had come from.

He shifted beside me, accommodating himself in my car. "It would certainly break the truce," he said as if I was supposed to know what that meant. "But it might be worth it." He flashed me a lazy smile, which I ignored, determined to never take a close look at his beautiful face ever again.

His smile faltered when I didn't give the reaction he had obviously been waiting for. "Or if the soul was utterly corrupted, I wouldn't need to wait for a Lightbringer," he mused then turned in his seat so he faced me and asked, "You haven't by chance killed anyone, have you?"

This time, I couldn't avoid my reaction, and my head flipped to the side, finding him studying me with a taunting grin.

"You must be kidding," I simply said and turned my focus back on the street. "And, *go away.*"

Again, his chuckle, full of the shadows swirling around him, filled the air as he leaned back in his seat once more as if he owned the car.

"Maybe I am." He gestured in the air before him and the shadows spread through the car like an extra layer of night. "Maybe I am not."

My heart raced in my chest as it got harder and harder to see through the spreading darkness.

"So you're going to kill me?" I shot at him, taking my foot off the gas and letting the car roll to the side of the road where no one could hit me. "Because I escaped? Is that what this is? Revenge?"

Another laugh, disguised by night, muted by shadows.

It had become hard for me to see at all, to hear, to breathe; that's how tightly his shadows were wrapping around me.

I didn't reach for the door, knowing that running would only make things more interesting for him. He had been circling me for months, biding his time as he watched me squirm at his glances and as I cried in his presence. There was no escape now.

"Kill me, then," I spat and took my hands off the steering wheel. "Come on, and kill me."

I wasn't sure if I was serious, if I truly was giving him permission to end my life and take my soul, but I heard the anger ring in my voice as if in the distance. Until ... until it hit me...

If he was here to kill me for my soul, it meant that he hadn't succeeded; that I still had a soul.

And within a fraction of a second, I broke free from my petrification and shifted into my ethereal body ... and then, I took flight, leaving the car, the night, and the Shadowbringer behind.

36. Leon

I couldn't remember the last time I'd taken a shower without rushing through the routine, without being half-petrified by fear about what would happen to Laney if I left her out of my focus for even ten minutes. So this was nice for a change. It was like the first real vacation in years ... even if it was a mere shower.

I had walked home, all the long miles, simply because I had nowhere else to be. No constant fear, no restless thoughts—just the cold November air and the blinding, pale light of the sun high up in the sky, dispersed and brightening the haze that hovered over Glyndon.

Now that it was dark outside, the shroud of growing night bringing back with more intensity the events of last night, I was determined to be clean when I went to see Laney again and looked into her electric blue eyes. So I shrugged out of my clothes and stepped into the shower without haste, wondering if this was what life could be like.

I braced my hands against the wall and let the water wash over my head and my neck, leaving the smeared paint on my face for last. It was a reminder that Laney's kisses hadn't been a dream.

Steam billowed around me like wafts of mist, the heat of the water almost burning into my skin, keeping me grounded in my corporeal body. It had become my first nature to float through the world in my ethereal body. Only when I was in school or hanging out with my mother was I in this shape any more. It made so many things in life easier. For once, I didn't need to shower that often, for not having a physical body meant that there was no sweat, no hunger—at least, not in the same way.

It also helped with the sleep issue. I didn't tire as fast or need as much time to recover when I remained in that form. So when I had held Laney last night, when her lips had brushed against mine, when her hand had twisted almost painfully in my hair, pulling me closer, her chest pressed against mine—

It had felt oddly real ... in a way I wasn't used to. My first kiss. A perfect, paint-smeared, emotion-driven, and passionate sensation that had made it hard for me to remain grounded in my corporeal body. Especially when Laney's touch was even more intense in our ethereal forms.

But it had been perfect. Almost ... normal. The way a first kiss should be. Full of memorable flaws, full of awkwardness, and still—perfect.

I grabbed the soap and squirted it into my open hand, determined to scrub my face until there was no trace of Laney's costume left on me ... only that memory of her lips on mine and how alive I felt.

"Leon?" her voice called me like an echo from behind the curtain of water, and I dove out of my thoughts. "Leon?" Again, but louder like she wasn't calling from somewhere in the sphere of our ethereal bodies but—

I turned off the water and turned, only to find Laney in the doorway, eyes wide as she stared at me through the misted glass. "I need to talk to you."

37. Laney

I tried to keep my eyes on Leon's face as he asked me to hand him a towel. Then, grateful to have something to do, I turned away and grabbed one of the fluffy, russet cloths that hung next to the sink.

I kept my eyes averted, forcing myself not to peek as he opened the glass door and let me place the towel in his hand. Once he had slung it around his hips, he climbed out of the shower.

"What are you doing here?" he demanded, his voice husky in the steam-filled room as he took my hand as in an old reflex, yet with a new gentleness that momentarily made me want to forget the Shadowbringer even existed.

The Shadowbringer. Right.

I let my gaze snap back to him, finding myself studying his shoulders and chest rather than his face for a brief, awkward moment until Leon cleared his throat.

When I looked up at him, despite the alarm in his eyes, a slight smile was playing on his lips.

"Cas popped up into my car and threatened to kill me," I heard myself summarize what had just happened, what I had barely escaped.

The smile on Leon's face was instantly gone. "He did *what*?"

It was clear he didn't need me to repeat myself but rather had no words to describe what was going through his mind.

But I explained anyway, how he had surprised me in my car, how he had told me that killing me would break the truce—whatever that meant. "Can he do that? Can he actually kill me and get away unpunished?" I finally asked, still standing there in my jacket and shoes, gesturing in the narrow space between us while Leon was scrutinizing my face with horror in his eyes, water dripping from his hair and running down his torso to soak into the towel.

I didn't know what answer I had expected, but when he said, "Let's sit down first," it certainly didn't give me much confidence my situation had actually gotten any better.

I followed him to his bedroom anyway, realizing I was still in my ethereal form, and sat on the edge of his bed while he headed for the dresser and pulled out a fresh set of clothes.

"Don't disappear," he told me as he vanished back into the bathroom, pointing at the bundle of fabrics in his arms, and closed the door behind him.

I had no intention of disappearing. Who knew what the Shadowbringer had planned for me next. It certainly wasn't anything I wanted to find out. We needed a plan. Something better than just Leon going back to his duty of twenty-four-seven protection. I was a Lightbringer now, and apparently, there was something more than just Leon standing between the Shadowbringer and the end of my life. A truce.

I fidgeted on the bed, eventually sliding out of my jacket and boots, and was folding my legs beneath me when Leon returned in his usual jeans and white Henley. It was hard to ignore the way his shirt stuck to his skin where he had dried himself off sloppily. He caught me staring, and I swallowed the urge to grab him by that same shirt and pull him down onto the bed with me.

"The truce," I prompted, struggling to regain focus on why I was here.

Leon sighed and prowled to the bed where he flopped down and leaned against the headboard.

"With all the people being born and dying every day ... every minute ... every second ... obviously, one Lightbringer and one Shadowbringer are not enough to keep up with the workload," he explained with exasperation on his tan features.

"Obviously," I confirmed and wondered just how many of us there were exactly.

"And while Shadowbringers serve for eternity, being granted immortality in exchange for their dark deeds, Lightbringers don't need to endure this longer than a normal human lifetime."

His words settled in my mind like dark stains as I realized their meaning.

"This is not a gift from God, is it?" I held his gaze as questions formed in his eyes. "I mean, the angels choosing us ... it is not a blessing. It is a curse."

Leon didn't respond for a long while, the coffee brown of his eyes turning darker as the seconds ticked by. "I am not sure it is either," he finally said, looking older than the teenage boy he was, the wisdom of generations surfacing in his gaze. "Are we blessed for the good we do? Are we cursed for the souls for whom we don't bargain hard enough? Is it even up to us to judge?"

"Are you saying we're just tools?" I interrupted his philosophical moment. "Because it most certainly feels like it." I gestured at him, at me, at the world in general. "Because if I can't even be safe from the Shadowbringer now that I have *manifested*, what good is it to feel so empty, to have felt what seems to be the perfection waiting for some of us if there is nothing we get in return?"

Leon closed his eyes as if to avoid looking too closely at the meaning of what I'd put into the room between us.

"At least the Shadowbringers get immortality," I pointed out, voice heavy with sarcasm. "What do we get? Fast track to heaven when we die?"

At that, Leon laughed, frustration in his eyes as he gazed at me.

"That's the plan," he said, watching my expression go blank at his words. "At least, that's what my grandfather used to say, what is in his notes ... what Lightbringers have been saying for generations and generations."

It took me a moment to comprehend his words. "You are saying I am going to heaven?"

Leon half-nodded. "Unless they were all wrong."

"Well, let's hope they weren't." It was all I could think of to say as Leon pushed away from the headboard and leaned forward to take my hand.

"We are," he corrected in a murmur, bringing his face temptingly close to mine.

I tried not to let my attention drift to the curve of his lips or the way his fingers played with mine between us.

"So if the Shadowbringer took your soul by killing you," he continued, his hands warming mine, which were still frozen from shock, "even if it wouldn't be the same for him—not a trophy, just as any other soul he would wrongfully take—he would break the truce that has been holding over centuries between our kind—or our allegiances. Heaven and hell."

I listened, trying to comprehend the concept of what he was telling me ... and realized just how little I truly knew.

"Gran was from a Lightbringer family," I pointed out, wondering if she had been destined for heaven from the start ... if Cas had been there to wrongfully take her soul. "The Shadowbringer was there when she died anyway."

Leon gave me an empathetic look and pulled my hand up between both of his to huff hot breath onto them before he folded them in-between his palms. "Your grandmother never manifested, Laney. She was treated like any other soul."

"Even if she was from the same line?"

"Like any other soul. Heaven, hell, or purgatory." He gave me a grave look as if he was expecting me to break at the news.

I didn't. Gran had been a good person. I knew she had. If Cas had been there to bargain for her soul, her being good obviously hadn't been up to the standards of whoever decided our fate. But what it was that Gran had done was for another time. I could ask Mom. Maybe she knew something I didn't.

What I truly wanted to know was what would happen if that truce ever broke.

"Then, it won't matter what you do in life. You'll be taken by either side as an act to prove their superiority. No bargaining. No purgatory. Either heaven or hell. Deserved or undeserved."

My already cold body went numb at his words.

"It will be anarchy of morals," he summed up. "And we will no longer fight with words."

The wind howled the entire night through the bare trees before the window, making my sleep light and full of shadow-tinted dreams. I'd returned home after a long discussion with Leon about what we could or couldn't expect of the Shadowbringer, considering everything that had happened.

It was unlikely he would throw a millennia-old truce into mayhem just over one soul he'd missed out on.

But the safety and protection program was rebooted nonetheless.

Only this time, I was sleeping at Leon's house rather than soaking his shirt with my tears in my own bedroom, and while his breathing was even, a warm stream of air coming and going on my forehead as he had wrapped his arms around me and tucked me to his chest, I wasn't remotely as much at peace as he was as we slept side by side.

Every sound outside reminded me that somewhere out there, a Shadowbringer was biding his time until he could take his revenge.

And then, there was the hard warmth of Leon's chest and abdomen against my side—

I turned my head just enough to get a glimpse of the side of his face. In response, he knotted his arms more tightly around me and folded one leg over mine, making me wriggle around until I could find a position where the weight of his thigh didn't threaten to crush my knees.

"You can't sleep?" he murmured drowsily and pulled me around so I faced him.

"I can't stop thinking," I whispered, snuggling into his arms, searching for his eyes in the darkness to find him gazing at me.

"What are you thinking about?" He lifted his arm from me and stroked my hair lazily before letting his fingers trail down my jaw and along my throat. He didn't even blink as his index finger pulled along the collar of the too big shirt I was wearing—his shirt—exposing skin that yearned for the heat of his touch.

"The Shadowbringer," I responded, voice shaky at the new sensation that ran through me. Not the electric current that I had felt before but a raging wildfire, the flames of which seemed to rise and fall where his fingertips traced my collarbone all the way to my shoulder, down my arm until he held my hand in his.

"Is there anything I can do to distract you?" he drawled, sounding perfectly at ease with the flames he was instilling in me, and led my hand to his lips, his breath tickling the inside of my palm as he turned it over and brushed it with his mouth.

What had I been worrying about again?

A gust of air escaped me as he dragged his lips all the way to my fingertips and kissed them, one after the other.

"You're doing a great job," I praised him, my words almost a sigh as I indulged in the mind-numbing luxury of his touch.

"Then what are you thinking about now?" he asked and placed my palm on his cheek, tracing my arm all the way back to my shoulder, along my back, between my shoulder blades where he splayed his fingers and pulled me toward him so our faces were so close we shared breath.

More, was what I wanted to say. *More. I want to feel you.*

But no word came out. Instead, my hand left his cheek for the benefit of his mouth where I brushed my index finger over his parted lips, tracing the soft curve of the top lip first, then the bottom—

My breath caught at the wet touch of his tongue as his mouth fell open, and he caught my finger between his lips. A chuckle rumbled through his chest as he beheld the look on my face and he released my finger, but not without repeating the wet stroke of his tongue over my fingertip, causing my core to tighten at the sensation.

Before the sound I'd been holding back could escape, Leon wrapped his mouth over mine and kissed me, his lips moving gently at first, waiting for the response of mine. But when my hand found his chest, fingers tracing the muscles down to his abdomen, his kisses deepened, a moan hatching from his lips as I opened for him and met his tongue with mine.

His hand slid down along my spine with light pressure, enough to trap my hand between our chests.

"Tell me if you want me to stop," he murmured between kisses and released my mouth, exploring my neck instead and driving shivers through my body.

I freed my hand in response and searched my way under his shirt, grazing along his waist, his hipbone, needing to feel his skin.

Leon chuckled and halted, lips halfway up to my ear. "You have no idea how many times I've dreamed of this," he whispered against my skin, goosebumps rising in response where his breath spread like a desert wind.

"How many?" I asked, arching my neck against his lips.

He didn't stop kissing me as he rolled us both over so that he was on top of me, his weight braced on his arms, the tousled mass of his hair brushing over my face as he moved. "Just every damn night for the past year."

"Are you even allowed to curse? You're a Lightbringer," I reminded him, trying to lighten the profoundness of what he had shared—a year.

At that, he stopped and lifted his face over mine, his eyes glinting in what little moonlight flitted in through the curtains. "I'll be damned if longing for you for a whole year puts me in hell," he whispered and brought his lips back to mine.

I didn't get to ponder his statement, for in my chest, right in the empty spot that didn't seem to disappear, a painful tug reminded me that I had a job to do.

38. Laney

Leon groaned as he felt it too, a second later.

"Really? Now?" he asked, eyes lifted to the ceiling and a grimacing exasperation on his features.

"It's not urgent," I whispered and knitted my fingers into his shirt, pulling him back toward me.

But Leon only pecked a kiss on my nose and rolled off of me. "It will be in a matter of minutes," he said with a voice that sounded way too professional, too mature.

There was some shuffling, and a second later, the light went on, flooding the intimate darkness of our moment with the light of reality.

"I don't know about you," he said with a smile as he took in the way his shirt was pulled and twisted around me so that it exposed my stomach up to my ribs and had slid over one shoulder, "but I want to be properly dressed when I go to work."

I frowned in response, finding that he looked perfect in his white shirt and plaid pajama pants as he got to his feet and strode to the desk by the window where a pair of jeans was draped over a chair. He didn't go to the bathroom to change this time, and I struggled not to comment as he pulled down his pants, exposing his long, muscled legs and the gray undershorts they stuck out from.

When he noticed I was staring, mouth probably hanging open—I couldn't tell, I was too busy ogling—Leon laughed and pulled up his jeans, buttoning them up before he returned to bed and straddled me with legs and arms. "Another time," he murmured a promise. Whatever that promise included, I didn't dare ask.

"I should probably get dressed, too, then," I responded unintelligibly and waited for Leon to climb off of me.

He straightened up above me without any apparent intention to let me get up. Instead, he dragged his gaze over my exposed skin. "You are beautiful," he said, breathless, and let his fingers graze down the line from my ribs to my navel, a smile on his features. "Incredibly beautiful."

It took me a while to sort my thoughts when he got up and held out a hand to help me out of bed, but when I finally managed, I headed to the bathroom to change out of his shirt and pants and into my clothes.

The tug in my chest and the ache were intensifying as whoever we were going to collect came closer to their final breath. By the time I'd rinsed my mouth and pulled my mussed hair into a ponytail, I knew it was time to go.

I wasn't scared this time as I zoomed through the night air, pulled by the call of the soul that was almost ready. I knew I could do it. I had done it before. I knew what to expect—even if I would probably never get used to the heartbreak after releasing the soul at the gates of heaven.

Leon landed the same moment as I did, our feet touching the ground soundlessly—but ours weren't the only feet. On the other side of the small room where an old woman was taking her final breaths, Lucas Ferham landed in his cocoon of shadows.

"You—" Leon took a step toward him, his body so tense I thought he would break apart.

"Nice to see you again, Lightbringer"—Cas nodded at Leon then gave me a long look—"Laney."

Ice crept through my skin as he flashed me a grin before assessing our target. There was nothing of the Cas who had helped me with Jo or the one who had eyed me from a distance in the school corridors. There was nothing of the Cas musing about the stars or the Cas who had kissed me, either ... even if that kiss had almost torn my soul from me. Just the cool, bored, bemused Cas who would risk the truce between our sides to take revenge.

"Let's see if you are a *real* Lightbringer yet," he mocked, the lazy grin from before spreading wider. "Let's see if you're ready to bargain."

"No," Leon hissed from beside me as I stepped to his side.

"Why not?" I asked, authentically wondering why I wouldn't. I'd observed him do it plenty of times. I had taken my first soul to heaven. Wasn't it time I did the whole deal?

"Yes, Leon," Cas drawled. "Why not?"

The old lady took a rattling breath, her eyes flying open as she was fighting for air. Her hand flung to her throat as if clawing at it would help her get more oxygen in. She couldn't see us, of course, but it didn't make it any less horrifying that we were witnessing her death—and maybe everyone deserved their death to be witnessed, no matter who they were, what they had achieved in their life. Maybe that was a gift in itself, that their last and final struggle was acknowledged ... seen.

"Stop, guys," I cut them off before they could get into a fight over my pride. "It's time."

And as if I had spoken a magic word, they stopped, both of their faces smoothing over, concentration taking over the masks they'd chosen for themselves.

The woman sighed her last breath, and her soul peeled from her body—a sight that still held me in awe, every time—until it turned into the silver star that one of us would inhale after we settled on a bargain.

I felt her then, the woman and her toll of good and bad. She had been selfless, good, and yet—my eyes snapped up to study Cas's face as I realized that he might have more claim to this soul than Leon and I.

A wicked delight had spread across his features while he was still reading the soul, determining the parameters of his offer.

I didn't wait to let him figure it out. "She comes with us, and you go to hell," I said matter-of-factly, wondering if either of the boys had noticed the silver frame on her nightstand with the picture of her holding a baby, next to a folder that had the simple words *Finding Mae* on it in an elegant script.

Mae. I picked up the photograph, turned it over, and opened the frame.

Mae, September 72, it said in the same handwriting. Her daughter.

I didn't know how I knew. Maybe it was the stack of pictures that seemed to have been taken by a private investigator that I found in the folder as I opened it, all showing the same woman from childhood to what she had to look like now.

"What makes you believe she deserves to go with you?" Cas bit at me, obviously surprised by my claim and not fast enough to pull up a bored face as he confronted me. "The woman is dribbling with guilt."

Even Leon nodded his agreement.

"Open your eyes." I gestured at the nightstand where baby-Mae and Mae of all ages was now distributed over the oval surface.

It took them longer than me to understand the woman was one and the same. A baby, given up by a mother who couldn't provide what she thought the child needed at that time—a mother who, for the rest of her life, had regretted her choice.

It was Cas who's eyes flickered with realization first, and I could tell by the twist of his lips that he didn't like one bit that I had bested him.

He darted around the bed, all of us leaving the soul hanging mid-air, suddenly busy with the images, when Cas pulled out a piece of paper with the same handwriting, just a bit more shaky than before. It was dated last night.

"*Mae*," he read, "*you were the most beautiful baby this world has ever seen. It killed me to place you into a stranger's arms. I was young, and your father was sent to Vietnam before you were born and disappeared there ... I had no one.*" Cas paused, glancing at me with eyes that seemed to be swallowing the world. "*I meant to reach out to you when you were older. But I never had the courage to face you and tell you that I failed you. Whenever I sent someone to find you, I got reports that you had a happy life. That you were loved. And that was all you needed ... and all I needed.*

I wish I'd had the strength to tell you once that I love you. I have loved you all my life, and I will even in death.

I hope this letter finds its way to you one day even if I'll never have the courage to send it.

With all my heart and all my love, my daughter.

Your mother, Carly Mae Jennings"

No one spoke as he lowered the letter and laid it back on the nightstand. For a moment, it seemed heaven and hell were in unison about the verdict, Cas's gesture softened as he stared at the picture of mother and baby. For one moment.

Then his face twitched back into the bored mask, and he gestured at the silver star that hung above the lifeless body of Carly Mae Jennings.

The woman had a thick dark streak of guilt darkening every facet of her shining soul. She had done something in her life that had haunted her even when she'd been alive. She herself had made her life a living hell. There was no way I was going to let her go there in her afterlife.

"She is coming with me," I repeated before he could even think of making a claim. "She has had purgatory all her life. She is done suffering for a choice she made decades ago when she herself had been abandoned." My voice was fierce, absolute, and much to my surprise, neither of the boys questioned me.

So I stepped forward and lowered my mouth to where Carly was waiting to be taken to her final home, and I was going to take her—but not without a last glance at the tiny, one-room apartment of the woman who had given up her heart. And as I readied myself to inhale her soul, the eyes of both Lightbringer and Shadowbringer followed the direction of my gaze, missing how my hand grabbed the letter from the bedside table and slipped it into my pocket.

39. LANEY

Returning from the gates of heaven tore me apart as thoroughly as the last time, only this time, I didn't have a night with Leon to piece me back together. It was Monday morning, and we were heading to school after a pit stop at my house where I had explained in three sentences to my mother that she had been right about Leon and that I might be spending more nights at his place in the future.

Her answering grin had been as much a relief as it had been disturbing. As if everyone but myself had known about Leon and me.

"What about Cas?" I asked, my tears finally ebbing as we pulled into the parking lot like we did on any normal day.

"What about him?" Leon asked and turned to face me after he parked the car.

A cold sense of fear crept back into my body at the thought of the Shadowbringer. "He didn't threaten me at Carly's," I pointed out.

"He didn't," Leon confirmed. "But you know he is bound to his mission when he's called by a soul, the same as we are." He gave me a stern look. "It doesn't mean a thing if he is tame during our missions. He can still wait around the next corner, once the soul is taken care of, ready to break your neck."

I shuddered at the thought of Cas's long fingers around my throat, the cold of his silver ring that would be cutting into my skin—

"I'll be there to prevent it," he promised and brushed his fingers across my cheek.

"Speaking of the devil." I jerked my chin at the stairs to the walkway leading up to the entrance.

Cas was there, his arm draped over Avery's shoulders, and grinning in our direction.

I braced myself for his stares and Avery's glares. But more than that, I braced myself for the question I needed to ask Leon before we got out of the car.

"This thing between us—" I started, unable to bring myself to speak the words that I was thinking ... if we were an item.

"What about it?" Leon asked, his eyes darkening just a bit as he cupped my face in his hands.

"Is this something you want people to know about—" I pursed my lips, wondering if there was a good way to ask if we were boyfriend and girlfriend.

Leon just chuckled at my expression, running his thumb over my lip before he leaned in to nip at it. "I love you, Laney," he told me, his voice amused. "Why would I not want the world to know about us?"

I nodded into his kiss before I detached myself from his mouth. "Time to face the world?"

After a final kiss, we got out of the car and headed for the school, hand in hand, the meaning of it entirely different compared to all of the times I'd shown up with his arm around me, tucked to his side. This was no longer him just protecting me from the dangers of the world. It was him showing with pride that we were together.

As we passed Cas and Avery, Leon lifted my hand to his mouth and kissed my palm. It was only when I looked up that I noticed that his eyes weren't on me. Instead, he was giving Cas a poisonous glare, which unsurprisingly, the Shadowbringer returned with bored nonchalance.

His eyes didn't remain on Leon for long but found mine, the storm-gray of his irises promising that this was only the silence before a storm.

It cost me all my strength not to bolt from him but muster a grin that equaled his lazy one and pin both him and Avery with a stare that, I hoped, felt like ice.

"What's wrong with her?" Avery asked as we were already at the door, and Leon had long dropped our hands between us.

I didn't hear Cas's answer, for Leon held the door for me and I slipped in—and out of the Shadowbringer's reach. For now.

The day went by without any coincidences. Cas didn't try to lure me into dark corners, Avery didn't mock me. No one commented when Leon kissed me goodbye before we headed to PE.

Jo sat with us for lunch, grinning more broadly than I had ever seen her do. I wondered if it had something to do with Leon and me ... until I spotted the boy from the party in the parking lot after school.

"I guess he changed his mind after the party," I whispered to her as I hugged her briefly, watching the color rise in her cheeks.

"Seems like it." She bounced out the doors, energetic in a way that I wasn't sure was normal for a girl with her condition. My chest clenched at the thought of what she was carrying around with her ... the burden of the secret, living with that fear that one day, medication and dialysis wouldn't be enough anymore.

Leon squeezed my hand. "Everything all right?"

I watched Jo passionately kiss the boy, who seemed as surprised as I at the public display, but he recovered quickly, pulling her into his arms. "Everything's good," I told Leon. It was. As long as Jo had happiness in her life, everything else would be bearable.

"It doesn't matter what it is"—Leon wrapped his arms around me as we started walking—"you can talk to me."

I leaned into his embrace and breathed in his scent. "I know."

The week sped by, the last leaves dancing to the ground and more than not, I feared seeing Cas, who kept hovering like a shadow at school. He never spoke to me. Never as much as indicated we had ever met. Even Avery seemed to forget I existed, or her minions, or anyone else but the Shadowbringer; so that I started fearing for her, too. What if Cas couldn't just take a manifesting Lightbringer's soul with a kiss? What if he had already taken Avery's? What did a living person without a soul look like?

I took a look in the mirror, wondering what I would look like today had Cas succeeded ... if I would even recognize myself.

However, he never once attacked me, never once threatened me since that day in the car.

"Will Leon be coming over later?" Mom asked from the hallway, already in her boots from the sound of her footsteps.

"Maybe," I responded, wondering when I would finally allow the two of them in the same room again since our relationship status had changed. Not that I was worried what Leon would say, but Mom...

"I thought I'd head over to his place later," I said sheepishly, grateful she couldn't see my face. We hadn't spent a night together since the one where we'd been interrupted, and my face turned pink as I thought of his promise. *Another time.*

"I never get to see him anymore," she mock-complained, her footsteps disappearing down the stairs. "I'm getting the car," she announced, and the door squeaked.

I donned my sweater and grabbed my jacket on the way out, ready for another mother-daughter-breakfast with raspberry Danish—not ready for the questions about Leon that would surely come.

Mom was waiting in the car, singing along with the happy tune on the radio.

"Ready?" she interrupted her performance to measure my tight face with her observant eyes.

I nodded at her and pulled my scarf up more tightly around my neck as if it could protect me from Mom's nosiness or Cas's potential attack.

Mom drove slowly, the first signs of frost on the street making people edgy.

"Your grandmother would have loved this weather," Mom said absently as she pulled the car into Santoni's parking lot. "You know, sitting at the hearth fire of her old house, doing sudokus and puzzles and telling scary stories over a cup of herbal tea."

There was obvious nostalgia in her voice as she remembered the grandmother I had only seen during the summers of my childhood.

"What stories did she tell?" I remembered little from those years.

Mom was quiet for a moment as she waited for another car to free a parking spot. "About the lure of hell," she said with a sideways glance, "and its messengers." She giggled like a child. "Stories her grandmother had told her when she was little."

My heart stopped for a moment there; at least, that was what it felt like.

"Messengers of hell?" I asked innocently, forcing a grin to cover my pending panic. "What is that supposed to mean?"

"I don't know," Mom shook her head from side to side, frustrated with the narrow parking spot, luckily, paying little attention to my curiosity. "Like angels of death and stuff."

Alarm bells were ringing in my head. Gran had known. She had told Mom but not me. Why hadn't she told me? She could have prepared me for this—I didn't have words for the mess she'd left me with. "Angels of death," I prompted and Mom shrugged.

"What do they do?" I asked, trying to control the urge to plead with her to tell me everything, every tiny little detail she could remember.

"I don't know, Laney. Raise hell on earth," she suggested with a laugh.

She was obviously not taking this seriously. If only she knew…

"Did they have names?" I asked, pretending to be curious for research purposes. "Like the archangels? Michael and Gabriel and—"

"Now that you mention it, she did say there was one named Lucas." She leaned forward, checking whether she was close enough to the curb before she cut the engine and turned to face me, her face that of a mother with not enough caffeine in her blood. "Let's get something to eat first, all right? I'll try to remember more, once I've got my sugar rush."

I forced an unconvincing smile and squeezed out of the car, careful not to hit the vehicle next to us with the door.

Angels of death. Lucas. Cas's face flickered before my eyes, and I could see it, that he was someone capable of doing just that—raise hell on earth. He sure had made my life hell.

I followed Mom into the store, ready to put on a cheerful face, and greeted the smell of freshly baked pastries as a welcome distraction from the questions that were circling in my mind.

Gran had known. How much exactly had she known? Why had she never told me if she knew the *gift* skipped one generation? Why Mom and not me?

We ordered our usual, sipping our coffee while we were waiting for the bag with our Danishes when a familiar voice called my name in a very unfamiliar tone.

I jerked around, at first not believing that Lucas Ferham could even sound like that—friendly, harmless, kind, excited, as if he was happy to see me.

"Hi, Mrs. Dawson," he said to my mother and held out his hand, making me want to smack it aside with all the mortified anger that wallowed within me.

Mom took it and shook it, her face full of questions. "And you are—"

"Cas," Cas flashed a grin that would have made any Hollywood actor jealous. "I go to school with Laney," he explained, looking like a normal boy as he chattered along.

Mom raised an eyebrow at me as I didn't change my expression but kept staring at him as if he were a giant whale, stranded in the small store.

"Laney likes to keep me a secret," Cas told my mother with a wink. Had he just winked at my mother?

"A secret?" Mom turned to me as if she found it mortally offensive that I had not told her about the handsome young man who had joined Glyndon High.

"Not true," I bit at Cas. "Believe me, Mom, he is no one worth knowing."

Mom squinted her eyes as if asking if I was serious, but I just grabbed Cas by his muscled arm and pulled him aside, telling Mom over my shoulder that he had a question about homework as we walked away.

I tugged him along, my fingers clawing into his biceps through his light leather jacket. Cas didn't complain. He didn't fight me off or tear away from me but let me lead him out of the store, around the building, and out of sight of the street.

There, I dropped his arm as if it were toxic and turned to face him, hands balled into fists and ready to give him a black eye if he did as much as set a toe in the wrong direction.

"What do you want?" I asked, not in the mood to dance around the topic.

Cas gave me a bored look. "I think I made that pretty clear the other day." He shoved one hand into the pocket of his jeans and leaned against the wall, folding his other arm over his chest.

"Unfortunately, my soul is not for the taking, Shadowbringer," I hissed at him. "You missed your chance, and now ... live with it."

I wondered if he actually was alive, since he was immortal, or if he was undead. Did he have a heartbeat? Could he bleed and hurt and die if someone injured him? Or was he the type of immortal that included indestructibility?

"What if I don't want to live without it, Laney?" His words made me cough in surprise.

"You think this is about what you *want*?" I asked, really pissed off at him now. "You think you can just roam the realms of the living and decide whose soul you'd like to take?"

Cas studied me with a look that didn't match the Shadowbringer I'd met. There was something like ... was that hurt in his eyes?

"You know I don't do that, Laney," he said, voice low, night weaving through his words even though the sun was peeking through the clouds above. He recovered in an instant, smoothing over his face, and winked at me. "You know I could try," he offered. "I could just *roam the realms of the living* and take whatever soul I want." He lifted one hand to his chin and rubbed his thumb and index finger along his jaw. "It's not so bad an idea, actually."

I considered if it would hurt him or me more if I threw my coffee at him.

"You can't break the truce," I reminded him.

"Can't?" he asked, challenge apparent in his eyes. "Or won't?"

"Both," I hoped.

He pushed away from the wall, taking a step toward me, all humor gone from his features.

"You got away, Laney." He spoke my name as if it was a curse, an evil spell. "I have been trying to get a trophy-soul for I don't know how many decades," he said, the wind, the birds, the sound of cars rushing by in the distance all drowned out by the shadows that coiled around him like tendrils of smoke.

"And why?" I wanted to know, exasperation flooding me as he stepped even closer, the shadows in his eyes darkening them to a solid black. "What would my soul have changed?" I held my ground—barely, but I held it.

"Because I am little more than a lesser demon without it," he hissed, those eyes turning deadly as he took another step and then another. "Little more than hell's errand boy."

"I don't know what that means," I said and hoped he would leave it at that.

Of course, he didn't. Cas huffed into the icy space between us, a laugh of unbroken darkness escaping him as he looked up at the sky as if pondering something, the pale sun making the bluish tint in his hair sparkle. Then, his gaze snapped back to mine, making a shiver run through my body, and he gripped my chin with his hand, forcing me to look up at him as he took a deep breath and brought his face directly above mine.

"I was going to trap you," he said, his tone dead. "I was going to let you fall for my allure, let you like me, desire me." His words hit me as if he'd slap me in the face. "And then, I was going to harvest your soul and take it back to hell."

The cold, calculated fury in his eyes was even worse than the steel of his grasp. I didn't dare move for fear he would crush me if I as much as flinched.

"Do you remember what your lovely grandmother said?" His breath was warming my face as he hissed the words at me. "Do you remember?"

I nodded once—as much as I could with his fingers locking me in place.

"What did she say, Laney?" he demanded. "What did she warn you about?"

I heard her words in my mind as if it had been yesterday.

"Speak them for me, will you?" a sugared deadliness rang from his tone that made me want to bolt rather than even squeak.

"Say it, Laney." His fingers tightened.

"Be careful who you give your heart to," I repeated Gran's words. The words that had been meant for me and me only.

"Exactly." Cas huffed a mocking chuckle. "Be careful, Laney."

As he spoke, it hit me... "She was speaking about you," I concluded.

Cas gave me a bitter smile. "Was she, now?" He let go of my face, leaving two painful points behind where I hoped it wouldn't show bruises. But his hands didn't remain gone for long. His fingers traced my cheekbone, the anger, the threat, the ... demon ... in his eyes suddenly gone.

I froze. I was safe, I told myself. I had manifested, and he could no longer take my soul as a trophy ... but he could kill me; break the truce and kill me.

"Even if falling in love with me would have been your worst mistake," he murmured as if he was sharing a secret with a lover, "I wasn't the only one she warned you about." For a moment, he was so still he could have turned into stone. Then he placed his palm on my cheek, making warmth spread where he touched me. "I won't kill you, Laney," he finally said, his eyes losing the darkness, the edge. "At least, not for a while." With those words, he let go of me and walked away, but not without a glance over his shoulder and a last word that was meant to destroy me. "I don't need to kill you, Laney. You might have already chosen your worst punishment."

40. Laney

I didn't dare move until he was out of sight and the echo of his voice had ebbed from my mind, leaving the pale November morning colder than I had ever experienced.

Worst punishment. The words returned as I made it around the corner, back to the store, stumbling over the curb and dropping my coffee on the concrete as I caught myself with my hands.

I cursed under my breath and picked up the cup to throw it into the trash when Mom rushed to my side, bag of pastries in one hand, coffee in the other.

"Did you get hurt?" she asked and set down her coffee on the roof of a car to help me.

My pride or my body? I wanted to say and didn't mean, almost hitting the sidewalk with my nose.

"I'm fine," I said instead and dropped the cup into the trashcan before I rubbed my chin where Cas had squeezed it like a lemon.

Mom opened the car, and we made our way home at the same speed we'd arrived.

"Cas seems like a nice boy," she said with an expression that was impossible to read. "Is he new in school?"

I frowned. "He is ... new, I mean." I grabbed the paper bag and opened it, filled with the anticipation of the scent of warm raspberry, and wasn't disappointed.

"Nice, too?" Mom asked, that expression on her face turning sheepish.

I rolled my eyes. "I honestly don't want to talk about Cas, Mom." I closed the bag as we stopped in front of our house. "Not in this life."

Mom didn't ask any further questions. She simply pulled out a coffee mug and poured half of her latte into it before she set it down on the table for me while I prepared two plates and extracted the Danishes. She didn't ask about Leon either, reading from the look on my face that I had other things on my mind.

"So ... Gran's stories," I reminded her as soon as she had taken her first bite. "She never told me those." I lifted the mug and swirled the coffee around in it, trying not to look too excited about learning more. "At least, not that I can remember. What's up with those angels of death?"

The radio was babbling in the background, making the silence that followed less awkward.

Mom sighed, suddenly looking old despite her youthful complexion. "I can't remember much, but I did take some notes when I was younger. Your grandmother kept asking me to pass on these stories to my children if I ever had any."

I watched her take another bite and chew. Gran had never told me, but she had asked Mom to tell me...

"Thanks, Mom." I left it at that and changed the topic, chatting about school, her work at the office, what we would like to do for Thanksgiving this year. All harmless and easy and nothing that could accidentally lead me to let slip that I had taken on the profession of carrying souls to the gates of heaven.

I sipped my coffee with the prospect of telling Leon about my encounter with Cas, but Cas's words were slowly digging into my mind, undermining my confidence that I was on the right path.

I wasn't the only one she warned you about. I don't need to kill you, Laney. You might have already chosen your worst punishment.

What if Gran had meant both of them? She had warned me about Leon the first time she had seen him. But what else had she known? Leon and I were on the same side. We were both Lightbringers, the messengers of the good, while Cas ... well, Cas was, as he had mentioned himself, little more than a lesser demon.

Leon had protected me, long before I had known what I was. He had been there for me all along.

Maybe Gran just hadn't understood what she had been seeing. Maybe she had mistaken Leon for one of the Shadowbringers.

Whatever theories I came up with, none of them made sense. None, but that Cas wanted to scare me. So that was what I chose to believe—at least, for now.

The man looked hardly older than my mother. So young. His hair still bright golden even when his skin had turned a pale shade of gray as death slowly settled within him.

Any moment now. I had watched it so many times with Leon. Had done it too many times under his supervision. Taken souls and delivered them to the doorstep of a bright afterlife, to where Gran had gone, delivered by Leon that first day I had realized he was something more than he let on.

Tonight, I had come by myself. No more Lightbringer babysitters. I had to be able to do this by myself. Even if Leon would have urged me to let him come along, I knew there had to come a time when I managed the whole transition all by myself. So I hadn't woken him when I had felt the tug in my chest, and he had kept breathing evenly beside me. I had simply pulled on my sweater over my pajamas and taken off.

As I gazed at the man before me, I wondered if Leon would show at all. Maybe he hadn't been assigned to this soul alongside me the way he had been with all the others. Maybe the angel whose essence was directing him in these regards knew that I no longer needed his help.

I took a step closer to the bed, glancing around the tidy bedroom; the neat arrangement of papers and pens on the desk in the corner, three pictures of the man—Max, I read on one of the frames with a younger version of his face on display—and a woman with wild, blonde curls.

Max had stopped breathing a minute ago, and his heart stopped beating around the same time.

A natural death. In his sleep. I didn't know the specific reason why he wouldn't wake up tomorrow morning, walk down the stairs, and head out the door, dressed in those comfortable-looking jeans and neat jacket he had laid out on the armchair by the window as if he had something to look forward to.

With a glance at Max's face, I knew that it was time. His soul would leave his body within heartbeats—mine, not his—and I lowered my face over his, examining the peaceful features of the man who hadn't felt pain or terror in his final moments. That was the way I wanted to go one day. Painless and easy. Maybe even picked up by Leon to escort my soul to see my grandmother again—if heaven was where I was headed. With the job I was now doing, I couldn't be sure.

Cas hadn't shown up, so I assumed I would be spared of seeing his beautiful face and the wicked nature that lay behind in stark contrast. *A lesser demon.*

Max seemed to be one of the souls that were destined for heaven without bargaining.

The silver glimmer of Max's soul appeared first, his shape peeling from his body in a translucent form before it collected into a small, star-like ball of light, a sight that still struck me with awe, every single time. I took a deep breath, about to let him settle within my chest, a shiver running down my spine as I thought of what I was about to do. The soul was hovering an inch from my parted lips when a voice, dark and gentle as night, asked from the corner of the room, "And you are sure your destination is where he belongs?"

I started, turning on the spot to face the boy I knew came with that voice.

He leaned against the wall by the window, one foot braced against the wooden paneling, features half-hidden in the shadows of the clouded night.

"Go away," I told him and turned back to Max—his empty shell. His soul was still within reach. All I needed to do take another deep breath, and he would be safe from Cas.

The angel of death, however, pushed away from the wall, shoved his hands into his pockets, and sauntered toward the closet, one dark eyebrow rising as he walked past me, glancing at the silver soul at my lips. His gait was laced with power and elegance as if he didn't have a care in the world—other than to prove me wrong. I was determined not to let him.

"What do you want now?" I asked, aware of the soul hanging in limbo before me and eager to take it where it belonged. If only it hadn't been for Cas's sudden entrance, I might have been there and back already.

"What, no threats today?" I taunted and hoped he'd make his offer soon so I could focus on the soul and not on the last words he'd spoken to me days ago behind Santoni's. He hadn't approached me since. Whether or not I was glad about that, I couldn't make up my mind.

With a swift motion, he withdrew one hand and laid it on the brass knobs on the closet. He winked at me, shooting me a smirk that made my stomach feel funny before he opened the door and jerked his chin at the contents without taking his eyes off me.

It took me a moment to realize what he was showing me.

My heart began thundering in my chest, my body turning cold—so very cold—at the assortment of newspaper articles, photographs of people, and...

I left the soul hanging midair and joined Cas at the open closet, wild panic flooding my veins as I recognized some of the articles.

"I know you know I am right," Cas prompted, turning so he faced the open doors with me.

Murder in Towson, one of the articles, *Child missing in Glyndon,* in another. There were about ten of them, collected over the past fifteen years, all pinned carefully to the plain wood, an image of the victim attached and a list of dates and times and activities beside each one of them as if Max had been studying their daily schedules—

"Oh my God," I whispered, and what had been sheer cold earlier turned into solid ice clamping on my body. "Is he—" I couldn't finish the sentence, knowing already that I must be right.

"The murderer," he completed it for me with a shrug. "More a serial killer is my assessment of the situation."

My chest tightened, and I gasped for air as my eyes darted back over my shoulder to watch the soul I had abandoned beside the bed.

"Laney," Cas's voice pierced through my momentary petrification.

My gaze locked on his in search of something that would help me focus ... and found a quiet storm in the gray of his eyes.

"I was about to take a murderer to heaven," I said, toneless, my realization reflecting satiation in the dark pit of Cas's stare.

"You were." He nodded, bringing his hand to rest on my arm—not a consoling gesture but played pity. "Now, what was I saying?" He let go of me, closing the door and making the proof of the dark side of the soul I had been assigned to disappear. "Right. The guy belongs in my resort."

He didn't wait for me to unfreeze as he marched up to the bed and leaned toward the glinting star, quivering with the movements of air as he rushed forward before turning to look over his shoulder. "You didn't touch anything in here, did you?"

I mechanically shook my head. In and out, traveling in my Lightbringer essence as Leon had taught me. "Why?"

"My fingerprints might not lead to anyone alive since the police started using fingerprints to identify people quite a while after I ... well ... stopped roaming the realms of the living as you like to call it," he said with a smirk. "But yours do."

With those words, he winked, turned back to the soul, and absorbed it into his chest.

I was too late to object—or maybe I no longer wanted to. When I could move again, Cas was gone, leaving me alone with the empty body of a serial killer. And I no longer knew if I should be upset or be grateful that he had come to steal this soul.

41. Laney

I was up with first daylight the next day, Leon's arms slung around me like a Kraken.

He hadn't woken when I returned, just turned over as I had slipped into bed beside him, thoughts spinning around the mistake I'd almost made.

Carefully, I reached for my phone on my bedside table and texted Jo to ask if she was up for a small adventure today.

Surprisingly, her response was instant, begging me to get her out of there. *There* being her parents' who were driving her crazy.

So, I slid out of Leon's arms, denying myself the urge to stare at his features relaxed in his sleep, mouth slightly open, hair mussed—

My heart ached just a little as I left him behind to take a shower and get dressed. But first, I opened the drawer of my nightstand where I had stored the letter I had snuck out of Carly's apartment and stuffed it into my bag.

I rushed through my morning routine, pulling my hair into a ponytail, and donned my clothes after a fast encounter with the steaming heat of the shower.

Leon was awake when I returned to grab my bag and leave a note for him.

"Going somewhere?" He smiled with all of the seductive force of his Leon-charms and propped himself up on his elbows.

"I'm heading over to Jo's," I told him. "I didn't want to wake you."

"You didn't," he reassured me, shaking white-blonde strands out of his face.

"I was going to leave you a note," I explained a bit awkwardly, wondering what exactly I would have written in it. *I'll be back later.* Or ... *Gone to deliver a letter I stole from a dead person.* Even worse, the thought of how I would have signed it. *Laney? Your Laney? Love, Laney?*

Probably neither of them. And most certainly not *I love you.*

For even if Leon had spoken the words, even if I was drawn to him, if I enjoyed his company so much it sometimes hurt, there was something keeping me from truly falling over that cliff.

Be careful who you give your heart to.

I studied him as he rolled out of bed like an athlete and padded over to kiss me good morning.

My spine tingled where he placed his hand on my back and pulled me closer, the other one cupping my face.

"I know we didn't make plans to spend the day together, but I could join you if you want me to," he murmured as he grazed his nose along the side of my neck, driving shivers through my body, and making me wish I hadn't already changed into my jeans and sweater.

Maybe it was better that I hadn't or I would end up going back to bed and standing up Jo.

Jo! I sorted my thoughts and caught Leon's face with my hand, stopping him from grazing below the collar of my sweater where his fingers had found purchase on the fabric. I couldn't, in good conscience, invite him for the adventure I had planned with Jo—even if it was more like a tiny road trip; nothing more than searching for the lost daughter of Carly Mae Jennings. The plan was to spend some quality time with Jo and find out how she was dealing with her situation. Having Leon there would make that impossible. Also, he would notice fairly quickly what was so easy to hide at school where we rarely had more than ten minutes of uninterrupted conversation during breaks—that Jo and I had a secret.

Actually, I had more than one, by now, Jo's illness being by far the one that had the least impact on him.

I hadn't shared with him about the incident with Cas at the grocery store or that Mom seemed to know more about our Lightbringer world than she herself was even aware of. I was determined to wait until she came back to me with her notes before I'd tell Leon just to make sure it wasn't a false alarm. But naming an angel of death Lucas ... well, it did make it look a lot like there was more to it than just coincidence.

And last, I wasn't sure if I could tell him I had snuck out last night and almost delivered a murderer to heaven. Had it not been for the Shadowbringer—

I didn't even want to consider what might have happened.

So in a sense, Cas had saved me last night. And that made me fear him even more.

"I'll drop by on my way home, all right?" I offered and had trouble not locking my free hand in his hair and pulling him back against my neck where his coffee-eyes had been wandering, mildly glazed.

"All right." His voice was husky as he dragged his gaze back to my face. "I have school stuff to do anyway. I'll be out of here in ten minutes." A broad smile graced his lip, making him even more surreal in his beauty. "Tell her I said hi. And call me if you need anything."

I kissed him briefly and twirled out of his arms before he could convince me with another kiss that I wanted nothing more than to stay in bed all day.

"See you later." I made it to my bag, picked it up, and was at the door.

"I love you," he called after me, but I was already out.

Mom was currently in the kitchen, cooking eggs, and turned, dishcloth in one hand, pan in the other as I stopped by the fridge to grab some juice.

"He loves you," she commented with a smile.

Heat rose in my cheeks. "That's what he says," I retorted, unable to keep a straight face. I was the luckiest girl alive to have someone like Leon love me. Involuntarily, my eyes darted toward the stairs, suddenly paranoid Leon could be standing there and overhear our conversation.

"I must say I'm not surprised." Mom dumped half of the eggs on a plate and offered it to me. "Eat with me before you head out?"

I knew Mom wouldn't mind if I left Leon alone in my room. She trusted him with my life—and rightfully so. He had saved it more than once.

Anyway, I took the plate and grabbed a fork from the draw by the sink.

"You're being safe, right?" Mom asked the second I'd sat down and taken a bite, having waited for me to have my mouth full so I was unable to object with my awkwardness right away.

I considered her timing as I dismissed my thought to hysterically laugh at her. Instead, I chewed, contemplative of her authentic concern for me and my future. I swallowed.

"It's not like that, Mom." It was the truth. Nothing even remotely dangerous had happened. His hands under my shirt being the farthest we'd gotten with constant interruptions from our missions, discussions we had to have about how to prevent the Shadowbringer from breaking the treaty—even if Cas had already told me he wasn't going to kill me, I hadn't told Leon that ... and I didn't fully believe Cas. That Shadowbringer was up to no good.

"I don't even need to know, Laney. You're old enough." From the look on her face, I could tell that she was hardly any more comfortable having this conversation than I was. That put me a bit more at ease. "All I want is to remind you to take precautions if you are having sex."

"You reminded me of that when I was thirteen, Mom," I pointed out, remembering our conversations back then with mortification.

Mom smiled. "I did, didn't I?"

I nodded and swallowed another bite. "Thanks, Mom, for caring."

"Don't thank me yet," she said, her lips splitting into a devious grin. "I am planning to have the same talk with Leon when he tries to sneak out of the house." She lifted the pan from the stove beside which she was leaning at the counter. "Why do you think I gave you only half?"

That actually made me laugh. "I'm sure he'll appreciate it just the same," I reassured my mother as I got to my feet and placed the empty plate in the sink.

I hugged her and swung my bag over my shoulder. "I'm heading over to Jo's for the day. Leon will be out soon. Don't scare him, please."

Mom only chuckled and patted my back.

The address on the letter was in Towson. I had checked it the night after I had delivered Carly to heaven's doorstep. Therefore, I knew where our trip would take us today.

"So what's that mysterious adventure you texted me about?" Jo wanted to know as she climbed into the car, waving at her parents, who had both agreed it was safe for her to go as long as we were back by tonight.

I'd promised them we'd be back in the afternoon and that I'd take good care of Jo, and they had smiled. "I'm glad our Jo confided in you," her father had said to me. "At least, there's one person at school who knows."

Now, we were driving past the white fences and fall-mangled meadows where, during the summer, herds of horses were grazing like the motive in an aquarelle painting.

"I need to deliver a letter," I told her with as much nonchalance as I could muster.

"To who?" Jo's eyes sparkled beside me.

"A woman named Mae." I pondered telling her more details, but that would only raise more questions. So I went with a half-truth. "Plus, there is a really bad zombie film that premiered before Halloween that I'd like to watch with you." We had seen the advertisement long before, and it triggered our idea to dress up as zombies. So it was something I was sure she'd agree to.

Her grin confirmed that I was right.

It didn't take us any longer than usual to get to Towson due to a lack of traffic. People seemed to have huddled up in their homes as the weather turned colder by the day, reluctant to leave their houses if it wasn't necessary.

So when I turned onto the street on the envelope, I wasn't surprised to find most driveways occupied with parked cars and lights on in the windows of the houses.

"There." Jo pointed at one of the brick bottom, wood top, two-story houses along the road that all seemed to look the same. "Seventy-four."

Jo had been my navigator, phone in hand, patiently narrating what I should be seeing at the next turn. Now, we had almost reached our goal, and my heart fluttered in my chest when I pulled over to park at the curb and noticed that the windows in seventy-four were all lit up.

"You have reached your destination," Jo chanted in a grand imitation of the synthetic voice of the navigation system. Her following laugh was like a balm to my soul. Jo was still the happy girl I'd gotten to know even if she was a bit less durable due to her condition. "Do you want me to come?" she asked when she noticed my hesitation as I took the letter in both hands and eyed the scripted words on the envelope.

Mae Christopherson. It was the name she now went by. From what I had been able to spot on the pictures in Carly's apartment, Mae was married. Again, I glanced at the windows, wondering if the moving figures were Mae and her husband or if I would be intruding while she had visitors over.

"I'll be fine," I told her unnecessarily. "It will only take me a minute."

Jo bobbed her head. "Leave the music on."

I left the key in the ignition, and Jo turned up the volume of some bouncy tune as I opened the door and got out on feet that were surprisingly reluctant now that I was so close to accomplishing what Carly had asked in her letter.

The bare trees and leaf-covered flowerbeds greeted me as I made it up to the white front door. I turned and glanced around before I rang the doorbell, giving myself another moment to find composure. I had no reason to be here, other than that I had seen the letter and I had taken Mae's mother to the gates of heaven. If Mae decided she never wanted to open the letter, it would be her choice. All I would do, I promised myself, was hand the woman the letter and leave. No explanations; they would only raise questions.

The neighborhood was nice enough to suggest Mae and her husband had made a comfortable life for themselves; not excessive, not rich, just ... comfortable.

After a deep breath, I was ready, finger ringing the doorbell, and waited with a pounding heart for someone to respond.

The response came so fast I almost stumbled back down the low stairs that led back to the narrow walkway made of stone.

"You must be coming for the piano lesson," a round-faced, middle-aged man said by way of greeting. "Mae is waiting for you in the music room."

He gestured behind him where I noticed a blue-noted melody float, accompanied by a charming alto voice.

"I'm ... actually..." I stammered, lost for words now that all I had to do was hand him the letter and tell him it was for his wife.

But he waved me inside so fast that I didn't have a chance to object, and sent me directly into the room where the music originated.

"You're late, Mary," Mae said without looking up, her heavy black curls moving as she swayed with the music her fingers produced on the piano that stood against the wall.

I listened for a moment, spellbound by the music until Mae stopped and turned, probably wondering if I was really there.

"You're not Mary," she noted correctly, brows rising in her mocha-colored face, her glasses half up her nose, and studied me, waiting for an explanation.

"I'm—" I started then decided it didn't matter who I was. At least, not to her. All I needed to do was give her the letter and turn around. "I have something to deliver to you," I said instead.

I held up the envelope and took a step toward her as Mae got up from the piano bench and pulled her shawl more tightly around her neck.

"You aren't wearing a uniform," Mae noticed, studying me there in the doorway to the cozy, wood-paneled room, resting her hand on the backrest of a leather armchair as she stopped a good three strides away.

"It wasn't sent via mail," I informed her, hoping that my nerves would hold through the next minute until I could leave the building again.

Mae's eyebrows seemed to disappear into her gray-streaked curls. "Who is it from?"

I put together all the courage I could muster. *For Carly*, I told myself. *You are doing this for Carly so she may rest in peace.*

Mae picked up the letter from my outstretched hand with hesitant fingers as I took a step toward her, offering the envelope.

"Your mother." It was all I needed to say before I left. Mae would figure out the rest when she read the lines hidden in the paper.

So I gave her a smile and turned to leave when Mae's footsteps rushed after me and her hand appeared on my shoulder, holding me back.

"You knew my mother?" she asked, eyes wide, her big, round eyes suddenly moist. "My biological mother ... I mean."

For a moment, I pondered whether there was any way it would be credible if I said I did—or if I said I didn't.

So I simply turned back to face her, a smile plastered onto my features that I hoped didn't let on how nervous I was.

"Her last thoughts were of you," I said, neither confirming nor denying anything. And when a tear ran over Mae's cheek, I added, "She knew you were living a happy life. Know that she is in a place where she will be happy at last, too."

With these words, I slid out of her grasp and strode back the way I'd come, waving at Mr. Christopherson who was just on his way to the stairs.

I didn't turn to comfort Mae as a sob sounded from the music room, or offer any explanation to her husband as he asked if I was already done with my lesson. Instead, I mustered a brave face and walked out the door, knowing that now, Carly's biggest regret weighed less heavily and she could find peace at last.

42. LANEY

Jo nibbled the rest of her popcorn on her way out of the theater a couple of hours later.

"Are you even allowed to eat that?" I asked, pointing at the salty pieces between her fingers.

"If I don't glut myself with anything else as salty as this and drink enough fluids," she answered, mouth full and chewing noisily.

It was easy to hang out with Jo. Even now that her life was full of restrictions, full of careful planning and medications. In some ways, her life was so similar to mine.

"Now, at least, I know what to say when Rakesh suggests we watch this movie together." She chuckled and blushed.

"Now you'll know that you won't miss anything substantial if you spend the entire film glued to his face."

We both laughed, and it was wonderful to see Jo happy.

"Honestly, Jo"—I hooked my arm into hers—"I'm glad the two of you are dating."

Jo nodded in agreement, her cheeks still tinted pink.

We were just arriving at the car when my phone vibrated in my pocket. I pulled it out in time to see Leon's call end. He had left several messages, asking if I was all right. They were popping through just now that the connectivity was back after we'd left the theater.

"Should I drive while you call him back?" Jo offered, dreading my concerned expression. "We can always switch later. For example at a diner … there was that small place at the edge of town that looked like somewhere we could pick up something for our parents to appease them for leaving them alone all Sunday," she suggested with a conspirator smile.

I just reached into my bag and extracted the keys, tossing them to her with a "Thanks", and dialed Leon's number as I climbed into the passenger seat.

Jo steered the car into the light afternoon traffic, the music tootling idly in the background, when Leon answered, relief in his instant "Hello" as if he'd been waiting by the phone.

"I was worried," he admitted, an uneasy tone threading his voice, the concern in it so familiar.

"Like a—" I paused and glanced at Jo, who was focused at the traffic light ahead, fingers drumming in beat with the music on the steering wheel. "Like a … you know…"

"Like a real boyfriend," he finished my sentence, his tone informing me he knew very well that wasn't what I'd meant but said it, all the same, just to say it—for the first time.

"Exactly," I retorted, wondering if my ears were the shade of tomatoes.

I recapped the film for him in a three-minute version, already eager to see his face again, to feel his laugh on my cheek as he kissed me in-between moments of conversation.

"When will you be back?" he finally asked after he'd given me a brief summary of his day—doing nothing. "Your mom really had a speech prepared this morning," he added. "I think I need to reconsider sleeping in your bed." A laugh followed that told me that he intended just the opposite.

"Sorry I didn't warn you." I chuckled to myself as I imagined Leon flushed pink before my mom while she asked him the same question she had asked me this morning. "I know you can handle yourself around her. It's not as if you haven't been coming and going for the past few years."

He laughed again at that. "True. Only, now, it's different." His laugh abruptly stopped. "Now I've something to lose."

"I'll call you when I'm home," I reassured him, glancing at the clock behind the wheel. "Definitely before six."

"Love you," he said instead of *goodbye*.

"Later," I responded, feeling a heat flood me that was a bit similar to panic. Speaking the words, despite the attraction between us, despite the trust, the feelings ... it would be like stripping naked in the middle of the highway. I wasn't ready. Gran's words of caution might have something to do with it, but mainly, I knew I wasn't ready.

I flipped the phone back into my bag and fell into my own thoughts, grateful that Jo had taken on the task of driving. Every inch of my body was so ... tired ... including my mind. Last night—the fact that Cas had saved me from a huge mistake, not filling in Leon about what had happened, and sneaking around with Carly's letter—had taken its toll. Maybe it had been the past months that had taken their toll, but I was too tired to ponder even that. I just wanted to close my eyes for a moment.

The screeching tires of the black van tore through the air before my lids could fall shut, followed by the sensation of being catapulted into space as Jo hit the brakes, causing the car to twist to the side before it skidded to a halt. I tried to focus, to orient myself, to see something—

What caught me was a familiar shape standing by the crossing, dark and lean, hands in his pockets, hair dancing in the wind.

The outline of the Shadowbringer was the last thing I saw. Then, that van hit my car.

And everything went black.

Fragments of words rather than words, let alone full sentences, filtered through the darkness.

"...leave ...... not now..." a voice older than time, younger than tomorrow, whispered in my ear. "...chance..."

During the pauses, I mainly heard my own heart pounding in my skull, too fast like the frantic wings of a butterfly with lead attached to its fragile legs.

"...need more time ...... not planned ...... hopeless..."

There was no way I could react to the words. I couldn't even react to my own wish of opening my eyes—did I wish to open them?

Something slid under my neck, making an explosion of pain erupt along my spine, in my chest, where one shallow breath was chasing the next. I could feel my body—that was good, I supposed. Even if it meant that all my limbs felt as if they were on fire.

The scent of oil and gasoline and blood marked the progress of time as it floated into my nose.

"Don't ...... only could tell..." the voice echoed almost like it was inside my mind—or fighting the angry, defiant pulse in my ears. "...do anything ... anything." I tried to hear all of the words, but they eluded me as if they were fragments of shattered glass that rained down; patched together, it made up a whole, but it could never be put back in that original state of completeness. "Hold on," finally, right by my ear, a whisper that was the sound of clear summer nights and cloudy, stormy skies, all at once, said, "For me."

Then, the voice faded, making way for the shouted orders of what had to be firemen or paramedics or police, I couldn't make out the meaning of their noises, only that they were coming closer and the voice that had whispered in my ear was gone.

I struggled to open my eyes, fought, with every shred of willpower—

But they remained heavy and unwilling and utterly useless, cutting me off from the world.

"Can you hear me?" one of the shouters asked so close to my ear that I felt I should be cringing away, only, the response my body gave was another fiery rain of pain, right from the top of my head all the way down to my toes, and not the movement I'd been hoping to make.

"Jo—" It all came back to me. The crossing, the van ... Cas on the sidewalk like the illusion of a dream.

"This one is awake," the voice by my ear reported, one careful hand probing along my arm as his attention returned to me. "My name is Malroy," he informed me at a normal volume. "I am going to be here with you the entire time while they cut you out of the car."

His words made some sense as I noticed the pressure on my legs and on my chest as if I had been folded into steel wrapping.

"Jo—" I repeated, and my eyes fluttered open for a brief moment, just long enough to take in the young face of the man crouching by the window of my car, tilting his head to the side so he could see my face. He was upside down ... no, he wasn't... The car had turned over and landed on its roof. I was upside down. Suddenly, the angry pounding in my head made sense.

I pulled together all of the strength I could find in the aching ends of my body and said to Malroy, "Get Jo out first." The words came out as a cough. I tasted blood. "It's okay if I die."

Malroy was about to object.

"It is," I cut him off with a voice so weak I wondered if I was speaking at all. "I'll go to heaven."

The next time I woke, the world was a fluffy cloud in which I was floating without a care. A metronomic beeping noise greeted me alongside darkness. A brace held my head in place, and I could only imagine that at least one of my legs must be in a cast. I didn't feel them any more than that they were there and that when I wriggled my toes, they actually moved.

With a whispered prayer of gratitude that I wasn't paralyzed, I let my eyes slide shut again. However, I didn't get to slip back into the dreamless state of before where pain didn't exist, probably due to very expensive pain medication.

The door opened, and hasty footsteps rushed to my side, accompanied by a discussion that seemed to have something to do with the timing of my waking.

"...should have been sleeping at least until tomorrow morning," one of them, a woman, noted. She was the first to arrive at my side. "Can you hear me?" She turned to me, a switched-off lamp in her hand, which she used to direct the other arrivals to their designated places.

I blinked at her, and inched my chin down as much as the brace allowed.

"Good," the doctor noted and dropped the lamp into the pocket of her white coat. "Do you know your name?"

I had to think for a moment, but it came to me quickly enough. "Laney," I answered, my mouth dry as sandpaper. "Laney Dawson."

The doctor and the nurses, who were checking what seemed to be an IV and the monitor beside my bed, all appeared to relax a bit at my coherent response.

"You have a broken leg and a couple of cracked ribs. Some really bad bruises. No internal bleeding, though. Organs are okay." She took a deep breath as if listing every injury had used up all of her lung volume. "You're lucky to be alive."

"You must have a special angel who watches over you," one of the nurses said from the foot of my bed.

An angel.

Lucky to be alive.

But I wasn't the only one who had been involved in the accident.

Jo and the driver of the van—

Jo—

"Can I"—I stopped mid-sentence and tried to clear my throat, but the hoarseness didn't disappear. So I continued, ignoring the fact that I sounded like someone was throwing pebbles into a paper box—"see Jo?"

The beeping from the monitor sped up as I waited for the answer. *God, don't let her be dead.* It was the second prayer within a minute.

"Your friend is still in surgery," the doctor informed me in a tone that was equally professional as it was sympathetic. "It may take another couple hours until she gets out."

One of the nurses checked the needle in my arm and gave me a compassionate half-smile while I did my best not to start screaming Jo's name.

"But she will get out, right?" I willed my words to be true.

The doctor only placed a hand on my forearm. "We are doing all we can to save your friend."

"I'll call your mother, honey, and tell her that you woke up," another nurse offered. "She left maybe fifteen minutes ago to take a shower and pick up some fresh clothes. She didn't leave your side from the moment they rolled you out of surgery."

I tried to speak again and failed, my throat too dry to produce a sound.

With a smile, the nurse held a cup with a straw to my lips. "Drink up, honey."

The liquid felt like the glacial lakes I had seen in geography classes or in fancy documentaries about the history of the world.

"Thank you," I said to the kind nurse, who shoved her seventies glasses up her nose and nodded at me with pink painted lips, which made a fruity contrast to her chocolaty skin.

"Someone called for you," she said only to me, leaning in a bit so that it made at least the appearance the others couldn't hear. "A boy."

"Leon," I whispered, and the nurse lifted her eyebrows, making the lines on her forehead deepen.

"He asked me to let him know when you woke up," she told me, and for some reason—I couldn't exactly say why—it felt like a question.

"Sure," I responded, wondering if my answer made any sense.

Then, my mind circled back to Jo and the last moments in the car and that she already had enough on her plate; the last thing she needed was ... this.

My eyes searched for the doctor, who was reading the chart at the foot of my bed, her middle-aged face reminding me of that of my mother when she was wearing her lawyer-face.

"She has kidney disease," I said to the woman who looked up, her hand lowering the chart. "Jo," I clarified. "Jo has kidney disease."

At that, the doctor glanced to the side at the nurse closest to the door, who flitted out, without a word.

"Why don't you try to sleep a little more," the doctor suggested.

Beside my head, the kind nurse placed the cup back on the nightstand. "It will be a while before your friend gets out of surgery."

"This will help you sleep," the doctor walked up to stand by my side and took a syringe from the kind nurse's hand. "Your body needs rest so it can heal."

I nodded. The dreamless sleep from before was better than the anxiety that rose in my chest when I thought about Jo—and the guilt that followed. It had been my car. I had asked her on that adventure. I had let her drive—

The sedative worked fast as the doctor administered it through the IV, and I was taken under by a pain-free heaviness that immediately let my eyelids droop.

The next time I woke, it was from a painful tug in my chest.

43. LANEY

My body was a weight, unable to move as I intended to get out of bed, my leg, trapped in a cast, my neck, useless in the brace, my arms attached to those tubes and needles, getting God-knew-what delivered directly into my veins. Pain killers, for sure. However, the dosage wasn't high enough to mute the pain that came with a calling soul.

Leon would go take care of the soul. It was a comforting feeling that even if I wasn't capable of moving, that soul wouldn't go unaccounted for by the side of the Lightbringers.

With a groan, I shifted just as much as necessary to glimpse at the window where a starless night greeted me. *Leon*, I called him in my mind, hoping that he would answer even though that wasn't the sort of connection we had. I wasn't sure if anyone had that sort of connection. I knew that, had Leon been in the hospital building, he would probably have heard me. But he didn't. The pain wasn't fading, and so I had to entertain the thought to at least try on my own.

I closed my eyes and attempted to shift into my ethereal form, but it didn't come as easily as I was used to. It took me several mind-wracking times to feel myself slither into the weightless version of myself where I wasn't bound to the principles of physics the way my corporeal body was.

With clenched teeth, I braced my palms and forearms against the bed and lifted my head then shoulders ... then I sat up, torso obeying effortlessly. I slid my good leg off the bed first. Then, when nothing in my body protested, I gingerly lifted the cast-wrapped leg—

Nothing. Not even a hint of pain. Only the tug in my chest that was getting more pronounced by the second. This was urgent. The soul was almost ready.

I could do this. I could. I had to.

With a deep breath, I stumbled to my legs and was surprised to find them holding my non-corporeal weight.

Gritting my teeth, I extracted the needles from my arm and applied pressure on the puncture hole for a minute just to make sure I wouldn't bleed—not that I knew if ethereal bodies could bleed. Then I took a deep, mind-clearing breath and took off, letting the essence of the angel guide me, letting it take me wherever the soul needed my assistance with transitioning into the afterlife—or an advocate against hell if Cas was there to claim whoever it was.

The journey was short. A blink of an eye rather than a minute like I was used to. And when I arrived, I found myself looking at a hospital room similar to mine. Only it was brightly lit and busy with doctors and nurses, and loud with orders and curses and loudest of all ... the sound of a flat line from the monitor attached to Jo's lifeless body.

"Jo!" The scream came out of me as I took a clumsy step with the cast. I didn't feel pain, I didn't feel a soul either, their alignment with heaven or hell, where on the scale between good and evil they stood. I didn't—

"She's gone," said one of the doctors, face grave as he set down the paddle of the defibrillator. The rest of the room mimicking him, dropping what they had been holding onto, lowering previously busy hands which now had no use. "Time of death, four-forty-three in the morning," the doctor pronounced the final words that sealed Jo's fate.

No. *Nooo.*

It couldn't be true. We had been laughing in the car only yesterday. We had been watching zombies on the big screen and nibbled popcorn. We had—

A sob hitched in my throat.

"Jo." I staggered closer, waiting for Jo's soul to hatch from her broken body, for my friend to embark on her journey so if there was nothing else I could do, at least I could take her to heaven where she wouldn't suffer, where I would someday—if Leon was right—see her again.

It was then that I saw him hovering by the side of the bed, a faint smile on his lips as he studied Jo's bruised face, hands which were reaching past the doctor who slowly retreated from the bed, braced on the edge of the mattress.

Had he been there the whole time? I had been so busy staring at Jo and the medical staff that I couldn't tell.

"Cas." His name slipped from my lips as I was still trying to comprehend that there was a messenger of hell leaning on the edge of my dead friend's bed. A Shadowbringer, ready to bargain for her soul.

Cas's head snapped up, a glacial expression replacing the smile on his face as he took in my appearance. All voices and noises faded from the room as my attention focused solely on him.

"What are you doing here?" I spat at him, and his eyes widened at either my tone or the cast he found on my leg sticking out from under the hospital nightgown. Or the brace around my neck, or the bruises I surely had on my face. I couldn't tell; he was looking everywhere at once, eyes swiping up and down my body, and the cold inside them faltered just a little.

"Got a job to do," he shrugged himself upright, getting out of the way as one of the nurses pulled a cloth over Jo's head, hiding her mangled face from the world.

My heart broke all over again. He wouldn't get Jo. I wouldn't allow it.

My eyes were squinted as I bore into Cas's, a new fire flaring within me.

It couldn't be long before her soul split from her body and I could carry her to where she belonged.

Cas studied me, probably reading from my face that I was mentally preparing to skip all the bargaining this time and simply inhale the soul of my friend so I could take her to safety.

"You can go now," I dismissed him, my lips pressing into a thin line the moment I had finished speaking.

Where was she? Why wasn't she rising from her body?

"You're not getting her," I told him acidly, hopping another step closer now that the last nurse was leaving, but not before she marked a cross over Jo's chest and said, "May God have mercy on your soul and take you into his realm."

It was the same nurse who had handed me the water cup. Only now, her kind features were torn in an expression of grief.

I shuddered at her words, for it didn't matter if God had mercy on her; Jo was going to heaven. I was going to take her, and no Shadowbringer could stop me.

Cas watched the nurse walk out and close the door behind her. "It's too late for that," he said, his eyes finally settling on mine, a thunderstorm brewing in the gray depths of them.

There was absolute silence in the room now that the monitor was switched off, that there was no IV dripping, no slouching footsteps defeatedly dragging from the room. Only Cas and me and the silence that came with expectantly waiting for a soul.

Only, Cas wasn't waiting for Jo's soul, I realized, as I noticed the flicker of silver behind his irises.

"No," I whispered, tone more deadly than any scream would have been.

Every muscle in Cas's body seemed to tighten.

"You didn't." I flung my hands in the air, helpless. It couldn't be true. He couldn't simply have grabbed Jo's soul without waiting for one of us. Jo wasn't evil. She didn't belong in hell. She didn't—

"Neither your precious Lightbringer boyfriend nor you came to claim her," he said with little compassion, or surprise, or anything humane at all.

I once more searched for the tug and the pain that came with it, but all I found was the hollow place that ached to accommodate Jo's immortal soul.

"You're lying," I claimed and took another step so that I could lean my thigh against the bed, gaining better balance.

Cas's eyes flickered, the silver so prominent now that I could swear it was calling out for me in there. The Shadowbringer, however, remained motionless like a statue, his gaze burning and aching all at once. Only when I leaned over the bed to stare into his eyes, to see Jo, did he unfreeze and brace his hands on the mattress the same way I had found him.

"Give her back." My words were so cold I could feel my blood freeze. Or maybe it was the knowledge that Cas had stolen Jo's soul.

I leaned even closer, head cocked as far as the brace on my neck would allow, until his breath warmed my face, tingling like a taunting breeze. I was so painfully aware of Jo's broken body sprawled between us that all I could think of was to release my right hook on the Shadowbringer once more. But something in his eyes, something more than the burning, Jo's desperate flicker behind his irises, caught my attention. It was the way his eyelids shuttered as if he was blinking away a tear. But there was nothing. No crystal clear droplet that would give away that he had—or had once had—a soul.

"I can't." The finality of his words clanged through me like distant thunder, making my bones and flesh go cold.

"What do you mean, you can't?" There was aggression in my own voice, accusation, desperation, and he straightened as if he was just now realizing that his shoulders had hunched, his neck bent—

I stared into those gray eyes as they hovered above me now, pupils wide, absorbing the plea in my gaze.

"Cas—" What could I say to him? What could I do to make him release Jo? How could I plead with an immortal whose job it was to take souls to hell? How could I reason with someone so ... wicked; so thoroughly evil that he would claim a good soul, given the chance, and damn it to an eternity in the underworld?

I didn't allow myself to even glimpse at the empty shell of my friend, who was resting in the soft hospital bed; didn't dare glimpse at the monitor where a couple of minutes ago, a flat line accompanied by a long, never interrupted beep, separating the screen of the machine into two halves, had informed the room that my friend's mortal life was over. I didn't want to look down at her cloth-covered, dead face—dead. Her body had stopped functioning. Her organs were now useless, heart had stopped pumping; her blood had stopped flowing in her veins, and her smart mind, her humor, her caring, loving self—

Cas blinked, his eyelids shielding that solid gray gaze of his for a moment that felt like an eternity before he sighed through his nose as if not allowing himself the full relief of a real sigh. When he reopened them, I saw it, flickering behind those wide, black pupils: the weak, silver pulsing of a soul. Jo's soul.

"It's too late, Laney." He took a step back and walked around the bed then stopped, eying me for a long second with a torn gaze as he prepared for his departure—while I was bound in shock.

Jo was in there, trapped. I had come too late. He had beaten me here, been here to breathe in my friend's soul, to tie her within his hollow heart until he could set her free in the burning fires of hell.

Hot tears shot into my eyes and I took a step, closing the distance between us, my hands shaking as I restrained them from shooting to his jaw, to push him back and tackle him, push him to the floor, and—

And what would I do? Tear her soul from him? I didn't even know how those small, silver lights managed to settle within one of us at all, so how could I force one out of someone. With my bare hands? With a suck of breath from his lips?

What options did I have?

My fingers curled, imagining throttling the angel of death before me.

All the while, Cas didn't move. He remained immobile, the preternatural stillness that distinguished him from everyone else in this world.

It didn't matter what he was, who he was, how long he had been playing this game for souls. How often he had succeeded in taking the innocent into his realm. This was Jo, crying for help behind his eyes, and I was going to do whatever it took to bring her to the side of the afterlife she belonged.

"Release her," I demanded, my lips curling back over my teeth in what I believed was an intimidating grimace. But my voice was weak. Defeated.

Cas didn't respond ... didn't as much as flinch at the promise of violence in my gaze.

"Do you hear me?" I gave one of my hands permission to grab him by the collar. And when my fingers dug into his black shirt, fingernails scraping over his neck as I closed my fist, he unfroze, and a smirk spread on his face. "Let her go," I growled the words, trying to keep my voice down. I wasn't even sure if I could hurt him in my ethereal form when I myself didn't seem to feel the pain of my corporeal body. But it didn't matter. I had to do ... something.

"You are too late. I took her soul the moment she left her body." There was no apology on his pale features, no plea for forgiveness. No. He was the same cold Cas I had met that first day in the nursing home, when he had wanted to take Gran away. The same errand boy of the devil, who had delivered countless beings into the underworld, earned or unearned. "Even if I wanted to, I can't," he continued, not even attempting to free himself from my grasp but glaring down at me, taunting me with that dark amusement that reminded me that if I didn't manage to save Jo now, she would be lost forever—damned was the better word.

"You can and you will," I dared him, unable to take no for an answer. *Whatever it takes.*

Cas studied me, Jo's silver light flickering in his eyes like a cry for help directly from hell.

"There must be a way ... there always is another way, Cas. Please." My words didn't come out fierce and determined but like the plea they truly were.

He just stared.

"Please, Cas." I felt my legs go wobbly, and instead of holding his shirt in my grasp, threatening him, I was now holding on to him as if somehow, by clinging onto him, I could keep Jo from slipping away. "I ... I'd do anything..."

He blinked once more, his features changing, the smirk vanishing as his features smoothed over to reveal the full extent of his beauty. His features were still, even, like a blueprint a Greek god had been modeled after. But it was an icy kind of beauty. One that came with the knowledge that it was there to hide the evil beneath.

"Having taken in the soul means that there is a soul on my tally that one day, sooner or later, needs to end up in my resort." He paused, pursing his lips as he glanced at the ceiling, tilting his head up so I could no longer read his face. Beneath my hand, his chest heaved a breath before he turned back to me. "*A* soul," he clarified, "not *Jo's* soul, not any one specific soul. Just *a* soul."

He waited for me to comprehend what he was trying to tell me.

A soul. *Any* soul—

"Take mine," I spluttered out before I could think it through. "Release her, and take mine."

Cas's eyes turned darker, the light gray almost slate in the shadows that clouded his gaze. "You would do that for her?" There was something in his voice that I couldn't identify. Some emotion that reminded me of those few moments when I had believed him to be better than he actually was.

I nodded, the last of my tears falling away. I would. For Jo, I would do anything.

Cas held my gaze. "If you do it, there is no way back. You're trading your soul for hers. You understand what that means, right?"

I wasn't sure if I nodded or shook my head. Cas explained anyway, "You are taking her place in hell one day ... when your mortal life ends."

So it wasn't today. Or tomorrow. I had some more years. Many, if I was lucky. Enough to figure out a way to reverse the promise if I made it. Leon would find a way. He always did—didn't he? Maybe. Did it matter?

Hell one day. But I could save Jo now.

"Do it," I croaked, my voice no longer holding up.

Cas stared, disbelieving of my willingness to take Jo's place, to trade my soul.

"We are talking about eternity in hell, Laney," he clarified. "Not about a vacation in the desert."

Something in his words made me believe he didn't want me to take the deal. Something, a shy glimmer of stars in the almost exclusive dark velvet of his voice.

I ignored it. Ignored the fear that was flaring in my heart, the anxiety for Jo, the prospect of what would be waiting for me once my own life ended.

As long as Jo's afterlife was where she belonged, in a place where someone like Gran would be looking out for her—

"I said do it." I tightened my grip on his shirt and forced all my determination into the look I gave him. All the determination of a girl in a neck brace with an unstable leg and a damaged face. And a mission to save her friend in any way she could.

Cas stopped breathing and nodded. Just one brief nod to indicate he had heard me. His eyes went vacant, and he coughed, the distortion of pain shooting into his features, veins on his neck standing out as he opened his mouth, and a translucent silver star floated from his lips.

"I hope you know what you're doing," he whispered.

And disappeared.

Leaving Jo's soul hovering midair where he had released her, and by doing so, damned me to take her place in hell.

44. CAS

The fact that she had given up her soul didn't bother me as much as the fact that she had won this round—even if she'd lost everything doing so.

My chest still ached from where I had accommodated Jo's soul and had almost spat my lungs out, reversing the settling. Those little soul-stars usually were easy to take or release, even if they didn't want to leave my chest once I delivered them to the antechamber of hell. But this one ... she had clawed at me with those spikes as if she were fighting for her life. Her afterlife.

And how lucky she was to have a Lightbringer as a friend and one so willing to make a sacrifice.

"What did you do?" Leon Milliari's voice came from the other end of the room from where I had launched myself into a corner and pulled my knees up to my chin, surveilling the empty space. Empty, not for the absence of things but for the absence of a living, breathing soul—

Until the Lightbringer disturbed my guarding of the dead with his bright and disdainful presence.

I ignored him.

"What did you *do*?" he repeated, skipping the distance between us as he traveled on the angel essence that was threaded through his mortal body.

Mortal. How easy it would be to snap his neck and be done with it. But the truce forbade it. And to be honest, I no longer cared. There was only one thing that mattered now, and that was the thread that seemed to originate in my chest and disappeared somewhere in a realm I could no longer touch.

Milliari darted toward me and grabbed me by the front of my shirt, yanking me to my feet with all of the force of his anger.

I let him.

"It was her choice," was all I cared to tell him. He knew as well as I did that he had owed me a soul. And not just any soul.

"You could have told her *no*," he objected. Ire lined his features, burned in his eyes, so dark that I wondered if he himself originated directly from hell.

"Or I could have let her make her own choice—wait, I did." I gave him a bored glance before I let my eyes wander back to the corpse of the girl who deserved heaven and was now taken there by the girl who had sacrificed her soul to make that happen.

"She is everything to me," the Lightbringer hissed, his fist pulled back as if he was going to throw a punch, but then it trembled, and he let it sink.

"And now she's mine." It wasn't difficult to say the words. He already knew they were true even before I'd spoken.

"Payment was due. I wanted to take her friend. You agreed."
I stepped out of his grasp, not needing much of my actual strength to free myself, and turned to look out the window. "A friend for a grandmother, right? That was the deal."

Leon growled behind me, bound by the truce and the truth of my words.

I could vividly remember the first time I had seen Laney Dawson in her grandmother's room at the nursing home. *You owe me*, I had told Leon Milliari. I hadn't specified back then, but he knew that giving up a soul like that of Mrs. Parker... It had been a sacrifice on my side to not even negotiate. It had been a result of shock that an emerging Lightbringer had gazed at me over her dead grandmother's body—and seen me. Even if it had been potentially just a couple of years in purgatory for the woman, tonight, Leon had seen the opportunity to cover his debt and offered to not bargain for Jo's soul so I would finally disappear from his and Laney's life. And I had bided my time and gotten something much more valuable than what I had expected.

"I didn't kill Jo, by the way," I informed him, just to be sure he had all the facts. "Even though I did have the pleasure of seeing their car spiral into the air and land on the roof." I faked a chuckle, and it came out dark as the shadows that were dancing around me. He didn't need to know that I hadn't just seen the accident but that I had dashed through steel and stone to grab Laney's hand and will her to hold on just long enough for help to arrive. That was my secret. A secret that no one would ever know. Not even Laney. "That your Lightbringer was involved was just ... let's say ... bonus."

I swear I could feel Leon was about to burst into one million sharp-edged pieces behind me.

Still, I didn't turn.

"You were supposed to take Jo," he growled. "Jo was the payment for my debt."

"And I did." The stars were almost invisible above the city lights as I screened the sky for something I could believe in. "Nobody told you to leave once we decided." He had shown up as expected, ready to fight for the soul of Laney's friend like a lion when ... when I had reminded him that he *owed me something*. And he had settled, after a moment of conflict on his features, telling me that I could have her if I promised to disappear from Glyndon.

Leon harrumphed. "I waited until you inhaled the soul," he pointed out.

"And how could we have known Laney would even wake to feel her friend's calling after you left? I was about to take off when Laney showed up." I agreed. "She's not looking good, by the way," I didn't fail to rub it in his face.

For a moment, the room was very quiet.

"You did everything right, Lightbringer," I reassured him and didn't like the sound of the words. They tasted wrong on my hell-tested tongue.

"Then why ... *why* ... is Laney on her way to heaven with Jo's soul?" Milliari's tone was lethal, hardly controlled.

"Because, Lightbringer, Laney traded her soul for her friend's." I turned and found him so close I could see the black specks in his irises. "Consider your debt paid."

He released a gust of air in my face. "You will pay for this," he growled, and if looks could kill, the one in Leon Milliari's eyes would have done just that.

But then, I was already dead, wasn't I? At least, to this world of goodness and hope.

I summoned my shadows and let them coil around me, ready to take off. "No, I won't. I never do. That's the benefit of working for hell."

Epilogue

LANEY

I didn't feel different when I returned from the gates of heaven what seemed to be hours later ... or no time at all. There was no pain, no emptiness other than the one I already knew from longing to return and walk right through those gates ... the gates I would now never walk through.

There was nothing to indicate I had struck a bargain with the Shadowbringer. Nothing other than the memory of Cas's palm against mine as we'd shaken hands after he released Jo.

My skin still seemed to tingle where our skin had touched.

The bargain was done, and there was nothing I could do right now. It would have to wait until tomorrow when I could tell Leon that I had ruined everything, until I could plead with him to help me find a solution. And if Leon forsook me for the choice I'd made—

Then, I would find another way. I would heal first so I was strong enough to confront the Shadowbringer. Then, I'd make a different, a better bargain.

The hospital bed was as I'd left it, and at the sight of it, I wondered how I'd get those needles back into my arm without help, wondered how to fake hearing for the first time that Jo hadn't made it through the night, how to make my features accommodate surprise, shock, everything that I no longer had in me now that the relief that I had managed to get her to heaven was the only thing that filled me—

It wasn't the only thing. For at the thought, grief overcame me, and my ethereal body faltered two steps from the hospital bed. Pain shot up my leg as it was suddenly holding my corporeal weight; my chest clenched, my head heavy as lead ... and as if I were a toddler unable to carry myself, I slumped to the ground with a gasp of pain.

"There you are." I looked up at the voice that drifted from the chair in the corner. "I've been wondering how long it would take you."

The kind nurse smiled at me, getting up and dashing to my side. She gingerly wrapped her arm under my shoulders and helped me up enough to bring my torso into the hospital bed.

I must have stared at her with the shock I thought I no longer had in me, for she said, "Don't look at me like that, honey. You think I didn't see you there in the other girl's room?" She folded me onto the mattress, her hands professional, efficient, and careful, making the procedure minimally painful, and then pinned the IVs back into my arm. "I recognize one of you when I see them."

"One of *us*?" I asked into the air between us as she bent over my face and kissed my forehead the way my grandmother had done when I was a child.

"You are what we speak of when we whisper *angels*."

Before I could say anything, she reached above the bed and pushed the button to call for the nurse. "My shift is over, Laney."

And as I watched her leave the room, I realized that mine had just begun.

About the Author

"Chocolate fanatic, milk-foam enthusiast and huge friend of the southern sting-ray. Writing is an unexpected career-path for me."

Angelina J. Steffort is an Austrian novelist, best known for her Wings Trilogy, a young adult paranormal romance series about the impossible love between a girl and an angel. The bestselling Wings Trilogy has been ranked among calibers such as the Twilight Saga by Stephenie Meyer, The Mortal Instruments by Cassandra Clare, and Lauren Kate's Fallen, and has been top listed among angel books for teens by bloggers and readers. Her young adult fantasy series Shattered Kingdom is already being compared to Sarah J. Maas's Throne of Glass series by readers and fans.

Angelina has multiple educational backgrounds including engineering, business, music, and acting, and lives in Vienna, Austria with her husband and her son.

Find Angelina on social media as @ajsteffort.

Made in the USA
Coppell, TX
29 June 2021